Along for the Ride

'There is so much I want to do to you, but we don't have the time.' He kept his voice soft, as if they might be overheard. Megan was glad he couldn't see her face in the shadowed enclosure. All thoughts of how they came to be together fell from her mind until it was only the moment before them.

'What would you do to me?' Megan kept her eyes on his as she picked the best spot she could find, an old curved tree with barren limbs just about the right height to hold on to. 'Tell me. I want to know.'

Along for the Ride

Michelle M Pillow

In real life, always practise safe sex.

First published in 2007 by
Cheek
Thames Wharf Studios
Rainville Road
London W6 9HA

A catalogue record for this book is available from the British Library.

www.cheek-books.com

Typeset by SetSystems Ltd, Saffron Walden, Essex

Printed and bound by Mackays of Chatham PLC

The paper used in this book is a natural, recyclable product made from
wood grown in sustainable forests. The manufacturing process conforms
to the regulations of the country of origin.

ISBN 978 0 352 34145 7

Distributed in the USA by Holtzbrinck Publishers, LLC, 175 Fifth Avenue,
New York, NY 10010, USA

To Dan, who every single book is dedicated to, whether it says it or not. You are my knight in colourful armour, the thorn in my backside and the love of my life. Now, please, go pick your dirty socks up off the living room floor.

Chapter One

'Ah, crap, what is he doing here?' Detective Megan Matthews frowned, leaning over to set her cup of coffee on the hood of Sam Chambers's squad car. She'd caught a glimpse of the all-too-familiar and unwelcome Ryan Lucas, and hoped by leaning over out of his eyeline that he'd not see her. 'Doesn't the department have any other photographers they can call? Does it *always* have to be him?'

It was late, but the streetlights and squad cars lit up the narrow street, shining down the abandoned alleyway now blocked off with yellow barrier tape. Part of a long trail of museum artefacts littered the alley, dropped by less than ninja-like burglars as they ran from the law – or, in this case, two museum security guards who were in somewhat impressive shape. The mess had created a crime scene that lasted for several city blocks.

Seeing one of the security guards smiling in her direction, Megan turned her attention away without encouraging him. She had put in a long day only to be called back to work the second she walked into her apartment. The last time she'd had a full night's sleep was over a month ago and the last time she'd had a day off was too long past to remember. For the most part, she didn't care. Her work was her life. She wasn't ashamed of that fact.

However, her job had seemed less important as of late. At 29, Megan was one of the youngest detectives on the force. She'd been on homicide for a little over two years before transferring to a special investigations unit. Now she worked on solving burglaries and the occasional kidnappings. Somehow, looking for stolen art wasn't as rewarding as apprehending a killer. But what could she do? The transfer was unavoidable, but not completely her choice. She blamed Ryan Lucas for it.

Ryan was new to their ranks as a forensic photographer, having come to them from newspaper freelancing. The annoying man literally entered her life in a 'flash'. With one click of a shutter release during the now infamous arrest of a serial killer, he'd made her immortal and also made it damn hard to do her job. Because of that photograph, she was now New York City's 'Little Darling Detective'. It showed her taking down Jersey St Claud, a man accused of killing seven women in just over three years.

Accused, my ass, St Claud is a guilty fucker.

Because of Ryan, her image had been plastered everywhere for months, turning up over and over again on the news during the initial arrest and pre-trial. She'd even heard of it being published in a few books, though she'd never seen it herself. Now with the trial coming up, there it was again. Images were powerful things and, because of the photo, she was often given sole credit for what had been a group effort.

Being a 'Little Darling Detective' meant she'd not had even the slightest hint at a decent date in just under a year. Her job was tense enough as it was, but take away any kind of recreational sex and she was a basket case. It was one of the reasons she'd asked to be transferred off homicide. The only men who wanted to be seen with a famous cop were the ones wanting to show her off like a dating trophy. She refused to be a novelty story they could tell their friends at parties. Then there were also the submissive types who wanted her to dominate them. Sure, she'd run into the kind before, but now it was worse. They all wanted the woman who took down crime with a single knee to the back.

'What, Matthews? Not happy to see your boyfriend?' Sam laughed. He was a pain in the ass, but she'd take a bullet for him nonetheless.

'Do me a favour. Try to distract him while I do a once through of the crime scene before taking off,' Megan said, ignoring the boyfriend comment. Denying the obvious fact that she had nothing to do with Ryan Lucas would only make the teasing worse. 'I'm beat and you all have this handled. Every cop in the city is on the lookout for the perps.'

In perspective, a few missing pieces of art hardly called for sleepless nights, although her artist sister, Kat, might disagree with that fact. However, Megan had seen much worse in the line of duty. What was a missing painting and a few ancient rocks compared to a person's life?

'You got it, boss.' Sam nodded, automatically pushing up from the car.

The one good thing that had come from Ryan's photograph was that she'd got a lot of respect from fellow officers. Not once did she live up to the hype of her publicity. She still came to work, still did her job and never asked for special treatment. Sure, the teasing had been hard at first, but she ignored it. Then, when it came time for public statements, she'd given credit to everyone from the police department to the FBI, downplaying her role in the arrest. In doing so, she'd earned herself some in-house kudos.

'Hey, superstar, where you off to so fast? Running off to solve the case without us?'

Megan flinched at the sound. Naturally, there were still a few jerks willing to annoy her. She turned, keeping a blank face, as she acknowledged him. 'Axel.'

Who in the hell called him?

Axel was the true definition of 'cop' – every stereotypical image that popped up when someone said the word. He had the buzz cut, the mirrored sunglasses, the thick moustache and bad aftershave. His daddy was a cop, his daddy's daddy was a cop, his uncles and brothers and even his brother-in-law were all cops. Deciding she didn't want to deal with him, she rudely turned and ducked under the tape.

'Whoa, so the little darling doesn't have time for average joes like me, eh?' he yelled after her, snickering in a way that made her skin crawl.

'Don't you have a bribe to take?' she mumbled back.

'Hey, those charges were dropped!'

Megan didn't answer. She grabbed a flashlight from her waist and shone the beam of light over the ground. Already, the little yellow photo markers were propped up, ready for Ryan to come through and snap his pictures. She stepped slowly around them. Each one indicated a piece of the stolen artefacts from one of the museums uptown. Her thick boots hardly made a noise as she walked over the uneven concrete. Seeing a glittering object within the darkness, she moved the beam of her flashlight behind a trashcan. It looked like a diamond earring.

'Someone bring me a marker,' Megan called.

'Here, I've got some.'

She stopped moving, closing her eyes. Wasn't Sam supposed to be distracting Ryan? Then what was the photographer doing alone in the alley with her? She didn't like him being around. Just his presence worked her nerves and distracted her concentration.

'Here,' Ryan repeated when she didn't answer. 'What do you have?'

'There,' Megan said, pointing with the light. She held it steady as he brushed past her to set the marker. 'Looks like an earring. Strange, considering what else they took.'

Ryan stepped through the beam and for a brief moment she got a good look at his face – not that she needed to see him to remember what he looked like. His hair was longer, falling to his chin in soft brown waves. The man had an endless supply of T-shirts and blue jeans, which always bulged at the pockets with the canisters that held rolls of film. She wondered why he carried print film when all she'd seen him use at crime scenes was a digital camera.

Megan didn't know why she noticed the small detail. Perhaps it was her training or maybe it was because Ryan kept popping up around her – at work and even a few times when she went to see her sister. Kat worked with her entomologist husband at the American Museum of Natural History. Dr Vincent Richmond had helped them solve the serial-killer case and Ryan had gone to take his picture for an article. Kat and Ryan hit it off, making it even harder for Megan to avoid the man. He was like a cockroach she couldn't get rid of.

OK, so maybe cockroach was a bit harsh. But he was a pain in the ass and she was too tired to deal with him tonight. Truth be told, Megan understood the friendship between Ryan and Kat. They were both photographers with laidback artistic mentalities. Megan has always been too edgy for such an easygoing lifestyle. She needed to be up and moving, needed the mental and physical stimulation, needed to be constantly challenged. Work did that for her.

Dazed from lack of sleep, she merely stared as he put the marker down by the diamond. When he turned to her, his dark-blue eyes struck her like a shock of cold water over the head. She blinked, coming out of her daze. Ryan would have been a handsome man, if she didn't resent him so much. He was athletic, but not too muscled. When he smiled, two dimples lit up his face and, when he spoke, his words were infused with hints of a lazy New York accent. It was enough to give a girl chills.

'Are you going to be at Sunday dinner?' Ryan asked, clearly trying to make small talk.

He always did that. Didn't he realise he'd nearly ruined her life? Well, her career, which *was* her life.

'Is there a department banquet?' Megan frowned. She didn't remember there being any city functions on her schedule.

'Sunday dinner with your parents,' Ryan explained.

What in the world did *he* know about Sunday dinner with her parents? Megan automatically knew the answer. Kat. Her sister had told him.

'Um, yeah, probably, if I can get away,' Megan said. It was Monday night and she really hadn't thought that far ahead in her schedule. Who knew what the weekend would hold. She did miss her family and hadn't been able to attend dinner the day before because of paper-work. At least now that her parents lived on Ninety-Sixth Street and Columbus, she did get to see them and her sisters more often.

Altogether, Megan had four sisters. She was the oldest of the bunch. Then there was Kat the photographer, Zoe the chef, Sasha the undecided college student and Ella the baby who was off serving in the Navy.

'You must be pretty excited,' Ryan said.

'Excited?' Megan repeated, confused. Maybe she needed sleep more than she'd realised because she couldn't, for the life of her, figure out why they were talking about Sunday dinner with her parents while in the middle of working a crime scene.

'Because Ella's coming home.' Ryan gave her a small smile.

'Oh, yeah.' Megan pretended to know what he was talking about. The news perked her up some. It had been a while since she checked her personal messages. Was Ella making it home Sunday? It would be the first time any of them saw Ella since she left for basic training.

'I'll be excited to meet her.' Ryan took the lens cap off his camera and made a few adjustments before aiming it at the jewel she'd found. His flash went off and Megan blinked hard, suddenly seeing bright spots in her vision. 'Actually, it'll be nice meeting the rest of your family. I've met Kat, obviously, and Zoe at her restaurant about a month ago when Kat and I were having lunch. I haven't met Sasha or Ella or your parents yet, but –'

'What are you talking about?' Megan broke in. Didn't this guy have a family of his own to go to? Why was he so worried about meeting all of hers? It's not like she wanted him in her life any more than he already was. And it wasn't as if Kat was going to date him. Kat was happily married and madly in love with her husband.

'Sunday dinner. Kat invited me to come,' he said, studying her. 'Hey, are you all right? You look...' He shrugged.

'Yeah, I'm fine.' Even to her own ears, her voice was flat and unenthusiastic.

'Anyway,' Ryan continued, again fiddling with his camera before moving to another marker to take the picture, 'Kat's got a meeting before dinner and she gave me the address to meet her there, but I was thinking –' he paused, clearing his throat '– that maybe we could go together.'

Megan blinked slowly, not answering. Did she hear him right? Did he just ask her out on a date – to her parents' house? Unable to answer, she actually felt sorry for the poor man. What kind of sorry loser asked a woman to go on a date with her mom, dad and sisters? It would have been mildly disturbing, if she didn't find it somewhat pathetic.

'You know... since we're both heading there anyway,' he said, as he took another picture.

Megan suppressed the urge to laugh in his face. He *was* asking her out on a date to her parents' house. The fact that she'd not had a real date since her picture hit newsstands almost made her say yes. But remembering that he was the reason for it made her answer, 'Um, no.'

'What? Why?' He lowered his camera to look at her.

7

Was he really surprised at her answer?

'I don't date co-workers,' she said, keeping her tone light as she did her best to be more civil.

'But we're not really.' Ryan moved to the next marker. The only way out of the alley was the way she'd come, which was also the direction Ryan was working his way over to. 'I'm not a cop. I don't keep an office at the precinct and it's not like our work can be compromised by the other.'

'Sorry,' Megan said, dismissing him, 'you're not my type.'

'How do you know?'

'A woman knows.' Megan started to edge past him, trying to make a clean getaway. The man was determined, she'd give him that. Most guys backed down after one of her curt rejections. Knowing it to be the kiss of death on any potential relationship, she lied and said, 'I'm looking for marriage, kids, you know, the whole familial package. The next guy I go out with will be "the one".'

If that didn't send him running for the hills, then he was crazy. No man wanted a woman who became so serious so fast, or one who was baby and marriage focused. Megan really wasn't either of those things. She had a good job and, if her fellow officers were any kind of example, cops made bad marriage partners. It was a natural side effect of the work. She knew as much going into the job.

'And how do you know you've found the one if you don't date around?' Ryan asked, though he did sound less sure of himself.

The man was persistent. Well, time to be extra dingy and turn him off completely. 'Oh, I don't know.' She heard a motorcycle engine roar behind her. 'A man with a motorcycle. A classic, not one of those street bikes we're always impounding.'

'Really?'

'Yep.' It was all Megan could do not to laugh. She sounded certifiably insane even to her own ears. Though the fact she was even having this conversation did decide it: she needed sleep, lots and lots of sleep. It was way too much fun teasing him. 'In fact, I would marry a guy like that with very few questions asked – so long as he was reasonably close to my age, disease free, liked children, unmarried, liked women, showered on a regular basis and had a good-paying, legal, steady job. The details are irrelevant. I know me and I know, with those few things, I would be happy.'

'All based on the type of motorcycle he had?' Ryan shook his head in obvious disbelief.

'It's not just the bike, it's the *type* of man who'd have a bike.'

'Kat mentioned you were sure of yourself,' he said softly. 'I guess she was right.'

At that, Megan frowned. He had talked to Kat about her? She took a step back, close to making her exit.

Ryan lifted the camera. 'Detective Megan Matthews, a woman who knows what she wants,' Ryan stated.

Megan wondered at the tone in his voice. He pointed the camera at her. Her mind raced as she wondered what Kat had said about her, what they'd talked about, and then she wondered why she even cared what they discussed. She took another step back.

'Say cheese,' Ryan said.

Megan opened her mouth, putting her foot down at the same time. A loud crunch sounded under her boot just as the camera flash went off. She stiffened in horror, looking down at the ground. As if staged as the ultimate humiliation, a yellow marker with a big number one on it stood next to her foot, pointing in Ryan's direction so he'd have a clean shot of it. Slowly, she lifted her boot, looking down at what she'd stepped on. It was a museum artefact – a carved deity that looked really ancient, really important and now really broken into five separate pieces.

This was a disaster. She, a New York detective, had stepped on evidence – evidence from a huge museum backed by generously rich patrons and known all over the world. And Ryan caught the deed on film. Again.

Lovely. Fucking lovely.

'You asked to go with her?' Kat demanded more than enquired, placing her hands on the diner's sunlit countertop. She lightly patted the solid green laminate as if to emphasise the importance of her questions. 'You didn't mess it up? You said it just like I told you? Word for word?'

Ryan nodded. 'I told her you gave me the address but had a meeting and asked if we could meet up beforehand.'

'And she said no?' Kat frowned.

The small diner was relatively new, just down the street from where Kat and her husband worked at the DJP Scientific Department of Entomological Research, a branch of one of New York's foremost museums. When Vincent worked through lunch, Kat would often come to the diner to get them both something to eat. And, whenever Ryan wasn't busy, he'd pop in and keep her company. The place didn't have much in the way of décor, just a few potted plants and classic red booths with green tabletops. A long counter stretched down one side, making a visual block to the waitress's workstation. They always sat at the counter, as both of them liked the rounded stools bolted to the floor. The seats were fun to spin on. Yeah, he and Kat had done that, too. But, to be fair, the two little kids sitting close to them that day had started it.

Ryan sighed. Maybe he and Megan really weren't meant to be after all. He'd tried everything to get her attention. Ever since he took her picture during the arrest of the 'Preying Mantis', as the press had dubbed Jersey St Claud, he couldn't get her out of his mind. She'd been so tough, so commanding, so in control of her surroundings. He hadn't meant for her photograph to become famous like it had, but what could he say? It was a great picture and just the kind of image boost the police department needed. Really, though, it was his editor who'd pushed the picture so hard. The man was friends with the mayor and giving her the front page had been a big mark of distinction for the city's whole political system. The masses loved to put a face to heroes and beautiful Megan Matthews was it. She was their new superwoman – beautiful, smart, law abiding and a perfect role model. Plus, it gave the citizens a sense of closure to the nightmare the Preying Mantis had caused before his arrest.

Megan was also frustrating as hell, an irritatingly perfect know-it-all who he couldn't get out of his mind. She had the kind of dark eyes that haunted a man with their mystery, a self-confidence that was only outdone by rare moments of true vulnerability. And he'd be lying if he didn't admit her aggressive domineering personality fuelled many late-night fantasies. What man wouldn't want to play cops and robbers with such a woman? He knew of a few choice places he'd like to be frisked – her hands on him, controlling him, touching him.

OK, so he was mildly obsessed with her.

'She's proving to be a harder nut to crack than I first thought.' Kat was the only Matthews sister to have settled down, though by the looks of her the woman hardly appeared settled. Her long dark-blonde hair was streaked with chucks of hot pink and electric purple. Pink shadow lined her eyes, matching the darker pink of her lipstick. Her clothes were just as eccentric as her makeup – platform shoes, a denim mini-skirt and a flowing camisole shirt that matched her purple hair. To see her, no one would guess she was married to a very studious well-respected scientist.

'Kat, I've told you before, don't help me if it's only to prove your sister wrong,' Ryan said.

'But I am so tired of her thinking that she knows everything. And –' Kat reached over to pat his hand '– she *is* wrong this time. She doesn't know a good thing when she sees it. Megan has always had to be responsible. Our mother's a flake. Our father worked all the time and Megan got stuck taking care of four bratty sisters. I think we ruined any decent date she had before she moved out of the house and who knows if she's dated anyone since then. She never brings them home and never mentions a boyfriend. Though, after the stuff we pulled as kids, it's no wonder she is the way she is.'

'I don't know, maybe it's time I gave up. I've tried everything – aloof, friendly, flirtatious. I put myself in front of her. I stayed away. I got myself invited to family dinner.' Ryan buried his head in his hands. He wasn't a completely pathetic loser. He did have some pride.

Didn't he?

What was it about Megan that made it impossible for him to walk away, even after a year? Even now the idea of her aroused him. He was embarrassed to admit he had a picture of her, which he'd taken one night while she investigated a break-in on the Upper East Side, on his nightstand – and not just for decoration either. There was no particular reason he'd picked that picture over others in his growing collection of her. But it did show her brilliant dark-brown eyes and the shiny texture of her hair. She always wore it back in a bun at the nape of her neck, but he could tell it would be long if she let it go. Still, there was something very sexy about the disciplinarian hairdo. Almost all her clothes were black – simple, form-fitting, curve-hugging black. Occasionally, she wore a white linen shirt under her leather jacket.

Ryan shifted in his seat, keeping his head down. He needed to stop thinking about Megan or he would be trapped on the diner stool all afternoon, hiding his erection.

'You have a romantic's soul.' Kat patted him on the back of the head.

She really was a nice person. Why couldn't he have fallen for someone like her? No, instead he chose the impossible Megan.

'It's because you're an artist.'

Ryan gave a weak laugh. The thoughts he'd been having all night had very little to do with romance. 'I'm beginning to feel like a stalker.'

'Not that again,' Kat scolded. 'Your intentions are purely honourable.'

Ryan gave a short chuckle.

'Well, OK eighty per cent honourable.' Kat laughed. 'There is a big difference between crazy stalker and pursuing a difficult woman who you just happen to like very much and who wouldn't know a good thing if it fell on her head and began beating her senseless.'

'Fine, but if I ever become the other one you let me know,' Ryan said dejectedly. He was tired, horny and pretty sure he could use a bath. Not to mention he had two memory cards full of images he needed to get loaded on to the computer and labelled.

'OK, enough pity party. I only have a few minutes before I have to go and we need to plot your next move.'

'I'm not buying a motorcycle,' Ryan said. 'Can't afford it.'

Kat laughed. 'You have to admit that was a pretty good line she used on you. Any normal man would run screaming for the hills to hear a woman say she was looking for marriage and babies right off the bat. No wonder my sister doesn't get dates.'

'What? You think she really wanted all that?' Ryan asked, confused.

'Oh, my poor, poor man. No, she doesn't want all that. Megan is too practical to marry a man just because he has a motorcycle. She was saying it to chase you off.'

'That's what I thought,' Ryan said, somehow at ease now Kat confirmed it. He'd be lying if he said her irrational comments hadn't bothered him at the time.

'Tell you what.' Kat stood up. 'Get some rest, 'cause you look like you've been run over by an evidence truck.'

'I feel like it. Huge crime scene last night and I was the only one available to photograph it. I worked until five this morning, and then had to boogie on down to the paper to meet with the editor I've been avoiding all weekend. I haven't been home yet.'

'Who? Walter? Is he still trying to get you to come back?'

'Yeah. You know he's desperate if he's up at six. He offered me a staff position. Guaranteed pay cheque.'

'That settles it. We need to get you and Megan together so you can quit taking crime photos and get back to your day job.' Kat grabbed the take-out bag off the counter. 'Go get some beauty sleep, Casanova. I'll call you later with a game plan later this week. You have a woman to woo on Sunday.'

'You are a handsome boy, you really should be married by now.'

'Thank you, Mrs Hartman,' Ryan said, forcing his smile to stay on his face as he opened his mailbox only to discover it was stuffed full with credit-card offers and an advertisement flyer for sexual-enhancement drugs. After shoving them into the side pocket of his camera bag, he locked the mailbox. 'But no one will have me.'

It wasn't that he didn't like the meddling old woman, he liked her very much. Her round cotton-ball hairdo and fitted apron reminded him of the type of grandma who baked cookies and knitted socks, the kind most kids loved to visit. But, as a widow without children, she had no kids to come and visit her. Maybe that's why they got on so well. Ryan didn't have a family either.

In fact, the small three-storey apartment building was a haven in the city, hidden and almost forgotten in the East Village. It was filled with the once lonely and forgotten, who became the collectively remembered when they moved in. With three apartments on every floor and ten tenants, they were a close-knit, if somewhat strange family.

On the first floor, Mrs Hartman was their grandmother figure, making sure they remembered to eat. Living sparsely, she managed to stay quite comfortable on the money her husband had left her. From what Ryan gathered, he'd been a corporate man of some sort. Also on the first floor were Ginger, a suspected call girl who hummed musical ballads, and a woman they'd all dubbed Mary who looked like Ginger's dowdy sister, though the two weren't related.

On the second floor, across the hall from his place, was Margie who was pretty in a depressed doom-and-gloom sort of way. The young woman was an orphan who kept to herself and bred African Grey Parrots. It was her main source of income and, instead of paying taxes, she gave her extra money to the church. Ryan didn't know if she'd been raised in a convent or if he'd just assumed she had because of all the crucifixes she hung in her home. Then there was Harry, the neurotic singer without a band who rarely slept and had a bad habit of talking more to himself than others.

Up top lived William the Pacer, who guarded the halls throughout the night with a baseball bat and acted as a self-appointed security guard and doorman. He drank a lot, which might have contributed to his cop-like illusions of grandeur. Pete and Rosa shared an apartment and broke up about as much as they got together. It was impossible to tell which one was living in the building at any given time, so they generally avoided using terms like 'your roommate' to either of the twenty-somethings. And, lastly, in the biggest area with access to the roof was Diederick Meier the Third. A rich boy with a house on the Upper East Side paid for by his parents, he came to their little sanctuary to get away from his wealthy upbringing. Ryan felt sorry for Diederick, perhaps more than he did any of the others. Out of them all, Diederick was probably the loneliest.

'You and Mr Meier both should have settled down. Got me some grandkids.' Mrs Hartman followed him up the stairs and Ryan automatically slowed his steps so she could keep pace. Without an elevator, they had no choice but to use the stairs.

'If I marry Diederick, how will we give you grandkids?' Ryan grinned, keeping his back to her.

It took a moment for her to process, but after a short pause she laughed and scolded, 'Oh, you naughty boy!'

'I'll have you know, I had lunch with a very pretty young woman today,' Ryan said, thinking of Kat.

'The married one?' Mrs Hartman asked knowingly. 'The cop's sister?'

'That's the one.' He reached the top of the stairwell and stopped.

'I have news for you, buckaroo, you need to actually date the woman, not the sister.' She reached out, grabbing his arm lightly and taking a deep shaky breath.

'Oh, so that's what I'm doing wrong.' He laughed.

Mrs Hartman smiled, then turned back to the stairs to head down again. 'Go get some sleep. I know you haven't been home all night. William already gave me the full report of last night's activity. I hope it wasn't anything too bad that kept you away?'

'Just a robbery. No one hurt,' he assured her.

'Thank goodness for that.' She took a slow step, holding on to the rail. 'I'll make sure Margie or Harry brings you something to eat later.'

'See, now why do I need a wife when I have all of you taking care of me?'

'If you have to ask, young man, you need more help than I can give. Ask Diederick, he seems the type to explain it to you.' Mrs Hartman giggled, sounding very young for her obvious age.

'You know, I could just stand in the entryway and talk to you.' Ryan watched her as she continued to make her way slowly down, keeping an eye out to make sure she didn't lose her balance.

'Ah –' she waved her hand in dismissal without turning around '– it's my exercise for the day. It's what keeps me in such fine shape.' She patted her plump side and gave a small chuckle.

'It's impossible to improve upon such beauty, Mrs Hartman,' Diederick's sharply accented voice said from below the white stairwell.

Ryan saw the man's shadow before the man.

'Like I told the other one, you need to focus your attention on the girls,' Mrs Hartman answered.

'That's not what you said, sweet lady. In fact, I think you implied I focus my attention *too* readily on girls.'

When Mrs Hartman giggled again, it was a cute, almost blushing sound. 'A suave man with your European accent should have no problem setting the ladies aflutter. I might be old, but I know a rogue when I see one.'

'Then I must find a woman to put me in my place,' Diederick agreed with her.

Diederick met his gaze and Ryan nodded once. The man understood as he stayed downstairs to wait for the elderly Mrs Hartman. 'Please, mademoiselle, allow me.'

To hear the Swiss-born man speak with a French accent was slightly comical, but apparently the man had learnt English from his French nanny as a boy. It made for some interesting turns of phrase when he spoke.

Ryan didn't wait for Diederick to join him before continuing to lug his camera bags to his apartment. It felt heavier than it should have, but he knew it was mostly due to tiredness.

Diederick's footsteps sounded on the wooden stairs as he took them two at a time. 'Mm, I've eaten at some of the finest restaurants in all the world and still nothing compares to Mrs Hartman's chocolate chip cookies fresh from the oven. If I wasn't worried about her overdoing it, I'd make her market them.'

'Did you bring me one?' Ryan asked, glancing over as he unlocked his apartment door.

'She sent you one.' Diederick laughed harder, passing the stairwell that would lead him up to his home and entering the hallway instead.

Ryan arched a brow.

Diederick lifted a half-eaten cookie. 'It is here to be eaten.' He shoved the rest of it in his mouth, still laughing.

'I'll remember that,' Ryan warned, though in truth he wasn't hungry for anything too sugary.

'So sue me.' Diederick shrugged. 'My parents can well afford to pay you.'

'Don't play poor little, pretty rich-boy with me,' Ryan said. 'I know you have your own money.'

'You like this?' Diederick held out his arms to the side, showing off his tight black crewneck sweater as he swayed one way and then the other. 'I am pretty, aren't I? You like that, don't you? Come on, it's OK. I won't tell Margie you're having sinful thoughts about me.'

'Oh, yeah,' Ryan replied very sarcastically. 'If I was a chick, I'd do you.'

'Sorry, buddy,' the man said, dismissing him. 'I love the *chatz*.'

'I'm sure you do,' Ryan drawled, pushing open his door then stepping inside.

'It means ladies,' Diederick yelled.

'Whatever you need to tell yourself.' Ryan shut the door, chuckling.

Even though his apartment was empty, it was comforting knowing that the others were in his building. Still, there was a nagging ache as he walked across the wooden slats of his floor. Faint, yet always there, it wound through him from his chest, a dull constant reminder of the life he didn't have. It started the day his parents died and remained with him. He wanted the feeling of family back. He wanted noise in the house.

Seeing Megan's picture on his worn coffee table, lying in a stack of artistic photos he'd left there, he frowned. Automatically, he looked towards his bedroom door where another one would be on his nightstand. Maybe it *was* obsession. But Kat assured him he wasn't overstepping any bounds and, in fact, she wanted him to do more, to be bolder, to risk it all.

'Are you worth it?' he asked, walking towards the bedroom. As he pushed open the door, his eyes glanced over his small plaid-covered bed towards the photo he'd spent many nights fantasising over. 'Or am I just crazy for trying?'

Ryan moved through to the bathroom adjoining his room. Though it was small, he kept the place clean. Well, he did on most days. He gave a small laugh as he kicked a dirty T-shirt across the black and white tiled floor, out of his way.

Turning a couple of knobs, he started the shower. It would take a few minutes for it to heat up. The clawfoot tub was deep and set high off the floor. Though it looked old, it wasn't, having been crafted out of acrylic instead of cast iron. Three shower curtains hung from the ceiling along an oval ring. They overlapped, but still allowed threads of cold air in when he showered.

Exhausted, he stripped off his clothes, leaving them bunched on the floor. Lukewarm water hit his flesh and he jerked the curtain shut. He grabbed the shampoo and squirted it directly on his head, lathering with one hand as he blindly set the bottle down. He missed the shelf and the bottle fell by his feet.

The water heated, hitting hard against his chest and stomach. Ryan turned and a few remaining trails of shampoo suds slid over his flesh. The light caress of them tickled, drawing his mind down towards his heavy erection. After lathering the liquid soap between his hands, he ran them instantly to his cock, soaping the length and massaging it. He'd not been on a date since snapping that first picture of Megan and it didn't take much to romance his body to full arousal.

The feel of his fist left him wanting. There was something to be said for the soft flesh of a woman against his, the contact, the sound of her voice. Megan's voice.

'Megan,' he whispered, taking himself in both hands, weaving his fingers over the hard length as he longed for her to do. He twisted and pumped in a fast steady rhythm with the image of dark lovely eyes in his head.

Her full lips would be so commanding, just like her personality. She'd be the kind of woman to take charge and Ryan longed to be dominated by her. And yet there was a small part of him that longed for her to trust him enough to let him take control over her. But he'd have to get her to actually say yes to a date first.

Bittersweet thoughts filtered through him; the sting of her rejection mixed with the pleasure of the building release. He cupped his balls, squeezing lightly. Her mouth, those eyes. Ryan grunted in pleasure, his knees weakening and his hips jerking as he came. Semen spilt into the tub and washed down the drain. He turned to the stream of now very hot water and let it wash the soap off his sensitive member.

'When did I become such a fool?'

Chapter Two

'Matthews, I'm sorry,' Captain Turner said from behind his desk.

Megan pulled her gaze away from the many certificates and honours hanging on his drab grey wall.

'But I must insist you take a vacation. No penalties, no citations inserted into your record. Just a nice, long, quiet, overdue and somewhat paid vacation for one of New York's hardest-working detectives.'

Megan couldn't move. This wasn't a vacation. She was being told to take a leave from the force for the sake of saving face. After being caught on film stepping on evidence, she had no choice but to give the captain a heads-up on what had happened. When the photo hit the papers, which it would undoubtedly do, they had to be ready. The unfortunate incident had happened a couple of days ago and the picture had yet to surface, but it was only Wednesday. No doubt it was being saved for the weekend editions when circulation would be higher.

Damn Ryan Lucas!

'I could always arrest him.' Megan didn't have to specify who.

'Ryan Lucas has been politely asked not to sell any photographs that might reflect poorly on the NYPD, but the truth is he can if he wants. Some kind of contract loophole.'

'Loophole?' Megan sighed heavily, not liking this situation one bit.

'Yeah, he doesn't have a contract signed.' The captain picked up his teddy-bear coffee mug, which read 'World's Greatest Cop'. If Megan hadn't known the gruff man had a four-year-old daughter, she would have thought it funny. 'Human Resources can't find one for him anyway. Technically, he's a freelancer. Even if he does leak the picture, we can't do much about it by way of firing him. All we can do is cut his assignments and put him into a position to ask for more. At that time, a confidentiality agreement can be negotiated. We can't force him to sign one at this point. We can ask, but, regardless, he took the picture of you before he would be asked to sign. Arrangements are being made to hire other photographers, but Lucas is dependable and, frankly, takes on much of the work. Like you, he doesn't seem to have a life outside of this place.'

Megan arched a brow. 'Subtle.'

'Glad to see your sarcasm hasn't left with your humour.' The captain gave a brusque laugh. 'Lucas is reliable and good at what he does. And, technically, the event did happen. He's not making it up.'

'It's hard to have a sense of humour when you don't have a job.'

'It's a vacation and you were due for one anyway. Count your blessings. I haven't left the city in ten years. We talked it over,' the captain continued, not needing to specify who 'we' were, 'and we think this is the best thing given the situation. Give all your cases to Axel. He'll make sure they're covered.'

Megan grimaced to hear the detective's name. Now she'd never hear the end of this. Axel would hound her about it for the rest of her days. But what could she do? This order came from the police chief, and quite possibly the mayor – if the chief had decided to tell him about it. Either way, it looked like she was off the job.

'Are you sure that's best? I can still do my job. I'll lie low, spend most of my time in the office shuffling paperwork. Don't take me off my cases. We're over-worked as it is and I don't want to leave the guys shorthanded.'

'Normally, that's exactly what I'd do with you. You're a good detective, Matthews. You have nothing to be ashamed of. We all make mistakes and you're not being punished for being human. But, with St Claud's trial starting, we can't have your reputation in question. A mistake like this could be blown out of proportion in the court of public opinion. You are a key witness. Now, turn your cases over to Axel, get some rest and in a month when you've finished testifying you'll be back on the job.'

Megan nodded. 'But what if the picture doesn't come out? Can I come back to work then?'

'No,' he answered, to her surprise. 'You're going to take this break. I can't risk anything else happening with you.'

'What if it comes out and everyone thinks I'm being punished for –?'

'No,' the captain interrupted. 'If it comes out, lie low and make no comments to the press. This is just a routine request for time off made weeks ago by a hard-working detective. The paperwork has already been backdated.'

'Fine,' she said, unconvinced this was the best course of action. What was she going to do with a month off work? Just the idea made her a little stir crazy.

'You saw St Claud's victims; you know this case better than anyone. Take a copy of the files with you to study if you have to. We've all worked too long and too hard to make sure this asshole goes down.' He studied her. Megan knew her face must have looked doubtful, because he ordered, 'You're going on vacation, Matthews, and that's final.'

Megan nodded again. 'Yes, sir.'

'Leave a message on my phone as to where I can find you if you leave town, just in case something comes up. But, unless you hear from me, I don't want you back in this building, understand? Who knows when you'll get time off again? Take it. Enjoy it and come back refreshed.'

Megan stood, nodded a goodbye and walked out of the office. There was nothing she could say to change his mind. Even if she could, he had bosses above him who obviously thought this was for the best. Though she saw their point, it didn't mean she had to like it.

'Well, the good news,' she told herself as she went towards the file room to order copies from the clerk, 'is that I won't have to see Ryan for a whole month.'

The bad news was she didn't know what to do with herself if she wasn't being a cop. Without work or cases to concentrate on, what did she have? She grimaced, as she thought, Stupid Ryan with his stupid camera. I wish we'd never met.

'Congratulations!'

Megan frowned at her mother's excited voice, slowly pushing her sunglasses on top of her head. Outside, the bright light was doing killer things to her hangover. She hadn't bothered to pull the glasses up when she stepped into the darker interior of the classic pre-war building where her parents lived. The structure was of Art Deco influence with an elevator in it, which was nice since her father was 53 and had a hard time climbing stairs.

In her parents' home, she leant over to hug her mother, ignoring the woman's greeting. Undoubtedly, Beatrice Matthews was congratulating her on having time off from work. Or, if her father had told her mother about the picture, then it was possible she was congratulating Megan on it not being in the weekend newspaper.

'Hi, Mom,' Megan said, pulling back from her.

Beatrice was a bit unconventional, as was evident by the décor of her home. Before Mr and Mrs Matthews had moved into the place, the apartment had been completely renovated with elegant mouldings over the door and entryways, new hardwood floors and stainproof carpet, a large window overlooking a balcony and sophisticated white curtains. Now those curtains were covered in pink lace, the wood floors and new carpets were hidden under oversized rugs and the mouldings along one of the main arches between the dining and living rooms were lined with framed family photographs and cutesy little poems about friendship and butterflies.

'I'm so happy for you,' Beatrice said, beaming ecstatically. Her blue eyes glowed with an ageless vitality. At almost fifty, she looked great, though, lately, she'd taken to wearing jogging suits, or maybe she only wore them on Sundays when Megan saw her most often. The one she currently had on was pink with tiny white flowers all over it. She also made her own hair products, which accounted for the darker brown colour of her naturally blonde-grey chin-length hair.

'Uh, thanks, but I don't know why you're getting all teary-eyed about it.' Wryness dripped out of Megan's tone. Of course, her mom would think getting time off was a good thing. But what her mother didn't understand was that it had been less than a week and Megan didn't have a clue what to do with herself. If she worked out any more, her arms were sure to fall off – that or she'd punch a hole through the punching bag. And, though drinking did have its appeal, she was sure her body would be pickled at the end of a month and that was one alcoholic coma she didn't want to have to crawl her way out of.

'Oh!' Beatrice swatted at Megan's arm, as if her daughter was being absolutely ridiculous.

'Hey, kiddo.' Douglas Matthews came from the bathroom, smiling as he saw his eldest daughter. He held out his hands. 'How's my girl?'

'Hi, Dad.' Megan leant over to hug him. In his ear, she whispered, 'Has Mom taken to using a different kind of tea leaf in her drink?'

Instantly getting the joke, he shook his head in denial, chuckling to himself.

'No, I use the same ones,' Beatrice said, her hearing as good as ever. The whole implication that she was acting so crazy she must've been drinking marijuana went completely over her head. 'Why? Do you need a reading? Are you unsure about the future? I can brew a fresh –'

'Um, no, I'm good, Mom. Thanks.' Megan turned quickly to her father before her mother could insist. 'Is Ella home?'

'No,' her mother answered for him. 'She called and said she couldn't make it. I worry about her, but every one of my girls has to follow their path. Besides, I did a reading for her and everything's going to be all right. I have a feeling she'll be home soon enough, safe and sound.'

Megan was sorry Ella couldn't make it, but she really didn't want her mother's predictions clanging their way into her hangover. 'Dad, you got any beer?'

'Beer?' Beatrice questioned, horrified. 'An occasion like this calls for champagne.'

'Mom, really, it's not that big a deal.' Megan followed her out of the entryway. 'It's just a few days off and no picture.'

'What? What do you mean no pictures? And you're only taking off a few days?' Beatrice frowned. 'But what about a trip? You have to take a trip. It's tradition.'

'Trip?' Megan hid her grimace.

Their mother insisted on taking a vacation with each one of her daughters every year – five daughters, five vacations. Well, except that Megan had been a little too busy for anything more than a night spent in a hotel room with her. Even then, she'd been called off to duty the last time.

Seeing her mom's excited face, she said, 'All right, I've got about a month off and I'll go on vacation with you.'

'With me? Really?' Beatrice nearly jumped up and down like she was on crack.

Ugh, I really need to get my head out of work, Megan thought. The comparisons were getting bad. Maybe a vacation is just what she needed. It would get her out of the city, earn her brownie points with her mother and hopefully take her mind off work. Anything had to be better than getting drunk and obliterating her exercise equipment.

'Yeah, Mom, really. And I tell you what. I'll go if you plan it. Hell, invite the sisters for all I –'

'Don't swear!' Beatrice scolded.

'Sorry,' Megan said, suddenly feeling like she was twelve. '*Please*, invite the sisters along and rope Dad here into it, too.'

'Sounds good,' Douglas said, not needing convincing.

'Where?' Beatrice asked, clapping her hands.

'Anywhere you feel like paying for,' Megan answered. Hey, she was on a detective's salary. She couldn't spring for a big trip. 'Oh, but no cruises and nothing too isolated. I have to be able to reach the department if they need me.'

'But . . .' Beatrice started, only to shake her head, stopping herself. 'Deal.'

'Deal,' Megan said, turning to ask her father about that beer.

'Girls! Sasha, Zoe!' Beatrice ran across the living room towards the balcony. 'Megan said we can go on her honeymoon with her. Isn't that wonderful? This is going to be so much fun!'

'Dad, about that drink . . .' Megan froze. 'What the fuck did she say?'

'He seemed really nice.' Douglas smiled. 'You didn't tell us you were dating anyone special. And do try to watch the language, dear. You are better than that.'

'Ah?' Megan didn't know what to say to her father, so

instead she ran after her mother. What had the woman done now? Read her future in the tea leaves and found her a Mr Right? Megan knew there was no Mr Right for her so she settled on arresting Mr Wrong. 'Mother, what have you done?'

Stepping outside on the balcony, she blinked at the brightness of the day until her eyes adjusted. There wasn't much of a view, just some old brick buildings, but it was outside and high enough that the air seemed fresher. Megan glanced around. First she saw Sasha and Zoe, both of them smirking in amusement which was never a good sign.

Sasha leant back against the balcony's rail. Her dark-brown knit sweater seemed a little too warm of an outfit, as it fluttered open in the breeze. The long length fell to her thighs like a jacket, showing the matching brown and cream layered T-shirts beneath. A contrast to her blue jeans and fall wear was Zoe in a yellow peasant skirt and cream tank-top with flip-flops.

All of the Matthews women had the same fair complexions. Zoe, Kat and Ella had their mother's blonde hair and Megan and Sasha took after their father's dark brown. After so many girls, their parents had resigned themselves to waiting for sons-in-law. Apparently, her mother decided to scheme for men in the family instead of waiting for the girls to find their own husbands. Wasn't Kat's marriage enough for the woman? Megan could just imagine who her mother would pick out for them.

'Megan.'

Megan glanced to the side at the familiar voice and grimaced as a little ripple of attraction caught her off guard. Ryan Lucas? Megan had forgotten Kat invited him to come. She knew there was a reason she didn't want to get out of bed that morning. Silly her for thinking it was because of the pounding headache. When she was at work, she was ready to handle him, but here? She didn't have an excuse to leave. Not caring if she sounded rude, she asked, 'What are you doing here?'

Ryan smiled cheerfully at her, taking her by surprise. He looked really sexy in a camel-coloured sweater and dark-blue jeans. Had the man finally run out of T-shirts? This was the first time since they met that she'd seen him in anything else.

Megan didn't move as he hurried across the balcony to greet her. Why was he looking at her like that? His eyes all soft and warm? The sun reflected off his dark hair, showing strands of lighter brown in its depths. He was clean shaven, a state she'd rarely seen him in. Usually, it was dark out and he had five o'clock shadow lining his jaw. Her hands shook as she reached to touch the side of her head. She could barely remember brushing her hair that morning as she pulled it back into the standard bun, let alone if she'd worn anything nice.

'Sorry, sweetheart, I couldn't wait to tell them about us,' Ryan said.

Did he just say 'about us'? Sweetheart?

She opened her mouth to protest the insanity, when his hand lifted to her cheek cupping her face in his warm palm. His dark-blue eyes focused in on hers, intense and bold. Instead of her words coming out, Ryan's mouth came in, covering hers in a kiss. A weak noise of protest started to form as she lifted her arms to shove him off, but then his tongue slid along her bottom lip and her knees instantly weakened.

'Let's give them some space,' Beatrice said behind her.

The sudden yet unexpectedly intimate contact kept her immobile and Megan ignored her mother's words. No man had ever dared to kiss her without her implied permission. Her senses became engrossed in Ryan's touch – the firm yet shockingly soft play of his mouth against hers, the warmth of his palm to her cheek, the heat radiating off his body to contrast with the slight breeze.

Her arms were to the side, held out from her body, torn between grabbing him and pushing him away. A hand skimmed lightly over her waist as the other one stayed on her cheek. Fingers curled around her ear, tangling into her hair. His parted lips wrapped around her bottom one, sucking gently at it. She waited for him to deepen the kiss, hoping the probe of his tongue would shake her into action.

Megan told herself she would just wait for the tongue. Men always tried to deepen kisses too quickly. When she felt the deep probe, she'd know it was time to pull away. She could retain her dignity and still be angry at him for daring to presume she wanted him.

'*Mmm.*'

She wasn't sure who made the sound. All thoughts dissipated as his hand slid behind her back, pulling her tightly against his taller frame. Unmistakable heat centred on her stomach. She wasn't sure if it was hers or his, all she knew was it had been too long since she'd felt it. A thick curtain fell around her senses, trapping her in the insanity of the moment, blocking out everything else. There was no balcony, no parents or siblings in the next room. This wasn't Ryan. It wasn't her. They were just two people, joined by the mouth, held in the growing turmoil of irrational desire.

And it felt so very good.

Her hands flexed at her side, her fingers stiff as she resisted touching him. His chest brushed hers, and she breathed deeply to ensure they touched again. Pleasure hardened the buds of her nipples and they ached to be free from her tight bra. She wiggled, trying to give relief to the arousal between her thighs. The smooth cotton of her panties became a frustrating barrier, blocking her sex from any stimulation beyond the distant echo of his mouth to hers. Waiting for the feel of his tongue turned to needing it. Megan opened her mouth, ready to accept his full deep kiss. She reached forwards with her tongue, barely thrusting past his lips when he suddenly drew back.

Megan gasped, frozen with her hands lifted to the side. Her aroused body protested by shaking violently. She blinked, stunned and confused as she stared at him. Her breathing deepened. He pulled further away, taking his warmth and the subtle smell of cologne with him.

'What . . . ?' she began to question, her voice a whisper.

Ryan didn't speak. If she had her guess, she would say he appeared as shocked as she was. Suddenly, he did something she didn't expect. He smiled at her. 'Mm, I missed you.'

Huh?

'Ah, look at you two,' her mother said behind her. The words were followed by a light clapping sound. 'I can tell you're going to be the first to give me grandkids. Just look at the sparks. I've never seen anything so electric between two people.'

'That's the plan, isn't it, sweetheart?' Ryan gazed at her.

Megan's eyes rounded. Was she dreaming? If so, she'd gladly go back to the fantasy of them kissing – no matter how distasteful it was that her dream included Ryan. Wait, no, she couldn't be dreaming. The slight throb of a hangover beat along her temple and there was no way her own mind would stop a kiss only to replace it with the sound of her mother's voice. Megan's subconscious didn't hate her *that* much.

'Kids?' Ryan prompted when she didn't speak. 'I know how much you want them. I, for one, want a huge family.'

'Oh!' Her mother's clapping got louder. 'I'm going to be a grandma!'

Megan instantly spurred into action. She turned to face her mother, horrified as the woman went screaming into the home to tell the rest of the family. Pointing back at Ryan, her mouth worked, opening and closing several times, before she finally managed to say, 'Don't move. You are under arrest for...' Megan looked around, confused, but then nodded once to support her claim. 'For impersonating a cop's fiancé!'

Hurrying into the house to stop whatever insanity her mother had started, she was accosted with an onslaught of surprise.

'Megs, you're pregnant?' Sasha asked. 'Why didn't you call me?'

'Ah, I can't believe it. Beggin' Megan's going to have a baby!' Zoe grinned.

Kat had arrived while Megan was out on the balcony. Her sister grinned at her, a mischievous look on her face. Megan frowned. Kat was up to something.

'Megan?' Her father's voice might have been much calmer than the others, but she'd have to be blind not to see the spark of tempered excitement in his eyes.

'I'm not pregnant,' Megan stated flatly.

Her father's expression fell some and she was sorry for it.

'But they're going to try,' Beatrice said. 'And all the women on my side of the family are as fertile as the rainforest.'

Megan frowned at her mother. 'No, we're –'

'I spoke too soon,' Ryan said behind her. 'I didn't know it was supposed to be a secret.'

'I thought I told you to stay outside,' Megan growled under her breath.

'Megan,' Kat interrupted. 'I just heard the news. Congratulations on your engagement.'

Megan arched an eyebrow.

'Mom?' Kat continued. 'Don't you think this calls for a reading? Why don't you brew the tea leaves so we can see what's in Megan's future?'

Megan's brow dropped into a grimace.

'Oh, you're right,' Beatrice agreed as she hurried off to the kitchen. 'I thought the exact same thing.'

'Walk with me, Meg,' Kat said, threading her arm and pulling her out to the balcony. 'You look like you need some air.'

'Kat,' Megan said under her breath, 'I don't know what Ryan told you, but I'm not engaged to him.'

'Don't be mad that he told everyone before you had a chance to,' Kat scolded, though she couldn't seem to contain her smile. 'I told him he could.'

'I thought you said you just found out.' Megan crossed her arms.

'It so happens that "just" is a relative word.' Kat gave a know-it-all grin. 'And I did just find out.'

'But we're talking about Ryan Lucas,' Megan hissed. 'How can you believe I'd marry *him*? You, out of all people? You know I don't –'

'I have a motorcycle,' Ryan said. Her senses must really be off because she didn't hear him following them.

'Um.' Kat let go of her arm. 'I'll make sure the two of you have some privacy. Apparently, Mom needs our help planning your pre-wedding honeymoon.'

Megan watched as Kat patted Ryan's arm on the way back into the house. A warm breeze stirred against them as they were left alone on the balcony. Megan glanced around, anything to avoid seeing Ryan. The sting of his kiss was too new on her lips. She hated him and she assured herself that fact hadn't changed, but their kiss had been incredible. Even now her pussy ached. Vibrators only worked for so long. Eventually, a girl needed the feel of the real.

'I give up,' Megan sighed. 'I have no idea what's going on here. I'd say it was a joke, but I don't find you lying to my parents about an engagement very funny. And I'd –'

'I didn't lie,' Ryan interrupted. 'We *are* engaged.'

'Did I wake up in another dimension?'

'You said it yourself. Details are irrelevant.' Ryan's smile stayed intact, but Megan watched him for other signs – those he wouldn't want her to pick up on. His eyes twitched subtly and his weight shifted on his feet.

'Excuse me?'

'We're relatively close to each other in age. I know because Kat told me your thirtieth birthday is coming up and I'm already thirty-one. I'm unmarried, always have been, and I have no kids. I own a classic motorcycle. The doctor gave me a clean bill of health last month and I haven't had so much as a cold for over a year. I shower daily, sometimes more depending on my workout schedule. I –'

'Are you crazy?'

Ryan lifted his hand. 'Ah, don't interrupt. I want to make sure I address all your points.' He furrowed his brow in thought. 'Let's see, motorcycle, close in age, unmarried, showered, disease free, like women – I do like women, by the way.'

'Good for you,' Megan drawled sarcastically. Was he serious? Like she'd even consider a psycho who quoted back the list she'd used to put him off. It had taken her a second to figure out what he was talking about, but, when she did, she was torn between horror and laughter.

'Thanks,' he said, as if she were really having a straightforward conversation with him. 'Let's see. I like kids. Then, last but not least, there's my job.'

Megan stiffened, instantly thinking of the crime-scene photograph he'd taken of her. 'What of it?'

'Only that I have a good-paying steady job, unless crime stops any time soon, in which case I can always go back to freelancing for the paper. They even offered me a staff position.' Ryan smiled at her, looking pleased with himself. 'So that more than takes care of your list of husbandly demands. I have a job *and* a backup job.'

Megan didn't readily speak. So that was his angle. He was blackmailing her. But why? What did he get out of it? A fiancée? Sexual favours? No, that seemed too crass. She glanced at the window leading into the house.

Seeing one of her sisters walk by, she came up with an idea. 'Who else have you told?'

'No one really. My parents both died when I was younger and I don't speak to my remaining uncle much. I think it's been five years since I've seen him. He needed money and, when he found out I didn't have any, he disappeared. He's not much on keeping in touch. The last I heard he was strung out somewhere in Amsterdam trying to get a job in the red-light district as a male performer. Apparently, even balding middle-aged men with a drug habit have a fan base there.'

That was it! That was his motivation. He was obsessed with finding a family, even if he had to hijack hers. Monday at the crime scene he'd kept going on and on about her family – how he'd met Kat and Zoe, but not Ella and Sasha. He wanted a family. First, he befriended Kat. Then, he tried to befriend her. When that didn't work, he turned to blackmail. Now the only question was, what kind of a psycho was he? A harmless needy loser? Or a dangerous sociopath who would see them all murdered in their beds so he could play house?

'I see,' she said at last. Megan didn't get a sociopath vibe off him, but that didn't mean he wasn't one. Those kinds of criminals often adapted to give the appearance of societal perfection, becoming just what everyone needed them to be. 'Very well.'

Ryan looked as if he didn't believe she'd said it. He wasn't very good at the blackmail thing. Though the look did make her think he was just a sorry loser and not a mastermind criminal. 'Yeah? Really?'

'It's what you want, isn't it?' Megan crossed her arms over her chest. Damn, but her nipples stung.

Unsure what she was going to do with this turn of events, she did know things would go a lot easier for everyone if the crime-scene photo stayed out of the newspapers. Not many things scared her and Ryan was no exception. At worst, she'd have to hold out until the trials were over. In that time, she'd study him, learn all she could about him and then deal with him accordingly.

'Hey.' Kat slid open the balcony door, her finger hooked through two teacup handles. 'Mom wants you both to drink these.'

'What is it?' Ryan asked.

'Tea.' Kat laughed and shook her head as Ryan started to decline. 'You have to. She's going to read your future in the leaves. She says it works better when the person who she's reading drinks from the cup as they think of their future and themselves, as opposed to her concentrating on the person or situation as she drinks it herself.'

'Is this for real?' Ryan glanced at Megan.

She met his eyes, not answering. She took the tea from Kat and gulped back the hot liquid. It burnt her mouth, sending fire down her throat, but she refused to let her suffering show. Her cup empty, she gave a small gasp. Then, mumbling under her breath, she said, 'I need a beer. If I'm going to be forced to do this, I might as well not remember doing it.'

Ryan's knees weakened as soon as Megan left him alone with Kat. His heart beat fast and he felt as if the wind had been knocked out of his lungs. Megan wasn't happy. Could he really blame her though? He'd weaselled his way into her life, become her fiancé, told her parents and talked about making babies.

I'm insane, he thought. There is no other way to explain it. I've gone crazy.

'I think it went rather well.' Kat slapped him on the back.

'Well?' Ryan choked. Tea sloshed over the side of his cup, running hot down the back of his hand. 'I can't believe I let you talk me into this. It's crazy. I just declared myself engaged to a woman who can't stand to be in the same room as me. She's in there getting drunk to forget I exist.'

'Hey, look on the bright side.' Kat tilted her head towards the edge of the balcony. 'She didn't throw you over the edge. It's a pretty good start.'

'This was a stupid idea. What were we thinking?' Crossing over, he leant to look over the side of the building. From the angle, it felt almost as if he could step upon the stone wall and walk down. Gravity pulled his hair as he watched people walking through the narrow street below. He wished he had super powers and could fly down into the oblivion of the city. 'She will never love me.'

'Love?' Kat asked. When he looked at her, her face paled. 'Oh, Ry –'

'I said *like*,' he lied. 'She will never like me. Not like this. Never like this. What were we thinking?'

'I'll tell her I did it. I told our parents the news before you got here and you were too confused not to go along with it.' Kat paused. 'No, that won't work. She'll ignore you again. We need something. What did she say? Anything?'

'She said OK.'

'OK? Are you sure it was OK?' Kat asked.

'She said, "Very well".'

'Oh, that's not good. OK would have been OK, but very well is not very well.' Kat frowned, rubbing the bridge of her nose. 'I'll need to get Zoe to help me and maybe Sasha. Mom's planning a big trip for everyone – everyone but Ella. She couldn't make it home after all.'

He said nothing.

'Can you get the next month off from work?' Kat asked.

Ryan nodded. 'The captain called me into his office this morning when I dropped off the museum crime-scene photos and said they'd hired some new guys to take some of my workload. They're training them to weed out the ones who won't stick with it. If I didn't know better, I would think I was being punished for something, but really they're just giving me a break since I've been doing the work of three men.'

'Perfect. I'll convince Mom to pick a place out of the city, somewhere romantic and secluded, so you two can get plenty of alone time. Vincent's his own boss and can do whatever he wants, so I'll make him come with us. You could use a guy around to back you up. If he complains about missing work, I'll just buy him a bug-catching net.'

'Where is Vincent, by the way? I thought you said he was coming today.' Ryan glanced inside, only to find Sasha and Zoe staring back at him, grinning. Zoe lifted her hand, wiggling her fingers in a little wave.

'Oh, something to do with dignitaries and African fire ants.' Kat waved her hand dismissively. 'All I know is I sent him a naked picture earlier on his cell phone, so he'll be home on time tonight.'

Ryan chuckled.

'Hey, a girl's gotta do what a girl's gotta do to get her husband's notice.' Kat winked. 'I know he loves me, but I swear I'm the only woman in the world who has to fight a bunch of bugs for her husband's attention.'

'Vincent would give it all up for you,' Ryan said quietly. 'I've seen it in the way he looks at you – once that distracted look he gets wears off, that is.'

Kat gave a small girlish giggle. 'It is adorable, isn't it?'

'Yeah. Adorable.' Ryan's tone was dry.

'Oh, sorry, forgot. I'll save that talk for the girlfriends.' Kat cleared her throat. 'OK, so here's the plan. We will go in. Ignore Megan for the most part. She's drinking and surly. The goal right now is to get to know my parents. Don't worry, they will all love you. Dad likes anyone who he thinks makes his daughters happy and Mom just likes everyone. We will have dinner, Megan will drink too much and you will get her home on your motorcycle.'

'I don't have a motorcycle.'

Kat grinned, reached into her pocket and pulled out a

set of keys. 'You do for tonight. I have a friend dropping his bike off in front of the building for you to use. This is the spare key. Just make sure you don't crash. Jack will kill me if anything happens to it.'

'I don't have a licence to drive a motorcycle,' he insisted.

'Well, don't tell Megan that. She's a cop and wouldn't think twice about having you arrested for it.' Kat giggled. 'Now, gulp that tea and get inside. If I know Mom, she'll have nothing but glowing things to say about your future with our Megan.'

Chapter Three

'Ohhh.' Beatrice's loud sigh fell over her family as she turned a teacup in her hand, staring down into its depths. 'This is not exactly what I ... Oh. Hmm. Well? Maybe, but, oh.'

Megan blinked, looking up from her place at the table. She slouched back in her chair, her feet sprawled forwards. The dinner Zoe had prepared for them – a masterpiece of garlic zucchini, baked tortellini and bread with basil-flavoured olive oil for dipping – had been devoured to the last bite. Megan especially enjoyed the intense ruby-red wine her chef sister had brought from the Italian restaurant she worked at. The liquor left her feeling warm and sleepy, not to mention the dulling effect it had on the arousal Ryan stirred inside her with his surprisingly expert kiss.

Her mother shook her head, worrying her lower lip as she stared from one teacup to the other. 'They could have gotten bumped sitting on the countertop. I should have read them right away.'

'Dinner was ready,' Douglas said. 'No tea readings during dinner.'

'That's *your* rule, dear.' Beatrice frowned, tilting the cups around, still studying them.

'It was a fair trade. I gave up reading newspapers at the table.' Douglas winked at Megan. She knew her father only read the papers to annoy her mother and get her to stop the nightly tea readings. 'Besides, Zoe's cooking is always well worth our full attention.'

Kat and Sasha laughed uncontrollably from the opposite side of the table. The two of them had been cracking jokes at Zoe and Megan's expense all night. It was clear they were drunk by the way they swayed in their chairs, hopping up and down excitedly each time they found something amusing.

Feeling Ryan's gaze on her, Megan turned to him. His soft eyes and easy smile caught her attention and held it. He hadn't said much to her since coming inside with Kat, but he said plenty to her parents until both of them seemed completely enchanted by the man.

Wine coursed through her veins, pleasantly hazing her senses. Her lids felt heavy, her muscles relaxed and the pressure of Ryan's touch haunted her mouth. He was everything she told herself she didn't want. Maybe it was the liquor, or perhaps the fact she'd been so long without a lover, but the thought of sleeping with Ryan made her heart beat just a little faster. She clenched her thighs together, as they again sparked to life, and tried to get her sex to stop aching. The more she fought her arousal, the more erotic notions curled in her brain.

Ryan's breathing deepened, matching hers. The sound of her sister's laughter faded. If she leant up in her chair, she'd be able to touch his leg under the table. His pants hugged his body, giving away the strong muscles of his thighs. Megan flexed her hand, pressing it to her own leg. She imagined what it would feel like to frisk him, standing behind him as she ran her fingers along the inside of his leg, reaching his balls. And then to push forwards, cupping his shaft in her hands until his cock became so hard it strained the material covering it.

Or maybe he'd frisk her, pressing her down like a dangerous criminal. One hand to her back, keeping her still, as he jerked her pants down to expose the wet lips of her pussy. His free hand would release his erection, stroking the length so it was good and hard. Megan tried to suppress the hunger, the impulsive desire, the ache of unfulfilled passions. She began to lean forwards, but Zoe's voice stopped her, dragging her hazy mind back to reality.

'Shh!' Zoe waved her hands at their two giggling

sisters to get them to be quiet. 'What is it, Mom? What do you see?'

'Yeah, Mom, what do the voices tell you?' Sasha whispered, not too quietly.

'Don't go to the light,' Kat added, causing another fit of giggling.

Megan took a deep breath, shaking herself out of her stupor. She'd forgotten Ryan's blackmail as she stared at him. But now, it came back to her as Zoe's words brought her attention to the teacups.

'I . . .' Beatrice frowned. She looked up at Megan glancing between her daughter and Ryan, shaking her head. 'I'll do it again.'

'Why? What does it say?' Megan asked, sitting forwards. By the look on her mother's face, the leaves said the truth. They said she was not destined to marry Ryan and bear him children. She didn't need a fortune teller to know that much.

'It's unclear.' Beatrice picked up the cups and hurried towards the kitchen.

Megan knew her mother was lying. For one thing, the woman was a horrible liar, perhaps one of the worst. For the second, in all the years Megan could remember, her mother never claimed she was unable to read what the tea leaves supposedly said.

'Mom probably doesn't want to be the one to tell Megan she's going to have twelve kids.' Sasha laughed, snorting as she fell over in her chair.

'Oh, can you . . . ?' Kat's laughter joined Sasha's in a fit of hyperventilation. 'Can you see Megan and . . . ?'

'Twelve kids?' Sasha finished. She lifted her hands in an obvious attempt to imitate her sister, waving them in the air and screaming softly in a panic.

'OK, I think you two have had too much wine.' Douglas reached over to take their glasses away.

Megan grabbed her own before her father decided to confiscate it as well.

'Mm, it's late,' Kat said, stretching her arms. 'Anyone want to share a cab? My rich husband is buying.'

'Me,' Sasha said. 'I'm a broke college girl.'

'I'll take you up on that. I'm a broke chef.' Zoe stood from the table.

'I've got a bike,' Ryan turned to Megan, 'and I haven't been drinking. I'll take you home, sweetheart.'

Megan instantly shook her head. Her blood was too heated with fantasies of him. Tonight was not the night to be alone with Ryan, let alone on the back of a motorcycle, straddling a hard leather seat as the engine vibrated beneath her. 'No, that's OK. I'll get a ride with Kat.'

'Mm, no, you two are probably only going to meet up later anyway,' Kat said. 'Ryan can give you a ride home.'

If her family wasn't looking at her expectantly, their tired eyes curious as to why she would refuse, she would have protested more. Megan thought of the picture, of Jersey St Claud. She could not afford her credibility to be in question because of a stupid mistake. St Claud was guilty and she was going to make sure he was put away for a long, long time.

All this because I stepped on a rock some cave dweller carved centuries ago.

'So long as I'm not keeping you from anything,' Megan said reluctantly. Slowly she stood.

'Nothing at all.' Ryan grinned, revealing the full depth of his boyish charm. 'I'm all yours.'

'Wonderful,' Megan drawled, tossing her glass back to finish her drink. Just wonderful.

Megan whistled, waving her arm as a cab sped by, but the car didn't stop. The street wasn't as busy as it had been during the day. A few couples walked, arm in arm, through the heavy spotlights of the streetlamps and into the surrounding shadows to fade away.

Her sisters' cab had just turned the corner and disappeared from view, leaving her alone with Ryan. Megan watched for another cab, but none came. Frowning, she began to walk along the street.

'What are you doing?' Ryan asked. 'I thought I was taking you home.'

'Listen, buddy, I might be obligated to go along with this, but that doesn't mean I'm going to ride on the back of your motorcycle.' Megan paused, shivering as she imagined how it would feel to have his body pressed to hers, her clit vibrating with the purr of the engine until she climaxed. She glanced at the only motorcycle on the street, parked before the building. Green and orange flames were painted over a deep-purple tank. It was a custom bike, one that clearly took many hours and a lot of money to build. Her voice weaker, but still harsh, she continued, 'And let you take me home so you can fuck me.'

For the briefest of moments, his expression said, 'Why not?' but he quickly hid it under a blank mask. 'Who says I planned on fucking you tonight? Maybe I'm not in the mood, especially after the way you acted all evening.'

'The way *I* acted?' Megan gave a short laugh. At least he didn't try to protest desiring her.

'I felt you kissing me back.' Ryan stepped up to her until their bodies were close. His words whispered along her flesh, a teasing caress that left her wanting more. 'And then you sat there, brooding and distant the whole night. I know you want me. I heard you moan my name.'

Had she said his name? Megan couldn't remember. How could she deny something she couldn't recall?

'I felt you squirm against my cock.' He grabbed her hip, jerking her hard against him.

Awareness struck her as she felt the stiff press of his erection. There was no family, no watching eyes to stop them this time.

Ryan rocked, moving his hips in a sinfully delicious rhythm. 'Maybe it's you who wants to fuck me.'

Megan tried to deny it, but a weak sound left her speechless. A car drove by, only to leave them in silence. She vaguely noticed a group passing in the distance, their bodies small blurry visions along the edge of her sight. The light from her parents' building outlined his head as he held her. A guard was inside, perhaps watching them even now on his security monitor.

'Let's find out, shall we?' Ryan's lids dipped low over his eyes. His hand slid between their bodies, tugging at her jeans until they were unzipped. Megan's head rolled back as he thrust his fingers forwards, bypassing her cotton panties to delve along her naked sex. Stunned that he'd made such a bold move, she didn't think to protest. A finger glided between her wet folds, blessedly pushing along her clit in a hard stroke. Her jeans kept him from touching deeper, but he'd found the centre bud and, for the moment, it was enough. Rubbing it in circles, he groaned, 'Ah, there's my answer.'

Megan didn't think, as she acted on pure instinct. Grabbing his shoulders, she thrust her hips forwards only to be rewarded with a deep gratification. Her mouth wide, she breathed heavily, leaning so that their lips nearly touched. She denied her mouth, instead reaching for his waist. Pushing his sweater out of the way, she unbuttoned his pants, tugging violently at them so they unzipped. It was Ryan's turn to moan as she grabbed his thick cock. Silk boxers caused her hand to glide as she fondled him.

'Ah, so what are we going to do about this?' He looked towards the street to where the motorcycle was parked.

Megan pulled away and his hand seemed reluctant to disentangle itself from her jeans. Grabbing his fly, she turned, leading him by his crotch towards a small alley along the side of the building. A combination of wine and passion made her stumble as her knees weakened. She caught herself, walking fast into the shadowed alcove of brick and cement. The place was unromantic, stale and dank and she couldn't care less. All she knew was Ryan's nearness, the longing for his kiss, the smell of his cologne.

Stopping a few feet in, where the streetlights didn't reach, she let go of him. Determined, she pushed her jeans off her hips. They fell to her ankles, trapped by her boots. Her body was so hot she didn't notice the evening temperature against her naked skin. Ryan made a weak noise, moving as if he would kiss her. But, Megan had other plans. 'I'll tell you what we are going to do about this. I'm going to turn around and you're going to fuck me. Afterwards, we are never going to mention it again.'

Megan turned, not waiting for an answer. Alcohol was thick in her veins, and, though it would be easy to blame her actions on inebriation, she was too pragmatic to lie to herself. She wanted this moment, whatever it was, however unwise.

She spread her legs as wide as she could while pressing her palms flat against the brick wall. Starved for fulfilment, her pussy was wet and ready. Besides, she couldn't think of any better position given their circumstances. It wasn't like she would lie on the dirty cement ground.

Ryan came up behind her, his hand stroking her outer thigh moments before the thick probing tip of his erection met her pussy from behind. The back of his hand brushed next to the intimate curve of her ass, as he moved himself along her folds, gliding up and down as he found the perfect angle for entrance.

Suddenly, he thrust, stretching her from behind, his actions as needy and raw as she felt. The position didn't allow for deep penetration, but that didn't stop him from withdrawing and pounding forwards with severe force. All her desires centred on her sex, even as her breasts ached to be touched, her body yearned to be free of clothes. The urgency of her need superseded such concerns and she met his hips, pushing back from the wall almost violently.

Heavy grunts sounded over the alleyway. A car passed on the street, briefly illuminating them with its headlights. Megan reached between her thighs, touching her clit, encouraging her body to find release. The arm holding her back from the wall began to sting and her muscles were tired, but she didn't care. She needed this too badly. It had been so long and she felt as if she might explode.

Megan gave a soft cry, frustrated and excited as she neared her peak. Ryan was holding both hips, moving in and out at a jackrabbit pace.

'Oh, oh,' Megan gasped for air. Finally, she met with sweet release as her orgasm caused her to shake. She worked her hands against the uneven wall, holding herself up as she came. Ryan kept moving, pumping in greedy abandonment until finally he grunted, pulling his cock out at the last minute as he spilled his seed along her inner thigh.

His hands fell from her hips and he stumbled back. Panting heavily, Megan reached for her jeans, weakly pulling them up. Only when she was partially dressed, her jeans zipped but not buttoned, did she say, 'This never happened.'

Her eyes met Ryan's. His hands stopped moving on his pants and all pleasure faded from his gaze. Megan stumbled towards the street, digging in her pocket and glad that the cash she'd stuck in it was still there and not lost in the alley. Without looking back, she hailed a cab. It stopped and she hurriedly got inside, barking a command at the driver. Only when it turned the corner did she allow herself to relax.

Sex had left her weak, but that wasn't why she trembled. How could she have given in to temptation? How could she have had sex with Ryan? Why now? After so long knowing him and denying any attraction to him?

'You all right, ma'am?' the cabbie asked.

'Just drive,' she growled, not wanting to make small talk.

Moodily, she glared out the window. The cityscape zoomed past, but she didn't see it. No, her mind was still outside her parents' apartment building, lost in the terrible deeds of what was possibly the biggest mistake of her life.

Ryan watched Megan leave him, not bothering to chase after her. What would he say to her if he did make her stop? Sated flesh did not necessarily make for a satisfied soul. Her cold words left him feeling empty, as did the emotionless way their bodies had joined in loveless passion.

Why had he given in to his desire? Why couldn't he have held off, seduced her? Why couldn't he have made her beg for him? Instead, she said fuck and he jumped to it, obeying like the lovesick fool that he clearly was.

'Nothing is going as planned,' he said to himself. 'Damn it, Ryan, you are an idiot.'

Glancing down, he fastened his jeans. The hard press of metal dug into his hip as he walked and he pulled the motorcycle keys from his pocket. Going to the bike, he debated leaving it where it was – in the safe viewing of the security camera outside Megan's parents' building. Then again, maybe a ride would do him some good. He could use a clear head.

He climbed on the motorcycle and leant over to stick the key in. It didn't fit. With a frown, he turned it over and tried again. There were no other bikes around. Ryan groaned. 'Ah, come on. I don't need this. Not tonight.'

'What the hell do you think you're doing?' a man yelled. 'Get off my fuckin' bike!'

Ryan flinched, instantly swinging his leg back over the motorcycle so he could stand. He turned just in time to see the angry fist that went with the enraged voice. It slammed into his eye, sending him reeling back on to the hard concrete. His neck snapped, shooting pain down his spine. He didn't move, his body tense as he waited for the beating to continue. The distant sound of annoying female laughter rang over him, followed by the revving of an engine. A strange relief washed over him as tyres squealed and the motorcycle zoomed down the street.

Holding his head, Ryan groaned, pushing up from the sidewalk. Already, the tender flesh around his eye tightened as if beginning to swell. He ran his hands through his hair, glancing back and forth over the street but there wasn't another cab within view. Somehow, the blackened eye was much easier to bear than Megan's hurried departure. Grumbling, he said, 'A perfect end to a fucked-up day. What the hell was I thinking?'

Chapter Four

'Hey, Rya – omigod . . .' Kat's words tapered off as she looked at Ryan's face.

Her hair hung messily around her shoulders and her cheeks were flushed. Since she wore a white lab coat, buttoned all the way down, and was standing barefoot in the long hall leading back to her husband's office, Ryan could easily guess what she and Dr Richmond had been up to.

Reaching for his cheek, she hesitated. They were too far apart for her to touch him anyway. 'I can't believe Megan hit you!'

'What?' Ryan automatically lifted his hand to touch the tender skin around his eye. As he'd first suspected, he'd developed a pretty mean bruise.

'I'm calling her. I guess I knew she would be a little upset, but to beat you up . . .' Kat frowned. 'You didn't hit her back, did you?'

'You think I could lift a hand to hurt –'

'You're right, I'm sorry, you would never hurt Megs.'

'Kat, no. You have it wrong.' Shaking his head, he reached into his pocket to toss the motorcycle key in his friend's direction. She caught it, frowning in confusion. 'This was a gift from the owner of the motorcycle I tried to ride home last night. Megan took a cab.'

'Jack hit you?' Kat's frown turned into a scowl.

'I have a feeling it wasn't your friend's bike. The key didn't fit and the owner decked me for trying.' Ryan gave a short laugh, moving slowly towards her.

Old floorboards creaked beneath his shoes and the musty smell – a combined scent of aged parchment and settled dust – grew stronger.

The DJP Scientific Department of Entomological Research was tucked away between two buildings and nearly impossible to find but for the plaque outside the front door. The small square foyer was empty except for a wooden desk with a borderline antique yellow corded telephone and wooden chair. Kat had decorated the white walls with large photographs of insects and what looked like a close-up of someone's waxed smarmy moustache. Every time Ryan asked her about the facial hair, she would laugh and change the subject.

'What kind of bike was it?'

'Not sure. It was purple, orange and green flamed. Looked like a custom job.'

'Jack can't afford a custom job like that. He has one of those old orange ones. I forget what they're called.' Kat made a face. 'And there weren't any other motorcycles there?'

'No. Not that I could see.'

'Don't worry, I'll have a word with Jack about that.' Kat's lips pursed tightly together in anger. 'So help me, if he forgot...'

'Don't worry about it,' Ryan dismissed. 'The walk home actually did me good.'

'You walked the whole way?' Kat asked in shock.

'Not the whole way. I took the subway. For some reason, I couldn't find a cab. It was the strangest thing.'

'What did Megan say when you found out it was the wrong bike? Was she mad? She didn't try to arrest you, did she? Did she think you were trying to steal it?' Kat sighed heavily, only to yell over her shoulder, 'Hey, bug man! Get dressed, I need you.'

Ryan grimaced. He didn't need to know Kat's husband was naked in the back room.

'I'm a step ahead of you,' Vincent said.

Ryan heard the man's voice before he actually saw the doctor. Though clearly rich by his carriage and clothes, there was an easygoing, almost absentmindedness to the entomologist. Vincent had been born into money and retained the enunciated speech pattern and stiff posture to prove it. But his brown eyes didn't hold judgement and he always had a ready smile.

As he neared, Vincent looked at his wife, unashamed by the adoration on his face. 'Have I told you I worship you, Margaret?'

Kat laughed, leaning up to kiss her husband briefly. 'You're lucky I like you, bug man. I look nothing like the dowdy Margaret.' Then, pushing her hand to his cheek, she turned Vincent's head towards Ryan.

Instantly, the man gasped. 'Megan hit you? When Kat told me what you two had instigated, I knew Megan would be upset, but –'

'No, no, she didn't do that,' Kat said. 'But I'm surprised she didn't.'

'Hey,' Ryan grumbled.

'What? You're the one chasing after her,' Kat defended. 'You had to assume there would be a few bumps and bruises along the way. It is Megan after all.'

'And handcuffs,' Vincent said almost thoughtfully.

Ryan stiffened in surprise. He looked at Kat to see if the good doctor was joking or not.

Kat looked momentarily stunned, but quickly got over it. Laughing, she said, 'Darling, I had no idea you were so kinky.'

'What?' Vincent blinked. Then, as if catching on, he said, 'No, I meant she would arrest Ryan for – hey, wait. Yes, you do know that I'm . . .' He paused, giving Ryan a sheepish grin. 'Never mind. We'll discuss it later.'

'Thanks.' Ryan chuckled, gladly taking the man's dismissal. Normally, he wouldn't care if the couple made jokes about a kinky sex life. If they were getting it on, more power to them. He wished them all the happiness and pleasure in the world. But the last thing he wanted under the current weight of his situation was to think about anything related to sex. After his deed with Megan in the dank alleyway the night before, he wasn't sure whether to be turned on by the memory or mortified by the fact that their first time together was so sordid.

'I believe you said I was needed?' Vincent prompted.

'Tell Ryan what he can do to win Megan,' Kat said. 'Give him some man advice.'

'Ah.' Vincent curled his lip in disbelief. 'Do you remember how suave I was with you?'

'Oh, yeah, good point.' Kat patted Vincent's arm, before telling Ryan, 'Don't have her look for poisonous spiders with you. That does *not* make for a sexy first date.'

Ryan arched a questioning brow.

'Don't ask,' Vincent said. 'She won't let me forget it as it is.'

'Oh, but I do have promising news.' Kat grinned. 'Mom called early this morning. She was up late last night and booked our trip. Before you protest, I told her you'd insist on paying her back for the ticket.'

'Thanks,' Ryan answered earnestly. Kat knew him well; he wouldn't want to freeload off her family.

'Though, I did give in and say she could pay for the lodging. I figured, since she was paying for all her kids as it was, there was no point in making you pick up an eighth of the bill just for pride's sake. And I got the sisters on our side. They are happy to help bring Megan down.' Kat laughed.

Ryan sighed.

'Oh, don't look at me like that. You know what I mean. Anyway, Sasha's free, so she will go with us right away. Zoe will meet us in a week. That's when she can get off work. It's all set. The parents love you. My sisters and I won't let Megs run you off. Vincent is there for moral support, aren't you, honey?'

'Whatever you say, dear,' Vincent answered, even as he gave Ryan an understanding smile.

'So get packed,' Kat said, 'because we are going to Montana.'

'Montana?' Megan questioned, scratching the back of her head. Her mother stood in the doorway to her small apartment. It was early afternoon, but Megan hadn't bothered to change out of her charcoal-coloured cotton pyjama pants and grey T-shirt with 'NYPD' across the chest. She stepped out of the way and shut the door behind Beatrice as her mother walked into her home. 'However did you come up with Montana?'

'You'll love it.' Beatrice grinned happily, as she dug into her oversized red leather handbag. It was more of a small suitcase than a purse, with a zipper along the bottom edge that opened to expand the amount it could carry. At Megan's coffee table, she began unloading the contents, taking out everything from a mini-first-aid kit and tissues to makeup and a small photo album of family pictures. 'I printed some information for you to look over.'

Megan flopped down on her couch. Her apartment reminded her of an unseductive bachelor pad. It was the kind of place poor male college students coveted, minus the keg and single co-eds. The cheap black pleather of her couch stuck to the back of her thighs whenever she was sweaty from working out. It matched her over-stuffed chair. Posters of 1990 cop movies lined the walls, held in place with thumbtacks. She'd only put them up to cover the yellowed paint. When she first moved in, she had a vague plan to renovate. It never came to fruition. The fact the tacky décor annoyed her mother was just a bonus. Beatrice offered to decorate it for her almost every time she came over.

'Where did I put them?' Beatrice mumbled, drawing Megan's attention back to the gigantic purse. 'Ah, here they are. Look.'

Megan didn't move as her mother shook a stack of papers in her direction. Beatrice wasn't fazed by her daughter's unenthusiastic response, immediately moving to sit beside Megan, as she flipped through the pile.

'There is horseback riding –'

'Do I look like I've ever been on a horse?' Megan drawled.

'I think you'd like it.' Beatrice placed a picture on Megan's lap. It was of a woman and two kids on horseback. 'You carry a gun and so do cowboys.'

'There is that.' Sarcasm dripped from her words.

'We can rock climb, ride bikes through the mountains, hike, raft –'

'Get lime disease from the ticks,' Megan chipped in. 'Get buried by an avalanche.'

Her words were a lot nicer than some of the scenarios her cop brain came up with. Seclusion, wilderness, people who lived isolated in the mountains – they were a recipe for crime and militias.

'Don't be silly.' Beatrice laughed, though the sound was strained. 'It is summertime and we'll have Vincent with us. If anyone knows how to avoid bugs, it's him. Besides, you will be busy with Ryan.'

'Yeah, Mom, about that . . .' Megan refused to think about screwing Ryan in the alleyway the night before. She'd spent all morning trying to push the memory from her brain. 'I have to tell you something about the engagement.'

'Oh, honey, I already know what you are going to say,' Beatrice said.

'What? The tea leaves?' Megan asked in surprise.

'No, it's the mother in me. I know you're feeling guilty about not telling us you were seeing someone, and for probably ditching us on Sunday dinners to go out with your man, but don't worry. Daddy and I are happy for you. Actually, I didn't want to say anything because I know you were busy, but your father hasn't been feeling very well lately and this news has done wonders for him. He is so looking forward to this trip. I think he's happy to finally have sons to go on vacation with. This trip is the perfect medicine – family all together and happy, seeing two of our precious daughters happily settled.' Beatrice gave a contented sigh, placing her hand over her heart as she gazed meaningfully at her daughter.

Megan swallowed. Her father was sick? OK, no guilt there. Even if her mother did have a tendency to blow certain things out of proportion – like health issues. It wasn't a far stretch for Beatrice to turn a simple cold into the Ebola virus.

Beatrice suddenly looked at her watch. 'Oh, I have to go pick up our tickets at the travel agent. You keep these –' she handed over the printed brochures '– and be ready to leave at four tomorrow morning. We'll meet at our house and all go to the airport together.'

'Four?'

'We have to get there early. You will be a dear and tell Ryan, won't you?' Beatrice asked. 'I forgot to get his phone number last night when I talked to Kat about the travel plans.'

'Um.' Megan frowned; she didn't have Ryan's number. She didn't even know where the man lived. Maybe that was a good thing. She didn't want him along, did she? Her body twinged with a curious sensation. Longing? Disgust? Passion? Disdain? She couldn't be sure.

'Bye, honey,' Beatrice said. 'I'll see you tomorrow.'

'Bye.'

Megan waited until the door closed before pushing the horseback-riding picture off her lap. Trust her mother to plan a vacation in one day. Frowning, Megan took the first page off the stack her mother had left. The print-out date in the corner was over a year old. Her mother probably had a huge file of possible vacations. 'Came up with it last night, huh?'

Megan shook her head and stood up. She crossed through the small living room to her bedroom, containing a queen-size bed with silver railing next to an empty nightstand. She grabbed a giant duffel bag out of the closet. A few T-shirts, hooded sweatshirt, jeans, pyjama pants and shorts was all she needed for the trip. Well, those and toiletries. She wasn't one to fret about packing and was done in less than ten minutes. She carried the bag to her living room but hesitated as she set it by the door. The strangest urge to pack something pretty came over her.

'Well, Mom does like to eat at nice restaurants,' Megan said to herself, refusing to admit it wasn't her mother she was thinking to impress. 'I might as well bring one dress with me. Just in case.'

'I need you to call your friend and tell him about tonight,' Megan announced without preamble as she walked past her sister into Kat's Upper East Side home. The penthouse was a vast contrast to where Megan lived. When people said Kat had married into money, they weren't exaggerating. Located on Seventy-Eighth Street, the beautiful pre-war building was lined with shrubs and trees. The home had more space than any two people could ever need, but Kat was doing her best to artfully decorate it with her photographs.

The living room was immaculately clean from the pristine white walls to the polished wood floors – something Megan knew Kat hadn't done. Vincent probably hired a housekeeper. The man doted on her sister, which was fine with Megan. He *should* dote on Kat. If he didn't, she'd beat the crap out of him. Kat might drive her to insanity, but Megan still adored her.

The living room was nearly thirty feet long and eighteen feet wide, with towering ceilings. Large casement windows looked southwards over the city. Floor-to-ceiling dark curtains accented the minimalist furniture. A wood-burning fireplace dominated one wall, centred between two built-in bookcases.

An oversized canvas filled one of the walls. Megan knew the work well. It was filled with pictures Kat had taken of the sisters throughout their lives. The younger years started in the middle and spiralled out as they grew. It was a testament to their lives, a work in progress. The newest addition was all of them at Kat's wedding – the bride in sexy white and the sisters in distinctly different dark-blue gowns.

Turning her attention back to Kat, Megan insisted, 'I need you to call your friend. Mom doesn't have his number and supposedly Dad's sick and is looking forward to having two men along on vacation.' Megan took a deep loud breath. 'Or something like that. Mom said it better. All I know is, I don't have a choice. So you have to call your friend.'

'Don't you mean your fiancé?' Kat giggled.

'I was drunk last night, Kat, but I'm sober this morning. I know you have an idea of what is going on here, if not the full picture. I can read it on your face.' Megan put her hands on her hips. 'I also know you get some sort of twisted sisterly pleasure out of seeing me squirm. Fine. Whatever. But don't pretend like you are innocent. I'm a cop and I eat pretenders for breakfast.'

'Ew. That doesn't sound very appetising.' Kat's disturbingly angelic expression stayed intact. Maybe that was why Megan was so good at reading people – she'd learnt to tell when her sisters were trying to pull one over on her.

'I know Mom told you the plans. Call your friend.' Megan glanced around. 'Tell him the plans.'

'What? You drove all the way here to tell me to make a call? Why not use the phone?'

'I . . .' Megan hesitated. 'I did call. You didn't answer.'

Kat reached into her pocket and pulled out her new pink cellular phone. She flipped it open. 'Funny, I don't see a missed call. Try another one, Megs.'

'Fine. I need a dress.' Megan knew she'd been caught in the lie, so she started another one. 'Mom wants me to bring one, but it seems the last one I bought went out of style when I was still in High School, unless you want me to wear my bridesmaid gown again.' She glanced at the large canvas only to see all five Matthews sisters' faces smiling back at her.

'A dress?' Kat grinned, just as Megan knew she would. 'Well, it seems you're not too adverse to Ryan, after all. Did something more happen between you two?'

Megan frowned as Kat lifted a playful brow. So, Ryan had bragged to Kat about what they'd done. 'So, we had sex. Big freaking deal.'

Kat's mouth fell open in surprise, but Megan didn't really see it.

'I'd been drinking. You saw me last night.' Megan ran her hand over her hair, smoothing it unnecessarily towards her bun. 'It's his fault anyway that I've been celibate and it is just as well he fixed the problem.'

'You've been celibate?' Kat's eyes rounded even more even though Megan wasn't sure how that was possible. 'Why?'

'Well, he took the picture and . . .' Megan motioned her hand in dismissal. 'Do you have a dress for me or not? I promised Mom I'd bring something nice to wear.'

'I can't believe it. I've never seen you flustered. You liked it, didn't you? You liked having sex with Ryan!'

Megan's first impulse was to yell at her to shut her mouth and pull her hair like they were teenagers. But she held back. Barely.

'Or is it that you like *him*?' Kat gave a loud short laugh and clapped her hands. 'Priceless.'

'Listen, Mrs Richmond, are you going to loan me a

designer original or not.' Megan was not amused by the teasing.

'I don't own originals.' Kat wrinkled her nose and stuck out her tongue. 'So neener neener.'

'Grow up.'

'Why? You're adult enough for the both of us.'

'I can't believe he told you. Ugh!' Megan reached out and pressed her hand against Kat's face, pushing back lightly to get her to stop her childish dance. Laughter sounded as her sister dramatically stumbled back only to right herself.

'Who told me what?'

'Ryan. I can't believe he told you about what happened. It's a little creepy, don't you think? You're my sister.'

'Uh, Megs, *you* told me. Just now. You are the creepy.'

'No, I saw it in your expression. You already knew. The man probably tells you everything.'

'Clearly not everything.' Kat giggled. 'Because I would have remembered that.'

'Forget I came by. Forget I told you to call him. Don't call him. In fact, I would consider it a favour if he missed the plane.' Megan turned to go. 'And forget the dress. I don't need it.'

Kat only laughed harder. As she shut the front door, Megan heard her sister holler through the thick wood, 'I can't believe it. The great Meg has finally –'

'Shut up, Katarina!' Megan yelled back, not caring to hear the end of the sentence. She hurried down the small hall to the elevator and pushed the button several times in her irritation. 'Come on!'

The elevator finally dinged and opened. Megan stormed inside, only to continue to take her anger out on the button to the first floor.

Three o'clock in the morning came too early, but Megan refused to spend the night at her parents' house just for an extra half-hour of sleep. But the root of her exhaustion wasn't lack of sleep, but more what had kept her from getting rest. Images of Ryan haunted her fantasies. She wished she could say 'haunted her dreams', but she'd been fully awake when the erotic thoughts occurred.

Unbidden, the feel of Ryan's body had curled around hers, hugging her like a blanket. In her mind, her hand became his hand, drawing up her T-shirt, cupping a breast, tugging her panties low on her hip. As she wiggled on the bed, pleasuring herself with the aid of her realistically shaped vibrator, she longed for the heat of Ryan's body over hers. Even as she orgasmed, the coldness of it left her unsatisfied.

Now, waiting to board their flight, she couldn't stop thinking about it. She'd purposefully taken a seat in the waiting area far enough from the rest of her family not to have to talk to them, but close enough not to be suspicious. But it wasn't her mother, who'd arranged for them to show up at the airport four hours before the plane took off, or her two giggling sisters, who were clearly plotting, or even her snoring father that caused Megan to keep to herself. It was Ryan. He sat next to Vincent, speaking in low tones, too low for her to hear. Megan pretended to sleep, keeping her eyes closed, but every fibre of her being focused on her 'fiancé'.

'Hey,' Kat said. Megan felt a kick at her foot. 'That's us.'

'Wake up, sleepyhead,' Sasha said.

Megan opened her eyes just in time to see her walk past. Just like her, Kat and Sasha wore T-shirts and comfortable sweatpants – Megan in black cotton with white stripes and flared legs, Kat in tighter brown cashmere with pink accents, Sasha in two shades of blue.

'Let's go,' Beatrice said, jolting with excitement as she urged them all to hurry. With hair and makeup firmly in place, their mother looked beautiful and awake and incredibly put together in her long-sleeve black blouse and leopard-print scarf. Megan never understood why people dressed up to get on a plane. Then again, she never dressed up to go anywhere.

'You ready?' Ryan's voice washed over her, sending chills along her flesh.

Of course, she knew she'd have to talk to him on this trip, but the sound of his voice took her by surprise. She blinked, looking up into his tired brown eyes. Stubble grew over his jawline, accenting his strong features. A lightening bruise encircled the bottom of one eye. Since she'd been blamed for it by Sasha that morning when he arrived at their parents' house, Megan knew he'd got the black eye from some misunderstanding.

Her gaze travelled down his arm to his hand. He turned his palm towards her, lifting it ever so slightly as if to offer it to her. She pushed up from the chair, not taking it. When she made a move to pick a small back-pack carry-on off the floor, he was right beside her, lifting it up before she could grab it.

'Allow me,' he said, his voice tight. Before she could speak, he walked away.

'The sooner we get on the plane, the sooner we can go back to sleep,' her father said, lightly touching her arm. He nudged her along with him to get into line. 'Your mother means well, but I think she got us here a little too early.'

'It's impossible to tell these days,' Megan said, wondering why she defended her mother, 'with airport security being so tight.'

'Is everything all right between you and Ryan?' Her father abruptly changed the subject. 'You seem distant from him.'

Megan looked her father over without appearing obvious. He seemed paler than usual and tired. Was there something to her mother's claim that her father wasn't feeling well? Or was it merely bad airport lighting and no sleep? Not willing to take a chance, she lied, 'No, everything is fine. I don't like flying and he's respecting my grumpiness by leaving me be.'

'Ah.' Douglas nodded, as if understanding.

'Tickets,' a flight attendant said.

'Oh, no, here, they're with us, too.' Her mother thrust two tickets at the woman and smiled brightly, as Megan dug out her driver's licence and flashed it at the attendant.

They walked with the other passengers to board the plane. The long hallway curved, separated into metal sections that eventually created a seal around the airplane's door.

Her father paused, letting her step inside first. 'I'm glad we're doing this,' Douglas said. 'It'll be fun. I only wish Ella could make it.'

'Me, too, Dad,' Megan agreed.

The first-class section consisted of a small area of cushy seats. Megan looked at them in longing, knowing what awaited them behind the curtain in their section. Towards the back, her mother motioned at them to hurry. Already Sasha, Kat and Vincent sat in a row of three, Kat in the middle flipping through an airline shopping magazine. Vincent gazed affectionately at his wife and Sasha stared out the small window.

Megan paused, looking from the empty seat next to her mother's purse, to Ryan standing expectantly in the aisle. Both spots were in rows of two seats. Which one would make for the worse travelling companion? Her mother or her pretend fiancé? Before she could snag her father's spot, he moved past her and sat down by his wife. Megan turned her full attention to Ryan.

'Do you want the window?' he asked.

Did he have to look at her like that? All soft and gorgeous? The light scent of his cologne caught her attention. A shiver worked over her, as desire threaded its way through her senses. She brushed past him, not saying a word as she took the window seat. Ryan was slower to follow, sliding in next to her.

A night of unsatisfying desires followed by a morning actively pretending not to notice him became almost too much to deal with. Megan took a deep breath, more aware of the heat coming off Ryan's leg than of the people moving about the cabin. Her family was seated slightly behind them and wouldn't be able to see her face unless she turned or lifted up in her seat. Aside from strangers, whose opinions she didn't care about, no one could see what they were doing.

Ryan's leg shifted and his muscular thigh drew her attention down. It was close and she wanted to touch it, to run her hand up to his cock, to straddle his legs as she rubbed her sex against his lap. A light moan escaped her.

'Megan?' Ryan asked.

Startled by the questioning sound, her eyes darted from his crotch to his gaze. 'I hate flying. I feel sick.' The words were weak, made even more so by the way she fumbled for the shade, pulling the hard plastic over the window to block out the light and hopefully hide her flushed cheeks. Her words weren't a complete lie. She did hate flying. Not because she was scared, but because it was like all the discomfort and unpleasantness of a fifteen-hour bus trip crammed into half the time. Either way, you got the same amount of travel lag, only on an airplane they gave you a bag of five peanuts and a tiny glass of soda.

'Hey, don't worry.' Ryan's hand brushed her knee.

Megan stared at the plastic cover, realising that she must indeed look frightened. But it wasn't takeoff that caused her to shake. She was scared of herself, of what she felt, of what she shouldn't be feeling for the impostor who invaded her life.

'Nothing will happen,' he reassured her.

Nothing? Megan took a deep breath, having a hard

time concentrating. Then, a strange fact came to her: Ryan had power over her and she secretly liked it. There was nothing she could do but wait and see what would happen next. Morally, of course, she resented being forced into an engagement, but, sinfully speaking, she kind of liked that he had the balls to even try blackmailing her.

'How can you know nothing will happen?' Megan found herself asking. She glanced to the strong hand by her knee, remembering what they felt like on her hips as he pulled and pushed with such gentle force. The moment should have been a cold and methodical memory so she couldn't be obsessed by it. Instead, it was all she could think about.

'Tea leaves,' he said.

It took Megan a moment to process his words. Eyes rounding, she looked at his face. He smirked in amusement. Unable to help herself, she gave a small laugh. 'You wouldn't joke about that if it had been your mother who tried to keep you out of the state volleyball game because the tea leaves said she should.'

'Did she succeed?' He leant closer.

Her voice dropped to match his. 'No. I went anyway and we won.'

'So the leaves were wrong.'

'They're never wrong. Just ask Mom.' Megan tilted her chin up. If only she had the power to freeze time. She'd keep him like this, his features shaded to perfection by the light coming in from outside. Tousled hair framed his face, just as it did when they worked late at a crime scene, and the brown of his eyes was sleepily seductive. Bedroom eyes. His lips parted and it would be so easy to slip her tongue along the edge, pushing them open wider. The man did know how to kiss. Airplane bathrooms weren't her idea of a romantic time, but maybe the mile-highers had the right idea.

'What happened?' he asked.

'I was drunk.' Megan knew it was a lie and hated herself for resorting to it, but how else could she explain letting him take her like a back-alley whore?

'At a state championship?' Ryan pulled back, frowning.

'What?' Megan asked. Crap! He is still talking about tea leaves. Concentrate, Megan, concentrate.

'You were drunk at state?'

'Of course I wasn't drunk at state,' Megan snorted. 'I was eighteen. That would have been illegal.'

'But —'

'I'm going to sleep now.' She angled her back towards him and closed her eyes. Crap, crap, crap!

It had to be lack of sleep. That was why she was so shaken. Resting her head against the wall, she tried not to smell him, as she willed the coolness of the plane to soak into her body.

'Megan?' Ryan asked softly.

She didn't move. Let him think she slept.

'Megan?'

Still, she didn't move. All of a sudden, hands brushed her hips. She stiffened in surprise, instantly turning to join her mouth to Ryan's. Her lips parted, inches from his, she stopped as the sound of her seatbelt clicking caught her attention.

'We're about to take off.' Ryan adjusted himself in his seat and grabbed a magazine from the small pocket in front of him. Megan held her breath, waiting, but he didn't look at her again. Leaning back in her seat, she closed her eyes, wishing for the plane ride to be over.

By the time they finished their layover in Colorado and were in line to board the second plane, Megan had imagined Ryan naked in every possible place. There were a few times she would have pulled him into a bathroom stall at the Denver airport had her sisters' banter not brought her back to reality. What was happening to her brain that suddenly all she could think about was ways to get Ryan alone and naked? The more she tried to concentrate on something else, the less she did.

'I keep thinking about the other night,' Ryan whispered into her ear from behind.

Megan blinked, surprised to hear the confession. Her family had already passed by the ticket counter and were on their way to board. They couldn't hear his words.

A hand touched her hip and this time she was sure it wasn't an accident – not like when he fastened her seatbelt, or when they stood in line at the fast-food restaurant for lunch, or when he and Vincent left to buy overpriced coffee from a kiosk.

Ryan squeezed her hip lightly, before grazing his fingers along the side of her ass. 'Do you think we might at least discuss our having sex?'

The flight attendant saved Megan from responding, when she said, 'Sorry, sir, we are not that kind of flight.'

Ryan's hand left Megan's hip and she hurried to board the plane. She couldn't get away from him fast enough. Wanting him was different to knowing he wanted her back and the information was almost too much for her to handle.

Damn you, Ryan, she thought, cursing him in her mind even as her thighs ached for his attentions.

Ryan watched Megan hurry away from him. Giving the flight attendant a sheepish grin, he shrugged as he moved to go after his sexy travelling partner. By the way his erection pressed against his jeans it was a wonder they didn't try to arrest him for bringing a loaded weapon onboard.

And loaded it was.

'Don't worry, sir,' the woman said knowingly behind him. 'We will land in Montana soon enough.'

Ryan gave a short laugh. Several times he had thought Megan might kiss him, but each time she had pulled back. Surely, she felt the electricity snapping between them, the potent sexual fire that needed to be quenched before it ignited them both. In greedy male arousal, he had fantasised about covering their bodies with a blanket so she could rub her steady hands up and down his stiff cock. He would be quiet, he knew he could be. No one would have to know. Too bad it wasn't night-time. Then everyone would be asleep and it could be her head beneath the blanket in place of her hand. Would she do it? Would the law-abiding Megan protest? She hadn't been averse to public lewdness the other night.

Ryan nearly stumbled as he followed her on to the plane, watching her ass beneath the cotton pants. Mumbling a half-hearted apology to the woman whose foot he tripped over, he hurried to take his seat. He opened the overhead bin, grabbed a blanket and threw it down on to his seat before stowing Megan's carry-on.

Seeing Megan's cool steadfast gaze lift from the blanket to look at him, all he managed to say was, 'The last flight was cold.'

Chapter Five

'Finally! I can't believe we're here.' Sasha groaned, throwing her purse down on the lodge-house floor. After the seven-and-a-half-hour flight, they'd been forced to drive another hour and a half in a rented SUV to get to the lodge Beatrice had booked. That trip included a brief stop at a grocery store for supplies. It was only a little after three in the afternoon, but it felt like midnight. 'Now no one wake me until this vacation is over. I just want to sleep forever.'

The large wood cabin consisted of a living room surrounded by beautiful floor-to-ceiling windows – a perfect showcase to a flower-speckled valley leading to the mountainous distance. No signs or fences marred the countryside and, apart from a well-worn path, Megan saw no other signs of human life.

She let her eyes drift over the knotted-pine walls decorated with old black and white miner photographs from the turn of the last century. The ceilings over the living room were high, only to lower over an open kitchen. Dark forest green and deep reds accented the furniture and gave a 'country' feel. A large stone fireplace dominated the wall opposite the kitchen.

'Wow, look at this place!' Kat instantly ran for the open stairway where, like the rest of the lodge, the steps were made of light wood.

'It's nice.' Vincent, who was stuck carrying in the ladies' suitcases along with the other two men, appeared less enthusiastic.

'And you wanted to stop at some crummy hotel, Sasha.' Kat stood at the top of the stairs where the hall was visible from the first floor. Her sister continued talking, but they couldn't understand her as she disappeared down the hall, hidden by what appeared to be a wall blocking the rest of the hallway from view.

'I don't care where I am, so long as I can sleep,' Sasha moaned in return. She stumbled her way to the couch, fell over and didn't move.

'I call the pink room,' Kat yelled from above.

'There should be a bedroom down here. Dad and I will take that,' Beatrice said, going to open a door next to the kitchen. 'Found a bathroom if anyone needs it.'

Even as she said it, her mother disappeared inside.

'I'll take this room,' Sasha said, still not moving.

'Megan, you should take the blue room,' Kat said. 'You're the pre-honeymooners and it has a big hot tub in the bathroom.'

Megan frowned.

'Don't worry, darling,' Kat continued loudly. 'We got a tub, too.'

'Uh,' Sasha groaned. 'Katarina, shut up! I'm trying to sleep.'

'Then go upstairs,' Beatrice scolded, coming out of her chosen bedroom. 'Megan, you and Ryan take the blue room. Kat and Vincent will take the pink. Sasha, you take whichever is left. You can share with Zoe when she gets here.'

'Sure, I get the leftovers,' Sasha pushed up from the couch, pouting.

'Some things never change.' Douglas laughed to himself. A large antlered buck caught his attention. 'Hey, any of you boys ever hunt?'

'Sorry, sir, the only thing I shoot is pictures,' Ryan answered.

'I hunt bugs,' Vincent offered, taking the stairs two at a time to join his wife.

'Ah, well, I have three other daughters,' Douglas said good-naturedly. 'Perhaps one of them will marry a hunter so he can tell me what I'm supposed to be doing.'

'Don't shoot the other hunters,' Sasha mumbled. She scooped up her purse and grabbed her suitcase, only to march up the stairs. 'See, I don't have to find a man to tell you that much.'

'Thanks for the help, honey.' Douglas chuckled.

'I'll go fishing with you, Dad,' Megan said.

'You know how to fish?' her father asked.

'Can't be that hard to do.' Megan purposefully kept her gaze from Ryan. The news they'd be sharing a room surprised her. She'd somehow convinced herself that her mother would be old-fashioned and demand they sleep in separate bedrooms. Megan knew it had been foolish thinking. Beatrice was hardly the typical mother.

'I know how to fish,' Ryan said. 'My dad took me camping when I was younger.'

'Great!' Douglas clapped his hands once. 'Fishing it is. I feel like a great outdoorsman already.'

'I'm going to rest.' Megan yawned, grabbing her bag. 'Morning came too early.'

'I'll get that.' Ryan took it from her.

Too tired to protest, Megan went up the stairs. Hearing her sister and Vincent giggling, she walked past the first closed door. The second door was cracked, leading to a yellow-wallpapered room. Sasha's unmoving foot hung over the side of a bed as she rested on top of a white-and-yellow-rose quilt.

The blue room at the end of the hall echoed the rest of the cabin with wood plank walls and wood-based furniture. A blue blanket cascaded over the back of a rocking chair, soft and plush. Megan kicked off her shoes, stretching her toes.

'Would you like me to run you a bath?' Ryan asked.

Run her a bath? Megan frowned, eyeing him intently. 'Listen, Ryan, we really need to talk about what is happening here. First off, you are not my maid. Second, I can take care of my own bath. Third – oh!'

Ryan pulled her arm, jerking her against his chest.

Before she could think, he pressed his lips to her throat, moaning softly as he held her tight. The hard length of him pushed against her, but her mind focused on one particular part – the thick arousal near her stomach. Grabbing her ass, he rocked his hips.

'First, we can play any fantasy game you want. If you want me to serve you, fine. If you want to serve me, perfectly fine.' He licked her pulse. His voice was soft, as if he was mindful of where they were. 'Second, I just wanted to get you wet and naked. Third, anything else we need to discuss can be done later when we're not tired and after we're no longer horny. Fourth, do we really need to list these things out? I'm about to lose count and all I really want to do at the moment is stick my hard dick into you.'

Megan shivered at his words, liking the confident way he talked about wanting her. Wiggling, she lifted her leg, parting her thighs so that his larger one could find better access to her sex. The caress wasn't as deep as she would have liked, but the sweet friction of her pussy against the stiff denim of his pants sent pleasurable jolts to her clit. Moisture gathered in her already wet loins and his hands dipped beneath the material of her sweatpants, rubbing along her lace panties.

'We need to talk about this,' she said just as quietly, breathing hard. Megan held his arms tight, keeping him from backing away. His thigh retreated and she automatically angled her hips for more.

'We will.' He unbuttoned his jeans, quickly unzipping the fly. The sound of it seemed abnormally loud. 'Later.'

Megan tugged at his shirt, wanting to feel his hot flesh. A night and a day thinking of nothing but kinky sex with Ryan had taken its toll. She couldn't concentrate, didn't care to. If she didn't find some sort of release soon she'd go mad.

Ryan's hands were just as desperate as hers as he pulled at her T-shirt. Their arms got in the way of each other's progress and Megan drew back, taking care of her own shirt and giving Ryan time to rid his body of his. A subconscious knowledge that this would happen might have affected her choice of underwear. The sheer black bra trimmed in white lace hugged her breasts while revealing every detail of her round hard nipples to his view. When she pushed her sweatpants from her hips, matching panties were revealed.

A low animal sound reverberated from the back of his throat. His lids fell over his eyes, almost predatory as he stared at her body. He walked her towards the bed, forcing her back with his aggressive presence. Light came in from the window, not hiding a single curve of his muscular form as it contrasted the folds of his chest. A small trail of hair accentuated his defined stomach, leading down to the part in his unzipped jeans where the tip of his erection poked out of his silk boxers.

As her knees hit the bed, it squeaked loudly. Megan flinched and their eyes met in silent understanding. There was no way they could use the bed if just a mild bump caused such a loud noise.

Still standing, she reached for his cock. Hot silk glided against her fingers and she thrust her hand along the ready length, exploring the turgid flesh. Ryan's lips parted and his chin lifted as a sigh of pleasure escaped him. Knowing he liked it only emboldened her. She gripped tighter, squeezing harder than before.

'Tell me you brought condoms with you,' Megan demanded.

'Yes. I even brought a note from my doctor that says I have a clean bill of health.' Ryan gave a short laugh, even as he continued to rock against her hand. His body jerked once, trembling over the entire length. He reached for her hand, pulling his waistband away from his stomach to free his cock, only to wrap her fingers over flesh instead of silk. 'Ah, your hands are so strong. I like it when you touch me.'

'Condom,' she repeated, aching to feel the sweet pressure of him inside her, stretching her like before.

He glanced around, before moaning softly. 'Downstairs in my bag. I'll go get it in a second, I just want to feel your hands first.'

Ryan pushed his pants off his hips, taking the boxers down with them to give her better access. His eyes closed in ecstasy and he bit his lip, sucking the fullness of it between his teeth. Eagerly, she dipped her hand lower, stroking the hard length. He wrapped his fingers around hers and forced her hand lower still, gripping his fist around her so she squeezed him tighter like before.

'It would feel better –' his eyes opened and he looked meaningfully at her mouth '– wet.'

Without giving her time to react, he lightly pushed her shoulder. Megan found herself on her knees. Sucking him off wasn't exactly what she had in mind. Her pussy ached for stimulation. She opened her mouth, trying to form the words, but Ryan already had the tip of his erection angled towards her face. He rubbed himself along her lips, stopping anything she might say. His bold demands excited her and she automatically obeyed by wrapping his cock in the wet heat of her mouth. There was something exciting about a man who could show what he wanted without embarrassment. She looked up at him, seeing the plains of his chest, his small nipples, the stubbled line of his jaw.

'Ah, yeah.' Holding the sides of her face, Ryan pulled her forwards, drawing her eyes to the small trail of hair on his stomach. Tight muscles flexed as he controlled her movements, pulling and pushing as he urged her mouth to move over his arousal.

Hearing his deep raspy breathing, Megan ran her hands over his hips, scratching his flesh as she moved to grab his wrists. She jerked his hands away from her face and tossed them aside. He slipped from between her lips.

'Please.' The word left him in a soft plea.

Megan drew small kisses along the tip of his shaft, torturing him with the light presses.

'Please, Megan.'

'Please, what?' She giggled, unable to help herself.

'Please suck me.' He thrust, trying to take advantage of her passing mouth. 'Suck me. I need to feel you. I need...'

He didn't finish. Megan gripped the back of his thighs, letting her fingers curl just beneath his ass. Ryan didn't protest as she took the lead over the rhythm. Her hips rolled in small circles, mimicking the bobbing of her mouth. Both of his hands found her hair as she did what he asked, working his erection back and forth into her moist hot mouth. Her teeth grazed him and he nearly choked her trying to go deeper.

'Not like this.'

Megan kept going, barely hearing his words. Her body ached and she drew her hand down to touch her sex, needing stimulation. Slipping her finger through the soft fold, she pinched her clit.

'Megan,' Ryan insisted.

Suddenly, she was on her feet, dazed and weak as she stood before him. 'What? Why did you stop me?'

'This is not how I thought it would be. Not like this.' He breathed heavily.

'Not like what?' she asked with a little more force than before.

'I...' He touched her face. 'Romance.'

Megan laughed. How could she not? Ryan had a woman on her knees, giving him head, and he was worried about it not being romantic enough? Without thought, she pushed him back, walking him until he was backed up against the wall. 'Romance is for people in love.'

Ryan searched her face, his eyes darting back and forth as he studied her expression. He didn't answer as he forcibly took her arms, swinging her around so their positions were switched. Her back hit the wall with a dull thud. She liked the rough command in him, the confident almost punishing way his mouth collapsed along hers. He pinned her into the wall, his tight body firmly trapping her against the hard wood.

Keeping her in place with his mouth, he reached for the crotch of her panties, hooking it with his finger to pull them off, out of his way. A knuckle skimmed over her sensitive clit, almost as if by accident. She moaned softly.

When the panties were gone, he lifted her off the floor. Her back slid up the wall, her bra catching and snagging against the planked wood. Fingers dug into her thighs, holding her in place. She knew she should make him wait for a condom, but, as his cock slid along her wet folds, probing without the aid of his hand to find entrance, she couldn't form the words to protest.

'Is this how you want it?' Ryan groaned, punctuating the words with a hard thrust. 'Emotionless. Unfeeling.'

This time he was able to go much deeper than the first, stretching her wide as he fucked her hard against the wall. He didn't kiss her, instead holding back as he stared piercingly into her eyes. Each plunge was stiff and sure, almost angry.

Megan didn't care. It felt too good. She held on, closing her eyes to his hard gaze as she let the sensations take over her. The feel of flesh was much better than her vibrator. Ryan's warmth, his strength, the sound of his harsh breath consumed her.

Her legs tightened along his waist, forcing him to slow his punishing pace. Automatically, he obeyed the silent command, gentling his hold. The strokes became easy smooth caresses inside her, almost worshipping in their tenderness. Keeping him deep, her body tightened as she found release. Megan whimpered, biting her lip to stop her cry of pleasure. She wanted to keep him inside her, but Ryan made a strange noise and jerked back. He dropped her legs and her feet landed on the floor, still shaking. Stunned, she looked up in time to see him gasping his release into his cupped hand.

She should have been thankful he had the presence of mind to pull out, but she was more irritated with herself because she hadn't thought of it first. Weak with the aftermath of release, she pushed away from the wall. Her heartbeat began to slow and her head to clear.

'I need to take a bath,' she said, refusing to look at him as she turned. What had to be the bathroom door was close and she reached for the knob.

'Don't want my smell on you?' he asked.

Megan stiffened, even as she pushed open the door. Every muscle was on edge. Her gaze focused on the other room. It was the bathroom. A light-blue toilet and matching porcelain sink were revealed. Short white curtains trimmed with lace hung over a closed window. Since she didn't detect a tub, she assumed it was behind the door, where she couldn't see.

'Ryan, don't.'

'What?'

'Don't pout and don't search for sentiments.' She was a cop and knew when someone was probing. Very aware of her exposed state, as she stood wearing only a bra, Megan forced herself to stay still. 'You chose this. Whatever your reasons, you chose it, Ryan. Sex is sex. If we have it again, that is all it will be – sex for common release, nothing else. I will never pretend to love you.' She placed her hand on the doorframe and glanced back.

He stood, glorious and naked, and clearly unhappy with her cold response.

'Now, I'm going to take a bath. I'm tired and travel worn. Getting clean will make me feel better.'

'I'm not a child. You don't have to talk down to me, Megan. You can turn off the cop voice.' He actually sounded upset.

She gave a short humourless laugh. 'It's the only voice I have. If you are looking for layers, peel an onion. With me, you see what you get.'

Closing the door behind her, she took a deep breath. Exhaustion and the day of travel had made her temper sharper than usual, but it was better Ryan knew where she stood. It was bad enough she had sex with him without having a talk to set ground rules first. What was it about the man that made her suddenly careless about such things? And no condom? She was a world-class idiot.

'I need to go back to work,' she whispered. 'Things make sense there.'

As she suspected, a large tub with built-in jets was along the far wall. It too was the same blue as the other fixtures. She ran the water, but didn't wait for it to fill all the way before stepping inside. Warmth encompassed her feet as she took off her bra. The sheer material along the back had been snagged from rubbing against the wall. With a loud sigh, she dropped it on the floor. One of her only expensive pieces of lingerie and it was ruined.

'Megan?' Ryan asked softly from the other side of the door. 'Can I come in to talk to you?'

'Not right now.' She lowered herself into the tub. The water wasn't too deep and she rubbed water over her arms in an effort to warm them.

'Please, Megan.'

'Not now.' She closed her eyes, leaning her head back. 'I'm too tired to deal. We'll have this conversation later.'

Too tired to *deal* with him? Ryan frowned. He was something to be dealt with? Aggravated, he slipped his shirt back over his head. The material was stretched where Megan had pulled on it and he tried to even the marks out by stretching it further in the other direction.

'What the hell does she want from me?' Ryan grumbled, careful not to speak too loudly. Then, taking a deep breath, he told himself, 'You promised yourself you'd give it this vacation. If she doesn't like you after this, it's over.'

Chapter Six

The early morning chill was welcome after a night spent sweating in the bedroom. Megan wished the heat could be attributed to carnal late-night activities, but in reality it was her mother's overuse of the fireplace combined with the heater. Ryan had nothing to do with it. He hadn't even been in the same creaky bed, choosing instead to spend the night on the floor.

Lifting her foot up on the railing along the big deck, she leant forwards, stretching her calf muscle as she got ready for a run. The blue glow of moonlight blended with the hint of dawn edged along the peaks of the distant mountains. Soon it would be light out. Megan hated to admit it, but she looked forward to the daylight and stretched a little extra to await its arrival. She had no problem walking down a dark New York alleyway, but this was wilderness, the wide-open untouched country. There were snakes, bears, wolves, raptors, deer, elk ... Did elk attack humans? She seemed to remember Ella saying something about big-game animals attacking when in their rut. Ella would know. She spent a good portion of her childhood watching nature shows on television.

'Wonderful,' she mumbled. 'I can see it now. I survive gang fights and serial killers only to be mauled by a sexually charged deer.'

'I don't think you have much to worry about. Deer murders aren't prevalent this time of year and I don't think you're their type.'

Megan jumped, startled by Ryan's laughing voice. Her heart sped ever so slightly. 'What are you doing up?'

'Same thing as you, I suppose,' he said.

She glanced over her shoulder. He wore shorts and a hooded sweatshirt with a front pocket. It was hard to see the details, but the dark colours were outlined by the soft light coming out through the window. He'd pulled back his hair to the nape of his neck.

'Care if I join you?' Ryan lifted his arms over his head, leaning to one side and then the other.

Megan almost said no but, looking over the valley set before the mountains, she thought better of it. 'Sure, company sounds nice.'

'Nice?' he almost choked on the word.

'Well, if a rabid deer comes along, I'll have something to throw at it so I can get away.' She smiled to soften the words.

'Happy to be your sacrifice,' he said wryly.

Megan laughed. She felt better. Her head was clear, her body rested and for the most part the jet lag was gone. 'Come on. I usually try to run at least a mile, longer if time allows.'

'I have no pressing engagements.'

'Five miles, then?'

'Doesn't need to be planned, does it?' He led the way to the stairs at the end of the long wooden deck.

'I guess not.' Megan followed him, stepping carefully over the uneven rocky path as they walked through the shadow cast by the deck. Coming around to a trail that cut through the valley towards the Rocky Mountain Front, Ryan moved to the side so they could walk beside each other. 'We should talk.'

'Do you really want to do that now?' Ryan asked.

'No.'

'Then, let's not. We'll be here for a couple of weeks. There is plenty of time for talking.' He began to jog, prompting her to do the same. It was an easy pace, but she didn't try to turn her morning exercise into a race. Going fast burnt energy too quickly and she wanted to make it to the distant mountains and back before breakfast.

Uneven dirt trails were a stark contrast to running over concrete sidewalks, but as the sun rose it became easy enough to see where she stepped. Ample grasses rolled over the Montana plains, covering the surrounding hills, distant trees and patches of dense shrubbery. It became apparent with the dawn that the mountains were way too far to reach by foot. Still, it was an awe-inspiring sight.

Yellow wildflowers dominated the flora colour scheme, enclosed within the blue-tinted grasses. Large flowers with arrowhead-shaped leaves mingled amongst shorter pink and yellow blooms. Bright-red bracts cradled tiny yellow flowers. Near the path, strange long-stemmed plants grew, feeling almost like velvet when she reached out to touch them as they jogged past. Then there were the giant brown cones with petals reminiscent of those of a sunflower, huge dandelions and what appeared to be dark-yellow snapdragons. Megan wasn't good with flower names, but she'd always liked the look of snapdragons.

Adding even more to the scene was the smattering of blue, purple and pink varieties. Though she tried, it was impossible to count the number of different flowers they passed. It seemed they ran by a new one every couple of yards.

Neither one of them spoke. Megan was glad for it. What exactly would they talk about? She didn't want to have the conversation she knew they should. Whenever the path narrowed, Megan backed away, allowing Ryan to go first. She looked forward to those times, when she could watch his ass moving beneath his shorts. Tan legs sprinkled with hair strode in steady rhythmic perfection.

Ryan slowed to a stop in front of her. Pointing to the sky, he said, 'Look. Golden eagle.'

Breathing hard, Megan shaded her eyes and followed his finger. 'It's not gold, it's brown.'

'No, that's just its name. I didn't mean the colour...' He trailed off as he caught her amused look. 'You knew that.'

Megan gave a soft laugh. 'My mom gave me brochures she'd printed off the computer. I had nothing better to do, so I glanced over them.'

'I wish I had a better lens with me.' Ryan reached into his front pocket, taking out a small black camera. He lifted it towards the sky. 'I'll have to come back out. The Oyster Plants and the Butter and Eggs are really in bloom.'

'Are we talking about breakfast or wildflowers?' Megan looked around. She could only guess which out of the thousands of flowers were the ones he'd named.

'Flowers.' He chuckled, following the bird with the small camera. He snapped the shutter several times. 'These probably won't come out the best. I can't get close enough. I'd love to have my macro lens.'

Megan stretched her arms, turning around to look at the cabin. It was a small brown spot shaded amongst a backdrop of trees. 'I didn't realise how far we went.'

'Tired?'

'Why, you going to offer to carry me?'

'Not on your life. You're the cop. I assumed you were going to rescue me.'

Megan snorted. 'Not likely. This isn't my precinct. Besides, if you remember, I brought you along to feed to the wild animals should they attack, so I can get away.'

'Don't run off on me yet.' Ryan motioned to the sky. The bird of prey dove towards the prairie, swooping gracefully to the ground. It disappeared briefly into the grasses only to lift once more with a small mammal clutched in its talons. 'I think he's found his breakfast.'

'Looks delicious,' she said dryly. 'Let's head back. My mother probably has our breakfast cooking.'

'Does she read the plates when we're done?' Ryan lifted his camera and snapped shots of random flowers.

Megan rolled her eyes when he turned the camera towards her. 'No, only the tea leaves.'

'Yeah, what was that all about last time?'

'She probably saw the truth.' Megan's smile faded. It wasn't hard to know what that truth was. There was no marriage, no kids, no relationship in their future and the reminder of why they were in Montana only served to kill the easiness that had formed between them.

'I'm not asking what that truth is, so don't expand.' Ryan lifted his small camera and aimed at one of the cone-shaped flowers. When he finished taking the picture, he held the camera out to her, as if offering it. She glanced down at his hand before turning her attention back to the cabin. Out of the corner of her eye, she saw him shrug and take another picture.

'Isn't it against your artistic code to use a point-and-shoot camera? Won't they kick you out of the photographers' club?' Watching him move, arousal unwound in her stomach. They were far enough away from the cabin not to be seen. But having sex in a grassy prairie filled with snakes and insects wasn't exactly the top of her list of fantasies. However, considering the field was all they had to work with, Megan was more than willing to try it.

'Ever haul around two full camera bags, a tripod and lights?' He shot her a quick smile. 'This is perfectly fine for basic shots – what was that?'

'What was what?' Megan frowned.

'That noise. Did you hear it?'

'Uh? That's not funny.' She glanced around.

'Bear.'

'Uh, that's really not funny.' Megan stiffened, but she heard it too. It was a light scraping followed by a series of short grunts. Her stomach clenched and she reached for her side, feeling for the comfort of her holster and gun. It wasn't there. Her hand shook and she balled it into a fist.

'It's just a cub, probably only a few months old since most are born in January, maybe early February.' Ryan started to lift his arm, but she grabbed it and held tight.

'Don't. Its mom will attack us. We should run away.'

'They hear better than we do. If we hurry, it will definitely know we are here.' He didn't look at her and didn't look as if he was ready to move any time soon. 'Besides, it's a black bear.'

'I know it's a black bear,' she argued. Glancing at the cabin, she saw it was still far away. There was no way they could outrun a wild beast. Her heart beat hard and heavy and she felt out of breath. Every muscle in her body was tight, ready for a fight. 'It's black and it's a bear. And you're forgetting the most important point. Its mother will eat us if she sees us looking at her baby.'

'You are thinking of grizzly bears. This is a black bear. See its shoulders? Smaller hump. And its face is less concave with pointed ears.' He pulled away from her hand, taking a step towards the cub.

Was he crazy? Going closer to the wild animal? They were still several yards away from it, but every instinct told her to put distance between them.

'Black bears aren't known for killing humans to protect their young,' Ryan continued. 'Food must be scarce this year for them. This one still looks pretty small. It can't be more than ten, fifteen pounds.'

'OK, all I heard there was, this bear is probably hungry and since food is scarce guess who's on the menu.' Megan reached for him again. 'Now, let's go.'

'I wish I had my telephoto lens.'

'I wish I had a sane boyfriend,' Megan mumbled. She caught what she said right after she said it. Holding her breath, she studied Ryan, worried that he might have heard her and taken it the wrong way.

Slowly, he turned to her. 'Boyfriend?'

'I meant fuck buddy,' Megan said, refusing to return his easy smile. It was hard though, trying to act tough and unaffected.

His eyes fell slightly, but he didn't comment on her chilly correction.

'There should be two.'

'Two what?'

'Bears. Two cubs are normally born at once, sometimes three.'

'Again, I'm not worried about the babies. I'm worried about the babies' mother.' Megan took a step towards the cabin, hoping he'd do the same. 'You don't happen to have some bear deterrent hidden in your pocket?' She glanced at his stomach, hoping to see a bulge of some sort poking at his sweatshirt.

'That's not bear spray in my pocket.' He gave a soft laugh.

'Ah,' Megan gasped softly.

Suddenly, the bear cub lifted its head and made a long resonating sound not unlike a human yelling for help.

'I wish I had my other camera,' Ryan whispered, holding up his small one to take another picture. 'This just isn't close enough.'

The bear was looking in their direction and Megan thought she saw movement in the trees behind it. 'Time to go, nature boy.'

'You're probably right,' he said. 'The mother normally stays with her cubs until they're close to eighteen months old. She might be near by.'

'OK, you know a lot about bears. Quit trying to show off.' Megan kept walking, deciding, if he wanted to get eaten, he could do it by himself.

'There are ten to fifteen thousand black bears in Montana.' Ryan moved to follow her, still looking in the distance. 'And they range in colours from black, cinnamon and blond.'

'I've never heard of a cinnamon bear,' Megan drawled, 'unless its candy shaped and chewy.'

They kept moving and Megan was glad to see the wild creatures didn't follow them. She began to relax. Ryan was a little slower and kept glancing back longingly. Megan thought she'd have to pull at his arm a few times to get him to continue on, but he kept going.

'You really must have a death wish,' Megan said. 'To want to hang out with wild bears.'

'It's no worse than what you do, hanging out with criminals. In fact, I'd say that was more dangerous.' He grinned, finally looking towards the cabin as he fell into a faster pace.

Megan glanced back, but the bear was thankfully no longer in sight.

'A bear? Really?' Sasha exclaimed, her eyes wide as she looked from the sweaty Megan to the equally damp Ryan. 'Did it attack you? Did it see you? Are you hurt?'

Ryan hid his smile. It was almost strange how all sisters could look so much alike, act the same in so many ways, yet have such different personalities.

'Did you get a picture?' Kat asked with excitement as her fingers twitched as if holding her own camera.

'Nature boy over here is as bad as Ella.' Megan brushed past him as she walked to the bar between the living room and kitchen. She took a piece of toast and piled it with scrambled eggs and bacon, making it into a sandwich. Her mother was there, holding a plate under her before she'd finished.

Breakfast was simple – eggs, bacon and wholegrain toast. When they had picked up groceries at a town on the way to the cabin, Megan's parents had sprung for the main supplies. Megan purchased beer, Kat and Vincent got wine and Sasha was in charge of sneaking and hiding the contraband from their mother – chocolate, soda, chips and white bread. Ryan bought his own provisions, a few candy bars and some gum, but mostly he found amusement in watching the sisters plot like children against their mother, giggling naughtily as they smuggled their bread into the car unnoticed.

Megan continued, 'I'm thinking of ways to get back safely and he's reciting the nature channel, telling me how bears see in black and white and eat stupid people who stand around watching them.'

'Ryan, dear, eat something,' Beatrice interjected.

Ryan smirked at Megan, as he walked to the bar to get his own breakfast. Megan inched away from him, but he pretended not to notice. 'I said no such thing. And you act like it was right on top of us about to bite. The cub was several yards out. We were in no real danger.'

'So you say,' Megan muttered.

'Yes, I do say. Besides, bears see in colour and eat greens, ant larvae, nuts and fruit. They only eat meat when they can't find other things. Food might be scarce, but the cub had a rotted log filled with ants.'

'I still say we should have run away,' Megan protested. 'Its mother could have been near by.'

Beatrice made a light noise in the back of her throat, looking distressed, but said nothing.

'Bears run over twenty-five miles per hour and they're one of the smarter mammals,' he said. 'I doubt you'd have escaped.'

'Aren't you supposed to play dead?' Vincent asked. 'I think I heard that somewhere.'

'Well –' Ryan began, only to be interrupted.

Sasha snorted. 'You're right. Nature boy is as bad as Ella.'

Kat stood, grinning. She came near where he was with the pretence of grabbing a piece of bacon. Softly, she mused, 'Smart man, huh?'

'I was trying to impress her with my brains,' he whispered. 'Too much?

'Just a little.' Kat patted him on the shoulder. 'But it's endearing that you try so hard for her.'

'Don't worry, Ryan. They call me bug man,' Vincent said.

'Bug Man and Nature Boy. Sounds like a couple of tree-hugger superheroes,' Sasha teased.

'Hey, you leave my superheroes alone.' Kat pretended to pout. 'Lest you forget we used to call you, *Sha-zow*!'

'Tell me, Sash,' Megan mused, pretending to study her plate. 'You still have that pink superhero cape you used to wear all the time?'

Sasha rolled her eyes. 'I was like five.'

'Yeah, when you first got it. I think Mom had to take it away from you when you were twelve. The poor thing was all tattered and worn.' Kat grinned, nearly snorting as she poked fun at her sister. 'You pouted for days.'

'Oh, yeah, remember when we convinced her it really could help her fly if she believed hard enough? And then we got her to jump off that little shed in the back yard.' Megan nearly dropped her plate in laughter. 'It didn't work, but you tried it five times before Mom made you stop.'

'Oh, yeah,' Kat agreed enthusiastically. 'Then we got Ella and Zoe to put plastic bags from the grocery store over their arms, convincing them it would work like a parachute.'

'And Mom couldn't figure out why her daughters kept trying to jump off the shed,' Megan finished.

'It was your father who was most worried,' Beatrice said.

'I'm ignoring you two,' Sasha announced, turning her

attention to Ryan. 'Where did you learn all that nature stuff anyway, Ryan?'

'My father.' Ryan picked up right on cue, helping Sasha change the subject, though, in truth, he loved watching them bicker and tease each other. It was endearing because, despite whatever they said, there was still the obvious love and affection between them. 'He was big into camping and wildlife. We went camping every summer when I was a boy. Never this part of Montana, but to Kansas, Colorado, New Mexico, lots of places.'

'I thought you said you didn't hunt.' Megan gave him a quizzical look.

'We never did hunt. We observed.' Ryan picked up a fork, holding his plate in one hand as he stabbed at the pile of eggs.

'And that's why you take pictures, isn't it?' Kat nodded in understanding. 'Because your father taught you to watch.'

'I taught *you* a lot of things, my dear,' Douglas said, looking up from the couch to join the conversation. He held a magazine in his hands. 'How come you didn't listen to one of them?'

'Because Mom was too busy contradicting your wisdom behind your back.' Sasha laughed. 'You'd give us scientific proof that there was no boogieman and Mom would read us real-life accounts of hauntings as bedtime stories.'

'I . . .' Beatrice hesitated. 'I was showing you there were two sides to every topic.'

'You were giving us nightmares,' Kat said.

'Not me,' Megan put forth with a shrug. 'I never believed the ghosts and knew that the boogiemen were nothing compared to real live criminals.'

'I for one vote that Megan can't talk about her job,' Sasha said.

'Then she won't talk the entire vacation,' Kat teased. 'I could be down with that.'

'Shut up.' Megan tossed a piece of toast at Kat's head. Her sister giggled, ducking. 'You left like fifteen messages on my phone about bugs when you were trying to get into Vincent's, ah –' she glanced at her parents before weakly changing what she was going to say '– Vincent's good graces.'

'Smooth, Megs,' Sasha teased. 'Really smooth.'

Ryan couldn't help but smile. It had been so long since he'd been around a family like this. Without brothers or sisters of his own, he hadn't been left with the bond to fall back on when his parents died. There was an easiness to the banter, unlike the dinner he'd shared with them at Douglas and Beatrice's house. He'd been too nervous about what Megan thought about him to relax.

'So, what does everyone want to do today?' Beatrice asked.

'Isn't there a dinosaur dig around here?' Sasha looked at her father.

'Yes, and preserved nests, too,' Douglas said. 'First ones discovered in North America. The area is filled with fossilised Maiasaura babies and adults, even the eggs, all dating from eighty million years ago. The palaeontology dig site at Egg Mountain has provided more biological evidence of the Cretaceous period than any other dig in the world.'

'How do you know that?' Beatrice busied herself picking up breakfast. 'I've never heard you talk about dinosaurs before.'

Douglas reached next to him on the couch and lifted up a few brochures. 'Found these on the coffee table.'

'Sounds interesting,' Sasha said.

'It would sound interesting to you, college girl.' Megan laughed, wiping her hands. 'Careful, Dad, or Sasha will change her major again.'

'Hey, I've only switched it a few times,' Sasha protested, though she didn't look insulted by Megan's joking.

'A few hundred,' mumbled Kat.

Douglas weeded through the small pile, reading the highlights. 'We don't have to do educational. We can hike, swim, visit the hot springs, horseback ride, camp –'

'Um, Dad, no offence, but this is about as much camping as I want to do,' Kat said.

Vincent laughed and whispered something into his wife's ear, causing her to giggle. She playfully hit his arm.

Ryan studied Megan, wishing things were so easy between them. He hated to be jealous of Kat and Vincent's relationship, but he was. Megan refused to look at him.

'I'll do whatever. Horseback riding or hiking could be fun.' Megan made her way to the staircase. 'I'm going to take a bath and change.'

'Trust Megs to pick something athletic,' Sasha said. The others didn't comment.

Ryan watched after her before catching movement out of the corner of his eyes. Kat was motioning for him to follow and Sasha eyed him expectantly. He glanced weakly at Megan's parents. They were busy reading over the brochures. Though Megan was an adult, he was still slightly uncomfortable with her parents knowing they shared the same room – even if her parents didn't care.

'You should shower, Ryan.' Kat smirked. 'You're all sweaty.'

'Katarina,' Beatrice scolded. 'Don't be rude.'

'No, Mrs Matthews, it's all right. I do need to bathe and change after my run.' Ryan followed Megan up the stairs.

'I told you, dear, call me Mom!' Beatrice yelled behind him.

Chapter Seven

Megan wasn't sure if Ryan's confident knowledge that she'd fuck him on this trip was upsetting, seductive or insulting. Tugging the towel tighter against her chest, she peered into the dresser drawer that held the contents of his check-on bag. He'd brought enough condoms to ensure they had sex at least twice a day the entire trip.

Hearing a splash, she glanced at the bathroom door. Ryan was in the tub, cleaning up after their adventure. Though hardly life-threatening, Megan was still a little shook up by the bear encounter. Wild beasts were not her norm and she wasn't a girl used to being out of her element.

She heard another splash. The idea of Ryan naked and wet, heat curling around his body as he washed the sweat from his skin, made her tremble. Maybe it was the mountains, nature, being so far removed from her job and the city, but her eyes were again drawn to the drawer. Reaching in, her hand shook slightly as she pulled out a condom.

Why was she so nervous when it came to Ryan? Was it just because she'd been without a lover for so long? Megan fingered the package, feeling the rubber slide around within. It wasn't like her to be nervous with men. Normally, she was confident and sure.

Logic told her they needed to talk first, to set ground rules, to clear up the matter of their fake engagement. But being with Ryan wasn't like most circumstances and he wasn't like most lovers, and their engagement was some sort of blackmail. The cop in her wouldn't let her forget it, but the woman inside her was willing to ignore it for the time being. There was something sexily erotic about his having power over her.

Sure, it was a little depraved to think that way, but she wasn't romantically minded Zoe, optimistic Ella, free-going Kat or over-thinking Sasha. She was her own person – instinctual, controlled, decidedly unromantic if not slightly pessimistic in her views. And, if her detective side needed an excuse, she could always consider it like an undercover assignment – doing what needed to be done to solve the mystery that was Ryan Lucas.

Comfortable with the logic, she walked to the bathroom door. A damp lock of hair stuck to her neck, still wet from her bath. She didn't care if she was already clean because she suddenly felt very, very dirty.

The door opened easily and she heard a startled movement in the tub before her gaze reached his. He appeared surprised to see her and she couldn't blame him, considering she'd not invited him in when she bathed.

'Did you miss a spot?' he asked.

'No.' Without hesitation, she dropped her towel. Ryan's eyes devoured her, lingering on her breasts before travelling down to her hips. His shoulders straightened as he sat forwards. Megan kept her gaze steady as she walked towards him. Her feet fell silently against the chilly floor tiles. 'You did.'

'Oh, did I?' Ryan stared up at her.

'Are you going to make room for me?' Megan asked, raising a brow.

As he moved over, the expectant gleam in his eyes caught her notice. Shades of uncertainty and hope spread over his features, as if he searched her for more than she could give. The raw intimacy of it terrified her. Ryan tried to hide the hopeful expression under a smooth sexy façade but it was too late. She'd seen it in him and had to wonder what it was he looked for in this strange relationship of theirs. Megan hesitated.

'Are you changing your mind?' He matched her earlier demeanour, lifting a playful brow in challenge. All tender sentiments were gone from his face, replaced by the confident, if not slightly cold lover. She wouldn't call him emotionless in his passions, but the way he looked at her now was more distant than before.

Was that a challenge? Had she been mistaken in the hopeful look? Was he daring her to play his little game? She just wished she knew what they were playing for.

Megan stepped into the tub, kneeling before him in the hot water. It was large enough for both of them to sit comfortably. Ryan pushed the button to turn on the side jets. The water began to churn, bubbling and rippling over the surface. She ran her hands over his thighs, caressing them up to his strong hips.

The heat from the bath stirred her already aroused blood. Every nerve ending tingled, reaching out to touch him. She wanted contact, wanted to feel him inside her. Dipping forwards, her breasts rubbed against him as she brushed her lips to his. Instantly, his tongue delved forwards, licking the inner edge of her lips as he moved his mouth against her. The easy light pressure deepened with each measured movement.

Hands slid over her sides, curving over her ass and squeezing. With a hard confident jerk, he pulled her against his fully aroused cock. Knowing he was as eager as she, that he wanted her as desperately as she did him, only pushed her desperation over the edge. She rubbed her sex along his shaft to stimulate her clit. Everything was so wet and hot and she couldn't quit from squirming against him.

Ryan massaged her chest, pinching her nipples. His mouth moved down her neck, licking her flesh, grazing his teeth as he pushed her back. With better access, his grip on her breasts tightened, his fingers slithering to encircle her tight nipples. The cool damp length of her hair against her back was an erotic contrast to the heat. He kissed her throat, then captured a nipple with his mouth, sucking and moaning.

Megan drew her hands along his arms, scratching his skin. Ryan made a weak noise, so she did it again, harder. She rocked her hips, keeping his shaft tightly locked along her soft folds without allowing him entrance. Though she wanted him, she forced herself to hold back, keeping him outside her body, waiting for the moment when she would be mindless with need.

'Megan,' Ryan whispered, sending a shiver over her with desperation in his voice. 'I need you.'

'What do you need?' she asked, taking a small measure of the power he had over her.

'You,' he groaned.

'Me?'

'I want to be inside you.' He took her by the hips and lifted her up. 'I love the feel of you on me.'

Megan panted weakly as the tip of his shaft found her ready beneath the water's surface. As she seated herself on his lap, impaling her body, his hands slid once more to her breast. The jets bubbled, punctuating their soft moans. She clutched the tub's edge on both sides of his head, using it for support.

'Mm, so tight,' Ryan mumbled, nipping at the breast lodged between his teeth. 'I can feel you clenching me.'

Megan tightened her muscles around his shaft, gripping him with her pussy. 'Like this?'

'Ah, you have to stop that or I'm going to come.' His actions countered his words as he dug his fingers into the tops of her thighs and kept her on him.

'Stop what?' Megan did it again.

'Oh, fuck, fuck.' Ryan's hands flew to the tub's edge, holding on as she rode him. He let her have control and she took it, setting a slow rhythm.

His eyes closed, his head back, Ryan was a gorgeous male specimen. Water clung to him and the overhead light hit the small bead, gleaming like diamonds along his tanned strong flesh.

Megan tried to hold back, tried to keep from coming as she enjoyed the build, but the pressure became too much. She jerked, her hands slipping only to find a hold on his shoulder. Unable to move by her own will, she let the orgasm have her, trembling with his cock deeply embedded.

'Mmm, I can't stop.' Ryan groaned, blindly reaching for her. 'Pull off. I can't keep from – ahh.'

The moan was pained and he tensed with the beginning release beneath her and, instead of pulling her off, his hips jerked up, ensuring his thick arousal stayed right where it was.

'Fuck, fuck,' he repeated over and over before groaning incoherently. 'You do things to me. You make me forget myself.'

Megan took several deep breaths, attempting to calm her racing heart. When the feeling gradually came back to her limbs, bringing with it her sanity, she pushed up. His body glided from hers. She felt him watching her, but didn't meet his gaze as she stepped out of the tub. Pulling her towel off the floor, she faltered briefly as she saw the unopened condom resting beneath it. She couldn't believe they had done it again. Where was her head at? Slowly, she walked to the bathroom door, not bothering to pick the condom up. 'You should hurry. They've probably decided on what we're going to do today and are most likely waiting on us to join them.'

Ryan watched her walk out of the bathroom. Did he just get used for sex? He would have been upset if he wasn't so sated.

It was all he could do to finish his bath. Not remembering if he washed his hair before she came in, he lathered it up and quickly rinsed. Everything about this woman was a mystery, one he wanted to spend the rest of his life solving. Getting out of the tub, he grabbed a towel and began drying off. The gleam of a condom wrapper caught his attention and he had a small sickened feeling in the pit of his stomach as he realised they'd forgotten protection again. What was it about Megan that made him lose all sense?

As he left the bathroom to get dressed, Megan was already gone, her towel crumpled on the floor. He dropped his own on top of it and hurriedly grabbed something to wear. If he wasn't quick, it was quite possible Megan would convince her family to leave without him and he needed every second he could get to woo the frustrating woman.

'We should talk.'

Megan glanced from the giant reproduction of a Tyrannosaurus Rex to Ryan and then back again. Under her breath, she said, 'I agree. We need to start using condoms.'

'That's not what I meant,' he answered. 'Though I do think we need them. It's only responsible of us.'

Megan didn't stay to chat as she walked towards the end of the large display to stand by her father and Sasha, who insisted on reading each and every plaque that hung by the reproductions. The two were taking the scholarly approach, while Kat forced Vincent to play with her in the kiddie area. The last she saw of her mother was as Beatrice headed towards the gift shop with her father's credit card.

'Tyrannosaurus Rex was named in 1905 by US palaeontologist Henry Fairfield Osborn. It means "tyrant lizard king",' Sasha said, reading the information plaque. 'Living in the late Cretaceous period, sixty-five to eighty-five million years ago, this meat eater was a fierce predator.'

'Interesting,' Megan lied, forcing herself to look towards the plaque and not to where she'd left Ryan.

'. . . humid, semi-tropical environment,' Sasha was still

reading. 'Until recently, they were thought to be the biggest carnivorous dinosaur.'

'Uh-huh,' Megan mumbled distractedly, chancing a quick peek to the side. Ryan was coming towards her.

'Giganotosaurus and Carcharodontosaurus are bigger.' Sasha made a small thoughtful noise, as if she found it to be utterly fascinating information.

'You don't say.' Megan was barely paying attention. She felt Ryan next to her and forced herself to listen to her sister.

'Their serrated cone-shaped teeth are continually replaced.' Sasha ran her finger beneath the words as Douglas leant over to read silently along. 'Their arms are only about three feet long with two fingers on each hand.'

Megan turned abruptly to Ryan and said under her breath, 'OK, you win. I can't take the info-junkies. Let's go somewhere and talk.'

As she walked away from her father and Sasha, the two of them didn't seem to notice the abrupt departure as they became engrossed in their discussion of what they'd just read. Megan knew she could only stand so much academic dialogue on dinosaurs. That's all the two brainiacs had talked about the entire drive to the museum. Stegosaurus this and Zuniceratops that. It was as annoying as watching two people speak Ancient Egyptian and having no way of beginning to translate them.

'Is something wrong?' Ryan asked.

'Why would something be wrong?' Megan grumbled. She stopped at a display unit set in the middle of the room. Two reproductions of vicious-looking beasts gnawing on larger small-headed creatures were surrounded by what looked to be ground-up car tyres. She picked up a piece of the black thick rubber only to toss it back down in disinterest.

'Dinosaurs not your thing?' he asked.

'They've been dead a little too long. I like concentrating on the present mysteries, not ones scientists have been trying to solve since the dawn of time.' Megan shrugged, turning her back on the creatures to look about in slight boredom. 'Don't get me wrong, I can appreciate the things; they just don't hold my interest for hours on end, especially when they're giant toy models and not the real thing.'

'There are some old bones over there.' Ryan pointed across the room to glass displays.

'We got plenty of old bones in the forensic lab back home.' Megan gave a small laugh. 'And those I get to touch, if I want to.'

'I'd offer to break the glass and get you one, but something tells me you wouldn't think twice about having me arrested.' His sheepish grin reminded her of the look he gave her when he'd been trying to ask her out on a date to her parents' house.

'Tell me something. That night at the big museum-robbery crime scene . . .' Megan paused, frowning.

'What about it?'

She'd been about to ask about the photo he took of her at the crime scene, but thought better of it. 'Did you actually think you were suave asking me on a date to my parents' house?'

'Well, I . . .'

'I mean, it's a little sad, don't you think? Asking a girl out to hang with the old folks?'

'I like to think of it as gentlemanly,' he said. 'Chaperones and all that.'

'Do I look like the type that needs a chaperone? I can more than handle myself.'

'Oh, don't I know it.' His look said it all. 'You more than proved you can handle yourself in the alleyway outside your parents' building. And in the bathtub. And –'

'Ah!' Megan punched his arm. 'That is real gentle-manly of you.'

'What?' He reached for her hip, drawing her closer. His tone dropped, becoming seductive, like a lover who shared an intimate secret. It was a rare occasion when any man ever used that tone with her. Part of her liked it, but a bigger part of her wanted to run away and hide. 'I only said I like how you handle yourself.'

Megan's breath caught. She pulled back, in what she hoped was an artful attempt to end the familiarity of the moment. 'I wonder what Mom's buying. She's been in the gift shop for a long time now.'

'Megan.' Ryan tried to stop her, but she didn't stay to hear what he had to say.

'So, how is it going between the two of you?' Kat slid next to Megan on the picnic-table seat. They had pulled over alongside the road on the way home from the museum. Sasha was busy reading the dinosaur encyclo-paedia their mother had bought her from the gift shop. Everyone else got a T-shirt and little geodes they could hit with a hammer and break open to see what kind of crystals were formed inside.

'Do you think Sasha will ever graduate?' Megan mused, intentionally changing the subject.

'Because I think you two looked pretty cosy earlier,' Kat continued.

'I wonder what her major is going to be.' The warm day borderlined on the hot side and Megan lifted her arms over her head, trying to draw whatever comfort she could from the cooler breeze. 'All she does is study.'

'I think you look good together, too. Both dark and pretty.' Kat leant her elbow on the table.

Green paint chipped from the top, weathered from years outside in the elements. Trees shaded the area, saving them from the direct sunlight. Small paths wound into the forest that was only metres from the main road. Ryan, Douglas and Vincent had disappeared, their father with a birdwatching chart, Ryan with his camera and Vincent with a bug catcher's net.

'Do you think she's scared to graduate? I know it sounds silly, but I've always gotten the impression she's frightened of starting her life for real so she keeps finding excuses not to leave school, like if she decides on a career she'll be stuck forever doing the same thing.' Megan stared at her college-bound sister, watching Sasha twirl a piece of her dark-brown hair as she followed the page with her finger.

'Ryan is a nice guy,' Kat said.

'I don't understand why she doesn't just pick a subject and go with it.'

'He's smart and just mellow enough to put up with your ways.'

'She's got so much going for her.' Megan refused to look at Kat and refused to acknowledge the whole other conversation her sister was trying to have with her.

'You need to take it easy on him. Don't worry, he hasn't complained. He wouldn't. But I saw his face when you walked away from him at the museum to join Mom in the gift shop. Whatever you said to him hurt his feelings.'

'I wonder how Ella's doing. Have you heard from her?' Megan turned a pointed look to Kat.

'You're not going to talk to me about this, are you?' Kat sighed heavily, shaking her head in what looked to be a cross between irritation and exasperation.

'I'm going to go see if Mom needs help with the picnic baskets.' Megan stood up.

'You know, Miss Megs, you can't run from the happy side of life forever,' Kat yelled after her. 'It's going to bite you in the ass someday whether you want it to or not.'

'How about them Yankees?' Megan answered, not bothering to turn around.

'Ornithologists say this area is renowned for its unusual bird species,' Douglas said, lifting his binoculars and pointing them towards a tree. 'But I'll be damned if I've seen a single one in these woods. I can hear them, I just can't see them.'

'We saw a golden eagle this morning,' Ryan said. 'Megan and I.'

'Did you?' Douglas lowered the binoculars in excitement. 'I would have loved to have been there.'

'I'll bet you have some luck back at the cabin this evening, when it's cooler,' Vincent said. His net rested against the bench he'd found along the path. Douglas moved to sit by his son-in-law. 'There was a hummingbird feeder on the deck. No hummingbirds, but there was a feeder.'

Douglas chuckled, before turning an expectant look at Ryan. 'Are you getting some good shots?'

Ryan felt mildly guilty about how he came to be on the trip. He liked both men a lot and found Douglas to be an interesting combination of doting father and distracted scholar. 'Yeah, I think so. I plan on taking my equipment out with me tomorrow at dawn.'

'I think he meant are you getting some good shots in with Megan.' Vincent laughed.

Douglas snorted. 'Out of all my daughters, boy, you sure did pick the spitfire.'

Both men didn't bother to contain their merriment, as they laughed harder.

'I suppose she can be a handful,' Ryan admitted reluctantly.

'Try two fistfuls,' Douglas corrected. 'Megan has always been strong willed and law abiding.' He made a soft noise of amusement. 'She used to throw the biggest tantrums if she saw me speeding in the car, or if I rolled past a stop sign. Got to the point I made sure to put her right behind the driver's seat so she couldn't see what I was doing.'

Ryan laughed. He noticed Megan always took the seat right behind her dad in the rental. Seeing movement out of the corner of his eyes, he instantly lifted his camera and waited.

'You got something?' Douglas asked, standing.

'Bird. Up there.' Ryan adjusted the zoom on his lens until he could focus on the small animal on a tree. It was high up, but the camera lens afforded him a good look at it.

'What does it look like?' Douglas asked, only to add, 'Vincent, get the chart.'

'Red face, yellow and black body,' Ryan said, taking a picture.

'I don't see it,' Douglas looked through his binoculars, angling them back and forth to follow the direction Ryan's camera had pointed. 'Ah, there it is.'

'Tanager, maybe,' Vincent said. The paper chart he held rustled in the wind as the bird took to flight.

'Let's see if we can find it again.' Douglas led the way deeper into the trees, away from the picnic area.

After a minute of quiet hiking along the worn forest trail, Douglas stopped. 'Look there. I think it's old gravestones.'

'What are they doing in the forest?' Vincent asked. 'There is nothing around here.'

'Might have been an old settlement near by at one time or a farmstead. I've run across these old sunken graveyards a time or two in Kansas as a kid.' Ryan walked into the trees, kneeling by a weathered stone. He ran his fingers over the top, shivering at the idea of how long the site could have remained untouched. The carvings were faded, the names long ago erased from history. There were only about a dozen gravesites, at least from what he could tell of the sunken markers. Some of them were overgrown with plant life and covered with years of fallen leaves.

'I should go get Kat,' Vincent said. 'She would want to see this.'

'Yeah, let's go get something to eat and we'll bring the girls back after,' Douglas said. 'Ryan, you coming?'

'Just a second, I want to get a few shots. You two go ahead.'

'Where's Ryan?' Kat asked, drawing Megan's attention up from the plastic bag filled with roast beef on whole-grain sandwiches.

'We found graves in the woods,' Vincent began.

'What?' Megan stood in instant concern, her brain humming to life as she automatically switched to detective mode. 'How old are they? You didn't touch anything, did you? The police will need the crime scene exactly like it was left so they can search for clues. Kat, quick, give me your cell phone. I'm going to try and call the local police department. Mom, I'm going to need some string, or rope to make a barrier. What? What is so funny?' Megan arched a brow at her father.

'It's an old sunken graveyard,' Douglas said. 'I doubt the police will be very interested.'

'Ha! You should have seen your face, Megan.' Sasha pointed and laughed, as if she'd been in on the joke when clearly she hadn't.

'Oh, neat, I want to go see.' Kat began walking towards the forest.

'Hold it right there,' Beatrice ordered. 'Let's eat before the bugs get it.'

'OK,' Kat mumbled, kicking at the dirt.

'Megan, go find Ryan and tell him to come get something to eat,' Beatrice ordered.

'Just down the trail,' Vincent said. 'On the right side. You can't miss it.'

'Kat can go,' Megan said. Her sister wanted to anyway.

'No,' Beatrice ordered. 'I told you to go. Kat will get distracted and we will never see them again.'

'She's got a point,' Sasha agreed.

Kat shrugged. 'Yep. Mom's probably right.'

'Fine,' Megan grumbled, going into the woods. 'I don't know why I have to get him. He'll come back when he gets hungry.'

'Thank you, dear!' Beatrice called cheerfully after her.

Megan lifted her hand and waved acknowledgement. Birds chirped in the distance, but were drowned out by the sound of her feet crunching on the leaves and twigs lining the trails. Her eyes focused forwards, she looked for movement along the side of the trail. Suddenly, a hand shot out from behind a tree and grabbed her. Megan stiffened, ready to fight, but held back as she saw Ryan's face. He tugged her into his embrace, holding her against his body.

'Worried about me?' he asked, making a soft noise of appreciation as he ran his hands over her hips. He glanced back. 'Are we alone?'

'Yes and no,' she said.

'You were worried about me?' A slow seductively cocky smile crossed his features.

'I meant, yes we are alone and no I wasn't worried.' Megan tried to pull back, but Ryan gripped her hips tightly.

'Mm, not so fast. I want to show you something.' His mouth was a hair's breadth away from her.

'I already heard about the old graves,' she said.

'Come see them,' he urged her, his gaze steady.

'Do I have to?' The breeze stirred gently at her back, pushing loosened strands of her hair towards him. They hit his chest, caressing him as she wanted to do. Her body ached with uncertainty in light of his tender look.

'Yes, you have to.' Ryan pulled her behind him, leading her deeper into the woods.

Megan saw the old rocks on the ground, nearly shape-less masses only recognisable by their arched appearance and the weathered engraving of a cross barely visible along the bumpy front.

Ryan pulled her body along his, letting her feel the beginning arousal that pressed against his jeans. 'I want to fuck you here.'

'What? Here?' Megan forced a frown.

'It is good luck,' he assured her.

'You made that up.' Lifting her hand to his chin, she rubbed her palm against the coarse hair on his jaw. The shade of the branches overhead cast his face into shadow and strands of his hair caught the narrow rays that managed to filter through.

'No, it's true. Honest.'

She lifted her other hand, pulling his face to hers to kiss him lightly. Her tongue traced the line of his mouth, while her hands pulled at the back of his head to urge him closer. His firm mouth moved expertly against her, giving her what she sought. The tight feel of his body drew her to him, until she melted against his length. She tried to get him to deepen the kiss by nudging his lips with her tongue. He groaned, opening his mouth to hers. A mutual flame coursed through their bodies in shared desire.

The isolation of the forest combined with the forbid-den imagery of what was around them. Megan pulled back, her chest heaving for air as she glanced around. The others waited for them and she found a secret thrill at the idea they might be caught. Even though she had the comfort of knowing her family would wait before sending someone in after them.

Ryan let go of her. 'Take off your pants. I want to fuck you right here, right now, in this forest. I don't want you to ever forget this moment, or me.'

How could she forget something like this? It was the story she'd be thinking of when she was eighty years old

MICHELLE M PILLOW

talking about the good ol' days. He motioned for her to follow, leading her into the forest away from the old stones.

Ryan took a condom out of his pocket and placed the corner of the wrapper between his teeth as he quickly undid his pants. Megan kicked her shoes from her feet, using her toes for leverage, only to stand on them to keep from walking on the forest floor barefoot. She tugged her jeans and panties down at the same time, standing exposed and naked. Then, slipping her feet back into the shoes, she waited as Ryan tore open the package with his teeth and spat the wrapper aside. He unrolled the thin latex rubber over the stiff length of his cock, stroking himself in the process.

'There is so much I want to do to you, but we don't have the time.' He kept his voice soft, as if they might be overheard. Megan was glad he couldn't see her face in the shadowed enclosure. All thoughts of how they came to be together fell from her mind until it was only the moment before them.

'What would you do to me?' Megan kept her eyes on his as she picked the best spot she could find, an old curved tree with barren limbs just about the right height to hold on to. 'Tell me. I want to know.'

'First, I'd kiss and touch every inch of your body. Then, I'd bury my face between your thighs and make you come.'

'Is that all you got? Surely you have wickeder thoughts than that. Aren't you artistic types supposed to be creative?' Megan arched a brow in challenge, even as she leant her back against the tree and lifted her arms. Spreading her legs in invitation, she smiled naughtily and licked her lips.

'I was only starting,' he assured her, coming to her ready body. He fisted his cock, running his hand up and down as he neared her. 'I'd only fuck you with my mouth after you were tied up, handcuffed to my bed and helpless to escape. I'd leave you like that, too, making you suck my dick as I straddled your face beneath me. And, with the taste of my cock on your lips and the flavourful cream of your pussy on mine, I'd kiss you until you were ready to be fucked again.'

'Ahh,' Megan panted. He took her by the hip, angling his arousal towards her sex. The cool rubber slipped between her folds as the tip probed her.

'You like that, don't you?' he asked, shading his eyes. 'You like being tied up and controlled?'

'I've never . . .' was all she managed to get out.

'Oh, so the little darling detective likes to be dominated. Interesting,' he mused. 'Is that what you like, Megan? Is that what you need? You need to be controlled, to be told what to do?'

Arousal hit her hard and she barely registered his use of the damned nickname the newspapers gave her. 'Ah, please, hurry.'

'Mm, maybe I should make you crawl and beg to suck my cock,' he whispered, his hot breath fanning her neck. His fingers ran passionately over her upper body to find a home on the soft curve of her breasts. He massaged the globes gently, peaking the nipples through her shirt. He grabbed her waist and lifted her up until she was face to face with him. With a barbaric growl, he leant to give a quick kiss to the top curve of her lush breast. 'I could keep you naked for a week on your hands and knees, body ready for me whenever I felt like taking it, your sweet pussy always at my disposal.'

'Try it and your little game just might backfire on you,' she assured him. To hear him say the words turned her on, to actually be forced to be a man's sex slave for a week was another matter. Submissive in the bedroom was one thing, being a full-time submissive was a completely different one that she would never agree to. She was too decisive a person to take that many orders.

'It's just talk, sweetheart. I would never do anything you didn't want.'

His very nearness empowered her. Ryan was so strong, yet so gentle. His lips devoured her neck, pushing her harder against the tree. Megan purred in the back of her throat. 'It might be you in chains as I make you beg.'

'OK,' he said, grinning as he pushed his hand between her thighs, denying her his cock. 'And what would you do with me, my sweet mistress, as you had me chained to your will?'

His chest grazed hers and she arched her back in pleasure. A sweet low moan escaped her lips as she gasped for breath, unable to answer. He held the back of her head captive by her hair. Forcing her chin into the air, he bit lightly at her ear. The hand between her thighs continued to stroke her – a mindlessly precise rhythm.

'Ah, take me,' she demanded, forgetting his question as the need became too much.

He groaned, the smile fading as his cock replaced his hand, teasing as he rubbed the tip back and forth over her swollen clit. His mouth ravished her throat in hot oscillations of desire. Her hands glided over the firm length of his tightly drawn flesh, needing to feel him. She caressed the deep folds of his muscles, wishing they had time to strip completely.

'I love the feel of you,' he said, 'and the taste.'

To prove his point, he licked her neck and groaned loudly. His words hummed delightfully in her veins, making her dizzy. She grabbed the branch above her head, lifting her body as she spread her legs wider. He thrust up, entering her hard.

'Every time I look at you, I want you.' Ryan's hips pumped in wild abandon.

Arching her back, she thrust forwards. His body slid into her with ease. Megan let out a loud moan of satisfaction. She seized the tree branch above her head for support, as his hands supported her ass, spreading her cheeks slightly. His movements became more fervent and the rhythm of his hips quickened, urging her to her climax.

'So good,' he whispered, stringing along unintelligible compliments as they neared release.

Megan bit her lip to keep from crying out, trembling with the crescendo of her desires. Suddenly, his throaty grunt joined hers as he climaxed, their joined flesh trembling in perfect unison. Her heavy breath mingled with his. As the shaking pleasure subsided, Megan's arms weakened and dropped from the tree on to his shoulders.

Her body sated, she was compelled to act. 'We need to get back before they come looking for us.'

'I know.' He brushed a kiss along her lips before letting her go. 'But first, I want to take a picture of us. Here in this place.'

Megan glanced down. 'You're crazy if you think I'm going to let you take a picture of me like this.'

'Don't trust me?' He quickly pulled up his pants.

She laughed, refusing to answer.

'Fine, put your clothes on. I don't need a photograph to remember how sexy your legs are.' Ryan grinned, eyeing her naughtily from head to toe. 'But, if you ever change your mind, I'll be more than willing to give you a private sitting in my studio. No charge.'

'No, thanks.' Megan shook her head, thinking, I really don't need any other compromising photos taken of me.

Chapter Eight

'Come on, Megs, get off your ass and dance!' Kat yelled as she jumped around the deck, twirling around Sasha who drunkenly pumped her arms. Stars filled the moon-lit sky, marred only by the drifting haze of grey clouds.

Vincent and Ryan laughed at the spectacle the two women were making on the deck turned dance floor. Cyndi Lauper's 'Girls Just Want To Have Fun' played loudly from the DVD player inside. Blue moonlight combined with the soft glow of firelight from the circular free-standing fire pit in the middle of the deck.

'Whoo hoo, shake it baby!' Kat ordered, pointing at Megan. 'Come on, big sista, dance with me.'

'I think I'll pass. You're being a big enough ass for the both of us.' Megan lifted her beer, angled it in a silent toast only to take a long drink.

It had been three amazing, if not slightly surreal, days since she'd made love with Ryan near the graveyard. Though things did not change between them, an easiness developed, if not somewhat of a silently agreed acceptance to follow the course of nature wherever it took them.

Often, the mood took them in their shared bedroom – never on the creaky bed, but on the floor, against the wall and even once on the rocking chair. It had been a precarious feat, one they agreed not to try again. He'd sat down with her sitting on his lap. In theory, the rocking motion of the chair should have been fun, but, in reality, it took a lot of muscle-straining work to get the rhythm right.

Twice, the course of nature took them during the now routine family picnics around lunchtime when they'd escape to a private place to be alone. There was something exhilarating about the mountain, the wide-open view. Even once, the mood took them in the early dawn hours with Megan kneeling over so he could take her from behind, hidden along the backside of the cabin where there were no windows, with only Ryan's sweatshirt to comfort her knees from the hard rocky ground. And the more they had sex, the more she became enthralled with the spontaneous forbidden passion of their acts.

'Spiritless wench,' Sasha yelled, drawing Megan's eyes back to her.

'Stop using old words, college girl,' Megan said.

'Read a book once in a while, tough chick-a-dee.' Grabbing Kat's hand as they half danced, half hopped in a circle, Sasha turned her attention to Vincent. 'Come dance with us, Vin.'

'Oh, he won't dance to this kind of music. It lacks class,' Kat said. 'But Ryan will dance with us, won't you?'

Both sisters sauntered over to him, not giving him a choice as they grabbed him by the arms. He didn't put up much of a fight.

Laughing, Ryan joked, 'Sure, I'll dance. I lack class.'

The music changed, blasting out another 1980s hit: 'Walk Like An Egyptian'.

Vincent slid into the seat next to Megan, taking a sip of his red wine. 'Man, I love your sister. Just look at her. She's amazing.'

Megan glanced at him, then followed his eyes to where Kat was bobbing her head back and forth, somewhat like a chicken, while thrusting one flattened hand in front and another in back. To Megan, Kat looked like a dork – a loveable dork, but a dork nonetheless. 'Yeah, amazing.'

Then, seeing Ryan dancing just as crazily as her sister, Megan couldn't help but laugh. He really didn't care what he looked like, as he mimicked their movements. Suddenly, the three dancers conferred among themselves, only to hurry into a straight line, one behind the other, with Ryan in front. Standing so their bodies couldn't be seen, Sasha and Kat wiggled their arms to the side to make Ryan look as if he had tentacles, as they occasionally poked their heads out on either side.

'You seem to be enjoying yourself,' Vincent said. 'Vacation going well so far?'

'Kat told you about what is going on, huh?' Megan's laughter died some.

'Oh?' The sound was unconvincing.

'Don't bother. I know she's in on this little scheme, just as I know you had nothing to do with it.' Megan sighed.

'Kat loves you, you know. She thinks Ryan can make you happy. That is why she did it.'

'It's not her place to decide, is it?' Megan took another drink from her beer, needing to change the subject. There was nothing Vincent could say to make her feel better about the situation. 'I tell you what, if I get dragged to another museum I'll gag – mountain folk, miners, dinosaurs, airplanes. Enough is enough. Besides, at the rate we're sightseeing, Zoe is going to miss all the fun.' The last word was drawled out and dripping with sarcasm.

'I don't know about that. If your mother keeps pushing to drive the four-hundred-mile scenic loop, I think there will be plenty of fun for everyone.' Vincent chuckled.

'Yeah, I'd hate for Zoe to miss out on the twenty-hour car ride Mom will turn that adventure into. And, between Ryan and Kat, it might even be longer if they keep stopping us to take pictures.'

Vincent gave her a wry look. 'As opposed to me holding us up so I can examine bug specimens.'

'Doesn't count.'

'And why is that?'

Megan grinned. 'Because you're sitting right here and we're bitching about the people who aren't sitting right here.'

'Ah, I see. So you won't talk about my bugs and I won't mention how I think your idea of climbing straight up the side of a mountain only to jump off a perfectly good ledge into unknown waters is a horrific way to spend an afternoon.'

'Exactly.' Megan took another drink of her beer, finishing the bottle. She leant over, setting it down on the deck next to her other empty ones.

Ryan moved to the back of the line and now Kat was the leader as the others' arms fluttered from behind her, turning her into some mythical creature with wiggling tentacles. Unable to help herself as the song ended, Megan tossed back her head and laughed. 'What do you say, Dr Richmond? Should we go show them how it's done?'

'Mm, one moment.' He grabbed his wineglass and drank the liquid down fast. 'OK, I might just be drunk enough now.'

'Hey Ya' started, an odd contrast to the older music they'd been listening to.

'Come here, bug man,' Kat ordered, crooking her fingers at him. 'Come dance with your wife.'

'Anything you say, my butterfly.' Vincent instantly went to Kat, grabbing her into his arms and lifting her off the ground. His dancing was reminiscent of a cross between a Tango and the Lambada.

'I always hear this song, but don't know who sings it,' Sasha said, taking Ryan's hand and using it to twirl herself around.

'They don't teach you pop culture in college?' Ryan gave Sasha an expression of mock horror.

'Outkast,' Megan answered, getting their attention. At their stunned look, she said, 'What? I listen to music. I'm hip. I know what's going down.'

'Oh, yeah, Miss Law and Order, you're real groovy,' Sasha teased.

'Shut up and dance with me,' Megan ordered. Cutting in, she grabbed Sasha's hand and began wiggling about the deck in what she knew to be an outrageous excuse for dancing. She did it on purpose, knowing if she were to seriously try it would be disastrous.

Sasha spun her around and Megan found herself twirled into Ryan's arms. She inhaled a deep breath, instantly pushing back. He grabbed her hand, automatically drawing her forwards so she was once more within reach of his embrace. Sasha put her hands in the air and skipped around the two couples, clearly not caring that she didn't have a partner.

Fresh air filled her lungs and Megan couldn't help but lift her arms to her sides, taking deep breaths. Ryan touched her cheek, a light skimming movement. He looked as if he might try kissing her, so she dropped her arms and began mimicking some of Sasha's dance moves.

Vincent and Kat moved fluidly together, as if sensing each other's body, knowing without words what the other would do. Megan wasn't so confident with Ryan. They didn't instinctively know each other's next move. So, when they danced, it reflected the newness of their relationship in each halted movement, each hesitant touch.

If Ryan felt the awkwardness, he didn't let on. Megan tried to look into his eyes, without appearing to gaze up into them. Being with him, in Montana, with no mysteries piling up on her desk to be solved, felt strange. She didn't feel like herself, not her normal, put-together, take-charge self. Here, it was easy to pretend this wasn't her life. She was someone else, someone free of responsibility and consequence. It had been a lifetime since she'd felt . . .

A flash illuminated Ryan's face. Megan blinked, seeing

spots along the side of her vision. She frowned, shaking her head as if she could recapture the drunken insight she'd been having. Since she'd felt...? Damn. It was gone and Megan was left with a feeling of something important she couldn't quite reach waiting on the edge of her mind.

Beatrice made a loud noise of joyous contentment. 'Ah, look at you all. If only my Sasha had someone to dance with.'

'Ugh, Mom, get Megan settled first, then work on the other two before you get to me.' Sasha didn't stop dancing.

'Smile for the camera!' Beatrice called.

'Mom,' Kat scolded as she ran towards their mother. 'Be careful with that, please.'

'What? Oh, I only dropped it that one time.' Beatrice sighed as Kat jerked the camera out of her hands.

'And broke an eight-hundred-dollar lens I'd spent months selling my blood to get,' Kat answered. 'I gave enough plasma to save the entire state of New York.'

'I can't believe you're still using that one on her,' Megan said to Kat. Ryan's arm was still along her side, holding her near him, but not too close. It had become like that over the last few days. She hadn't noticed the exact moment that he'd started touching her without direct passion, but it felt normal that he did. 'You got it used for fifty dollars at a police auction.'

'Megan!' Kat gasped, her eyes wide in mock distress, as if to ask, 'How could you rat me out like that?'

'Katarina Matthews, er, Richmond,' her mother scolded, remembering her married name at the last second. 'You may be grown, but I'm still your mother and I can ground you if I want. I can't believe you made me think... Oh!'

'Ha ha,' Megan taunted playfully. Sasha giggled. Ryan's grip tightened on Megan's hip and, though she refused to look at him, she was very aware of every place their bodies touched. 'Kat's in trouble. Kat's in trouble.'

Sasha joined in the singsong chanting and Megan used it as an excuse to artfully pull away from Ryan's hold. As soon as she did, she wondered why she had. Her skin missed his heat. Who was she kidding? She missed him holding her.

'Kat's in trouble. Kat's in trouble,' Sasha and Megan repeated, their voices growing in volume.

'Shut up!' Kat yelled, reminding Megan of when they were kids. 'Shut up or I'll tell Ryan that you came to my house looking for a sexy designer gown to wear for him while we were here!'

Megan's chanting died mid-sentence and Sasha's voice tapered off soon after.

'Megs?' Sasha gasped, covering her mouth like a naughty child.

Megan's jaw dropped and she eyed Kat in shock. How could her sister have said that? And in front of Ryan? 'I ... I ... No, but, I ...'

Kat nodded, pursing her lips tightly together. 'Not so loud-mouthy now, are you?'

'But, I ...' Megan looked helplessly at her mother. How could she use the 'Mom wanted her to dress up so they could go to a nice restaurant' excuse with her mother standing right there, able to deny her claim? She felt the eyes of her family on her, of Ryan, as they waited for her to speak.

Her mind raced with panicked thoughts. Omigod, Ryan will think I wanted him to be here. That I was excited to be with him. Hurry, think of something quick.

'Megan?' Ryan whispered softly. Or did she just imagine she'd heard his voice over the ending threads of the song. Her heart was pounding and everyone was staring at her. Even her father's face appeared on the other side of the window, his figure outlined by the soft firelight inside the living room's fireplace.

'Yeah, well,' Megan pointed at Kat through the sudden silence. 'Kat's pregnant! With a baby!'

Another song began, but Megan couldn't process what it was over the soft almost whining melody. Stunned, she watched as her world seemed to spin and slow. Each expression was etched on her mind as she looked from face to face.

Kat gasped. 'Megan!'

'Butterfly?' Vincent made a weak noise of hesitant excitement. 'Kat, is it true? A baby?'

'Yippee!' Beatrice yelled, jumping up and down like a maniac. 'Kat, sweetheart. Oh, I have to tell someone. Douglas, Douglas!' Their mother ran into the cabin. 'Douglas, hurry, I need to use the phone. I have to call someone.'

The deck exploded into a sea of chaos as everyone started talking at once.

'Megan!' Kat screeched.

'Oh, butterfly, is it true?' Vincent asked, pulling Kat to his chest with a happy smile. Her face became muffled in his chest and her hands lifted to weakly pat his arms as he rocked her back and forth.

'Congratulations,' Ryan said, going to shake Vincent's hand. 'This is wonderful news. I know you'll both be wonderful parents.'

'Damn it, Megan,' Kat said. 'How could you tell?'

'Congrats, sis! I can't believe I'm going to be an aunt.' The music inside had stopped with the commotion, but Sasha did a little happy dance anyway.

'Butterfly, what's wrong? Don't you want to have my baby?' Vincent looked hurt.

'No, yes, but yes, of course I want to have your baby,' Kat assured him, torn between glaring at Megan and trying to comfort her worried husband.

Megan swallowed. She couldn't believe she'd said that.

Shaking, she didn't move from her spot as she stared at Kat.

'I need to speak with my daughter,' Beatrice yelled into the phone so loud her voice carried outside. 'I don't care if she doesn't have phone privileges. I don't care if you are the US Navy, I'm her mother. I didn't spend fifty hours in labour to be told by you I can't talk to my daughter. This is a family emergency. Her name is Ella Matthews.'

'Kat,' Megan finally managed. 'Oh, Kat.'

'Megan, how did you even know?' Kat stepped towards her.

'I saw the pregnancy test this morning in the . . .' Megan motioned weakly in the direction of the upstairs bedrooms. 'Ryan was in our bathroom, so I . . . It was in the trash.'

'Always playing the detective, aren't you?' Kat whispered, her eyes wide. 'How could you tell them?'

Mortified by what she'd done, especially in light of Kat's expression, Megan wasn't sure what to do – a feeling she wasn't too familiar with having. Kat's anger, Megan could have handled, but the look of complete shock and utter disbelief was worse. Her sister looked as if she'd been betrayed and that betrayal was a light Megan had never seen in Kat's eyes.

'Kat . . .' Megan tried to think of the right words.

'It was *my* secret to tell,' Kat said, so soft the others couldn't hear.

Her sister turned her back on them and that's when Megan realised the seconds had been drawn out, seeming longer than they had been as her guilt swam inside her. Vincent looked mildly worried, but the others didn't seem to have a clue what was happening between Kat and Megan. There was more than what was being said in words. Kat was pissed off and doing her damnedest not to show it in front of everyone else.

Shaking her head, Kat forced a smile to her face as

Vincent walked with her inside. Her expression was strained as Megan watched her through the window. Vincent shook Douglas's hand excitedly. Sasha ran to open another bottle of wine. Beatrice continued arguing with whoever was on the other end of her phone call to Ella.

'Huh,' Ryan said softly. Megan turned to him, stunned to find him still with her on the balcony. He lifted Kat's wineglass. 'Cranberry juice.'

'She wouldn't drink, not with the baby.' Megan turned back to the window, watching the scene inside. Her pregnant sister didn't look at her. 'Not Kat. She'd never harm another soul. It's not in her. She's not like me. She's sweet.'

'Why don't we go inside with the others and celebrate?' Ryan tried to pull her arm. 'So you told her secret. I'm sure she'll get over it. Good news always has a way of keeping people happy. She probably had some grand plan as to how she was going to announce it. You know Kat.'

Megan jerked away from him. 'You go, Ryan. I've done enough damage for one night.'

'OK, so we'll stay out here together and –'

'Ryan, go.' Her tone was harsh, but she didn't try to soften it. She turned her back on him, facing the mountain range that wasn't visible in the dark distance. 'I don't want you right now.'

For a moment, he didn't speak. Finally, Megan saw him nod his head, from the corner of her eye. 'I see.'

The sound of his footfall hit hard upon the deck. Megan bit her lip, rolled her eyes towards the expanse of the starry heavens in an act of self-deprecation before saying, 'I didn't mean it like that. I don't want to be with anyone right now.'

There wasn't an answer and when she turned, his name on her lips, she found that he'd gone inside and was taking a glass of wine from Sasha. Megan crossed her arms, her body shaking. She had really put her foot in it this time.

Her head ached, but, if Megan had any doubts about her run-of-the-mouth accident the evening before being just a dream, Kat's cold stare directed at her cleared up the confusion. Her sister sat, wrapped in a blanket on the couch. The television played softly in the background. Since there was no reception, Megan knew she was watching one of the very few DVDs available to guests but thought better of asking what it was called.

Rays of late-morning sunlight streamed in from the picture window, but Megan was too hungover to notice the pretty scenery. She'd come inside the night before only after her mother's insistence and continued to drink herself into a near stupor. Sadly, she didn't even remember going to bed, only that she'd awakened in her clothes in the early hours to puke her drunken guts out. Ryan hadn't been there.

'Where is everyone?' Megan asked, knowing instinctively that Kat wouldn't answer her. By everyone, she really meant Ryan, though her father, Vincent and Sasha were missing as well.

It was her mother who answered. 'The guys have gone fishing. They should be out of our hair all day.'

Great, Megan thought grumpily. In light of her queasy stomach and throbbing temples, she wasn't too disappointed about being left behind.

'And Sasha?' Megan asked, just as her sister came out of the downstairs bathroom.

'Sasha is bloated and crampy,' Sasha answered, moaning dramatically as she picked a coffee mug off the counter and stumbled to the couch to sit by Kat. She tugged on her sister's blanket until Kat let go and they both could snuggle. 'Mommy, can you hand us the remote? It's too quiet. I can't hear what they are saying.'

'Oh, poor things.' Beatrice shook her head, instantly

falling into the motherly role at Sasha's childish endearment. Calling her 'Mommy' was a free pass to getting whatever they wanted. 'It's a good thing we've decided to spend the day in.'

Realising she still stood in the kitchen in front of the coffeepot on the bar, Megan grabbed a clean mug and finally poured herself a cup. As Beatrice handed Sasha the remote control only to lean over and tuck the two girls in, Megan had the strongest urge to join the two of them on the couch so she could get in on the motherly pampering. Knowing Kat would probably like nothing more than to throw her out the window if she tried, she instead chose to sit across from them on a chair.

'Mommy, can you get the window, we're getting glary spots,' Sasha said. She gave Kat a mischievous smile, clearly aware of what she was doing. By the look on Beatrice's amused face behind them as she went to draw the curtains, their mother wasn't unaware herself.

'Thanks, Mommy,' Kat and Sasha sang out in unison. Now that the room was darker, it was easier to see the television screen. Couples danced in a line, dressed in period clothing that had to be over a hundred years old in design.

'I thought the only movies they had were westerns and musicals,' Megan said, hoping Kat would answer.

'Kat brought this one,' Sasha said.

'What is it?' Megan asked, taking a sip of her hot coffee only to flinch as it burnt her taste buds. She leant over to put the mug down on the coffee table. Their mother had disappeared into her bedroom.

'I dunno,' Sasha answered.

'*Pride and Prejudice*,' Kat said, her tone flat as she refused to look at Megan. 'And why don't you stop talking before you ruin this for me, too.'

Megan held her breath, stunned that Kat had said it. Out of all the sisters, Kat had always been the most tolerant, the most accepting towards her and the most forgiving. But her words hurt, cutting deeply at her core. If she didn't have work and if she didn't have all her sisters, she was left with nothing. Having Kat mad at her was a fate worse than being transferred to vice to play prostitute for the rest of her career. Megan dug her back into the chair, slouching. There was no way this day could get any worse.

'Guess what I have,' Beatrice called in excitement. 'Since the guys are gone and we're stuck here all alone without a car. I thought we'd do makeovers. Who's first for the spa treatment?'

Megan tilted her head, seeing that her mother carried two large black bags. Spa treatment was her mother's way of politely saying waxing legs, plucking eyebrows, filing nails and lying around with seaweed mud herbal gunk on their faces – or whatever Beatrice's latest facial concoction was.

'And I think Megan should go first.' Beatrice winked at her.

Megan could barely suppress her groan at her mother's proposed torture. She'd been wrong. The day was definitely looking to be a lot worse.

'Great.' Megan forced a smile, trying to hide her sarcasm. 'Can't wait to get started.'

'I don't understand why we can't catch a fish as long as our outspread arms, like the guy in all the brochures,' Vincent said, lifting the squirming fish he'd caught with one hand. It was only five inches long. The creature opened and closed its mouth, as if gasping for air. 'OK, then, back you go, little guy.'

'Don't want to keep him?' Douglas asked. 'I think it would have made a fine hors d'oeuvre.'

'Perfect, one tiny hors d'oeuvre for seven people.' Ryan laughed. He'd been trying hard to enjoy himself, or at least to act like he was enjoying himself. Megan's comment the night before stung. She'd said she didn't want him, like he was some plaything for her to screw while she was on vacation with nothing better to do. He'd been foolish to think she really liked him.

'It wasn't tiny. The way I remember it, the fish was this big,' Vincent said, holding his hands out to signify what equalled the size of a dolphin.

Ryan chuckled. 'Don't you worry, buddy, I seem to remember the same thing.'

'Speaking of things not being what they appear,' Douglas said.

Ryan's smile faded. Did the man know the truth about his relationship, or lack there of, with Megan?

'Don't worry, son. Sasha explained everything to me,' Douglas said.

Ryan looked at Vincent, who appeared as stunned as he felt. Clearing his throat, he tried to apologise. 'I never meant for things to get so far out of hand. I mean –'

'Think no more about it, boy. I've lived with women my whole life.' Douglas chuckled. 'And I can tell you this much. Find a hobby that takes you out of the house at least once a month, because those mood swings women get only become stranger with age and there isn't a damn thing you can do to make it all better. When a woman gets her time of the month, that's our sign to run as fast as we can – like today.'

Ryan sighed in relief, giving a slight smile. 'Yeah, thanks Douglas, I'll keep that in mind.'

'You do that, son, you do that and I promise you that your marriage will be much happier for it.'

Chapter Nine

Ryan let loose a long breath. Under normal circumstances, just looking at Megan made his dick hard. But this wasn't an ordinary circumstance and his dick wasn't just hard, it was about to take off into orbit.

Megan slowly walked down the stairs, her eyes down as she watched each step. He felt like an oversexed teenager going to the prom, seeing the stunningly gorgeous vision who would be in his arms and hopefully into the back of his car or some cheesy hotel room by the end of the night.

Her hair was piled halfway up on her head, only to fall in long curls over her back. Hot-pink and brown tulle gripped Megan's waist and chest so tight he couldn't help but greedily lick his bottom lip at the way her cleavage jiggled with each downward step. There were no straps holding the bodice up and he imagined how easy it would be to dip his finger down the front to pull out a hard nipple. Sheer brown covered the bodice, stopping as it reached the ribbon tie belt and full skirt decorated with lace appliqués. High heels made her legs look extra long and delectable.

They'd been in Montana for seven days, the last three of which were spent estranged from the beauty before him. Zoe had arrived that morning and this outing was to celebrate her joining them. She had driven to the cabin in her own rental car, a small two-door that made strange clanking noises when put into gear.

Now, as he again looked at Megan's tanned chest, he couldn't seem to recall exactly why he'd been denying himself the pleasure of her body. So what if she was using him? His cock was pleading to be taken advantage of.

Her sisters were just as prettily done up – Sasha in a shiny chocolate-brown halter gown, Kat in a draping blue silk print kimono which looked fetching next to Vincent's finely cut suit, and Zoe in an Ancient Greek patterned silk twill dress. Beatrice wore more of a black pantsuit with leopard-print accents, a wild contrast to Douglas's tweed jacket. Since the best he could come up with was a pair of dark dress slacks and a lightweight black argyle V-neck sweater, he felt severely underdressed.

'Oh, I want a guy who looks at me like that,' Zoe said with a girly sigh.

Ryan blinked, realising she referred to the way he was staring at Megan like a love-crazed maniac. Perhaps that was because he *was* a love-crazed maniac when it came to his sweet confident detective. Thank the stars his slacks were loose and his boxer briefs were tight. With Megan in that dress, he was in for a very difficult night.

Hunting Season, though listed as a fine dining establishment in the local phonebook, was hardly what veteran New Yorkers would consider a five-star culinary experience. Like everything else in the state, there was a down-home country feel to the restaurant's motif. Megan liked the warm comfortable ambience more than she did some of the places Zoe dragged her to in the city.

'The wine list is actually pretty good,' Zoe said, studying the wine book the host provided for her, after a long speech about how they were very lucky to get into the normally booked restaurant. Zoe merely smiled at the man, as it had been her cunning that got them the table in the first place. Apparently, she'd name-dropped a few high-profile chefs that she'd worked with in New York.

'I think I'm going to go with one of their local microbrews,' Megan said.

A fire burnt low along the far wall in the stone

fireplace. Though full, everyone talked in hushed tones and the dining room wasn't loud.

'Go figure that,' Sasha drawled. 'Megan drinking beer. You are such a cop.'

'Thanks for clearing that up. It would explain why I'm craving doughnuts to go with my beer.' Megan rolled her eyes only to stop on Ryan. His dark gaze studied her intently. It was the same expression he wore when he'd seen her walk down the stairs, the same expression Zoe had called him on. Out of all his looks, she'd come to know this one best. He was horny and he was plotting ways to get her alone.

'We should let Vincent order the wine,' Zoe said.

'Oh, easy,' Sasha warned, grinning into her menu. 'The last time we talked about this, Megan went into a diatribe about underage drinking.'

'Well,' Megan said, frowning. 'It is illegal.'

'Ah, but Vincent only drank underage in Europe.' Sasha giggled, knowing full well she was trying to rile her sister. It was working, too. Megan felt the hairs on the back of her neck prickling.

'To tell you the truth,' Ryan said. 'I never much understood what wines went with what. It all tastes like liquor to me.'

'I like the warm fuzzies we get when drinking it,' Zoe said.

'Ah-ha!' Kat pointed at her. 'The real reason you became a chef!'

'You caught me. I'm working my way up to a thankless middle-management job for the free cooking spirits.'

They all laughed. Megan's eyes met Kat's briefly, smiling. Her sister quickly turned away, her happy expression fading some. Megan felt a pang of guilt renew itself inside her. She felt horrible about telling Kat's secret, but every time she tried to go near her sister, Kat would find a way to ignore her.

'This conversation reminds me of that night Kat brought Vincent to meet us. She was so jealous of Megan,' Zoe teased. 'She told him that Megan was allergic to pasta just to get him to take her out on a group date instead of meeting Megan alone for dinner. She weaselled her way in.'

'That's right!' Sasha laughed, clapping her hands. 'I almost forgot about that.'

Megan glanced at Ryan sideways, as she took a drink of the water that was already set out on the table. He studied her intently. 'So, you and Vincent were dating?'

'What?' Megan choked.

'No, we were talking about work.' Vincent turned to his wife. 'I don't think you ever told me you were jealous of my having dinner plans with Megan.'

Kat grabbed her triangular dinner napkin off the table and threw it at Zoe. 'Thanks for ratting me out, sis!'

Zoe laughed. 'Well, at least now he knows that Megan wasn't really allergic to pasta. Um, you did know, right?'

Vincent chuckled, nodding.

'Yeah, you all laugh it up,' Megan warned. 'I'm the one who got stuck with an omelette while the rest of you had that gourmet masterpiece.'

'Hey, those were gourmet eggs,' Zoe joked.

'Yeah,' Sasha drawled. 'They came from the butts of Upper East Side chickens, not the pesky Bronx fowl.'

'Sasha!' Beatrice warned. Their mother's scolding only made their laughter worse.

'What?' Sasha shrugged with a look of fake innocence, clearly not caring that she was in trouble.

'Not at the table, dear,' Douglas said, his tone low and even. 'You know better than to call them pesky.'

They laughed harder.

'Oh.' Beatrice shook her head. 'We try to go somewhere nice and see what happens?'

'We all have a good time?' Megan asked, grinning.

Her mother instantly lightened.

'Like old times growing up,' Zoe added.

'And we get to be with the people we love,' Kat said.

'And we –' Sasha glanced around the table, searching for what to say '– we get to make the restaurant people sing happy birthday to . . .' Again she looked around, her eyes narrowing on Ryan. A mischievous grin curled the side of her lip. 'Ryan.'

'What? No, it's not my birthday,' Ryan protested.

'Oh, don't be shy, Ryan,' Kat said.

'I don't think they sing here,' Zoe put in. 'It doesn't seem like the singing type of place.'

'Oooh, you lucked out, buddy,' Vincent said. 'Though I have to say it's nice to have someone else to take the hit for me. Every time we go out to eat, I seem to celebrate another birthday.'

'Yeah, what are you? A hundred?' Zoe teased.

'Hey, free ice cream and cake,' Kat defended.

Megan watched, but Kat wouldn't look at her again.

'Welcome to Hunting Season,' a waiter said, appearing across the table from where she sat.

Megan ignored him as she looked at Ryan. He'd shaved and had his hair combed neatly back into a small ponytail at the nape of his neck. He lifted a water glass and took a sip and she swore she saw his tongue dart along the edge of the cup. When his eyes lifted, she was sure of it.

'Dreamy eyes will have a micro-brew,' Zoe said.

Megan gave her a look. It seemed her sister was making up for lost teasing. 'The darkest one you have, please.'

'Same,' Ryan said.

A white linen cloth covered with a cut piece of glass over the top of the long rectangular table blocked her hand from view as she slid it under the table and on to Ryan's knee. He tensed under her hand and she slowly rubbed along his inner thigh.

'Can I interest you in an appetiser?' the waiter asked.

'Mm.' Megan leant into Ryan. She couldn't resist playing with him. It was the same mischievous feeling she'd had in the alley as he took pictures of the museum crime scene. Gripping his thigh, she whispered into his ear, 'Yeah, how about an appetiser?'

'Yes,' he breathed.

The waiter looked at Ryan expectantly.

'The ... ah...' He paused, lifting his menu. Megan watched his throat work, wanting nothing more than to lean in and kiss the sexy spot right beneath his ear. 'Snake.'

'Texan rattlesnake cakes,' the waiter said. 'Excellent choice, sir.'

'Ew.' Sasha wrinkled her nose.

'Interesting. I like trying something new.' Zoe nodded in approval.

'I was thinking the same thing,' Douglas agreed. 'Try something new, my wife always says.'

'And now you listen?' Beatrice eyed him in disbelief. 'What does snake taste like, sir?'

'Chicken. They always say it tastes like chicken,' Sasha mumbled. 'So why don't we just eat chicken?'

'Ignore her,' Zoe told the waiter.

'And for the main course?' the waiter asked, his hands behind his back. He didn't write their orders down. 'Perhaps, some of our regional cuisine? We have a nice selection of aged steaks. Or, if you prefer, there is a terrific grilled salmon with lemon glaze, lobster bisque, penne pasta with scallops and cream sauce.' The waiter continued, as if reciting the menu he'd clearly memorised.

Megan again leant into Ryan, daring to drift her hand higher until she could feel the potent heat coming off his semi-aroused cock. 'I think I know what I want for my main course.'

Ryan adjusted the menu, continuing to stare at it with renewed force. She looked at it, so her family would think they discussed what to eat. It didn't matter, since everyone else had begun to place their orders and had their attention diverted to the task.

'Oh, yeah?' Ryan's breathing came hard and he gripped the menu tightly. His voice weak, he asked, 'Aged steak?'

'Mm, not quite. I prefer my meat young and hot.'

'Veal Parmesan?' he whispered.

'I want your hard dick in my mouth,' Megan said, sliding her hand over his inner thighs. 'I want to suck it until all the sweet creamy filling comes out.'

'Omigod, um, oh, wow, I, um,' he mumbled incoherently under his breath. Louder, he said, 'Porterhouse.'

'How would you like it cooked?' the waiter asked.

'Rare,' Megan said for him, smiling innocently.

'Oh, no, Megan, you can't order rare meat. It's not safe,' Beatrice said.

'Medium,' Ryan said, thought he still sounded shaky. Then, quickly, he added, 'Baked potato, ranch dressing.'

Megan pulled her hand away, giggling to herself. 'The pasta with scallops.'

'That was a dirty, dirty trick.' Ryan's breath fanned her neck and his hand slid under her gown over her bare leg only to discreetly pull back before reaching any real level of sexual intimacy. She clenched her thighs together, his playful stroke as tormenting as him thumbing her clit. 'And you are going to pay dearly for it.'

The evening rolled along with laughter, easy conversation and heaping piles of food. At one point the chef came out to schmooze with Zoe. For Megan, the only blight was Kat's refusal to look in her direction or talk to her directly. Ryan's heated looks sizzled with tempered passion and halfway through the main course she felt guilty for having felt him up with no way to finish what she'd started. By the end of the meal, the guilty feeling was gone, as he'd brushed his leg and hand casually against her several times. Aroused, it was all she could do not to grab him by his shirt front and drag him towards the bathroom stalls. The fact that sex in a public bathroom was about as appealing as swimming in the bacteria-filled Hudson River kept her from doing it.

After dinner, as they walked out to the car, Ryan's arm slipped around her from behind and pulled her gently back against his chest. As he lifted his free hand, she saw a set of car keys in it. He waved at her family, saying, 'Goodnight, everyone. Thanks for dinner. We'll be back at the cabin tomorrow. Zoe, thanks for letting us use the car.'

Zoe waved, giving an impishly cute grin. 'No biggie.'

'What are we doing?' Megan asked, as the doors to the SUV slammed shut. Sasha's hand showed out the side of the window, as she waved to them.

'I called and made us reservations at a hotel here in town tonight.' Ryan let go of her and, whistling softly, twirled the keys around his forefinger as he went to the driver side of Zoe's small rental car.

Megan looked around. The town, settled in a valley, was at the base of the Rocky Mountains, much closer to the majestic rocks than their cabin in the wilderness. Tiny compared to New York, Miner's Pass was a long main strip of businesses. Hunting Season and its adjoining lodge were the biggest establishment and appeared to attract the kind of wealthy crowd that normally frequented quiet out-of-the-way luxury haunts. The other businesses were geared towards tourists – bait shops, curios, country general store boasting five-dollar T-shirts – with the occasional sign for a realtor or insurance agent poking out from their woodsy-looking depths.

'OK,' Megan said as she opened the car door with a frown. 'Why are we staying here in town? We have a room already.'

'Because,' Ryan said, starting the engine, 'our other

room is in a house full of your family and we need to be alone.'

'We do?' Megan hid her smile, as she fastened her seatbelt. Feeling him up under the table had obviously gotten him a lot randier than she realised if he was going to such lengths to get her all to himself. So, Mr Lucas planned on getting her alone so they could have wild crazy, loud sex all night. She was wholeheartedly supportive of his sordid plan.

'We're going to talk,' he said, as he read a small piece of paper in his hand only to glance back and forth at the road signs.

'Talk?' Megan gave a small sultry laugh. She wiggled in her seat, parting her legs in subtle invitation.

'Yes, talk.'

'I like talk.' He sounded so serious, but she wasn't fooled. If he had anything to discuss with her, it probably consisted of some choice dirty little words. 'What do you want to talk about?'

'Not here, let's get to the hotel.'

'How about . . . ?' She bit her lip. 'Rattlesnake really does taste like chicken.'

'Curious, wasn't it?'

'Mm, very. I'm so glad we had this talk. Now, I want to show you something else that you might find fascinating.' Megan grabbed one of his hands, and brought it to her leg. He glanced down, moaning softly. She manoeuvred in her seat so her knees were angled in towards him. Inching her skirt up, she exposed her knees.

'I need my hand.' To prove his point, Ryan lifted it off her and looked at the paper, reading more directions. The car slowed and he turned the corner. There were no stop lights and only a few yield signs on what looked to be the main roads.

Megan grabbed his wrist and placed his hand back on her body, only this time on her naked flesh. The paper scratched and she took it from him, tossing it to the floor. 'I need your hand, too.'

'I don't know where the hotel is.'

'Right at old log cabin, left at Miner's Cove, one mile and follow the signs from there,' Megan said. At his look, she shrugged. 'I'm a detective. I read the paper when you held it up.'

'That's more of a secret agent thing to do, isn't it?'

She pushed his hand higher up her leg, wiggling in her seat in anticipation. His fingers neared her sex. Megan hesitated, before grabbing her seatbelt and unbuckling it. The need to have his hands on her outweighed her need for safety. Ryan turned a corner. She slid her hips to meet him. Warm fingers bumped along her sex.

'No panties,' he said, as if to himself.

'I took them off at the restaurant for you, but you didn't go exploring.' She closed her eyes to the passing houses.

'Your family was there, it wasn't the time.'

'They didn't suspect a thing. Trust me, covert operations are my speciality. I did grow up with four sisters after all. How else do you think I got all the dirt on what they were up to?' Megan moved, rubbing her sex against him. 'Oh, yeah, I think you need to see what you can get out of this secret agent, Mr Lucas.'

His fingers curled against her and she wiggled until he could thrust one inside. Holding him in place, she rocked her body, tweaking her own clit as she rode his hand.

'Enjoying yourself?' Though the question was supposed to be cocky, she heard the breathlessness of his words.

'Just keep driving,' she moaned. Outside, the houses turned into dark valley and the flash of dim streetlight stopped pulsing through the window. Tugging her breast, she worked a tight nipple over the top edge of her tight bodice. The pressure of the gown combined with her pinching fingers sent little jolts of pleasure down to her wet pussy, like a thread tying the two together.

'Tell me how I feel to you,' she demanded, wanting to hear his voice.

'Wet, hot,' he breathed heavily, making weak noises in the back of his throat. One hand gripped the wheel and he determinedly looked at the road.

'You can do better than that.' She pushed down, gasping at the magnificent sensation it caused.

'You feel like the fires of hell.'

Megan gasped, stunned.

'Mm, yes, hell.' He stroked her gently. His fingers moved with a deft precision born of sudden urgency, cupping her sex as she rocked on to him. Her fingers were there, moving with his, parting her soft folds and encircling her clit. 'And you, my temptress, are torment-ing me with the feel of moist velvet on my fingers without hope of sinking my cock in you any time soon.'

'Ah, right there.' Megan's body tightened as the orgasm built. She gripped the seat behind her head, using it for leverage.

'Your pussy is like hot silk and so moist and slick against my finger.'

'Ahmm,' she answered, beyond words as she came. Ryan's hand kept stroking, fuelling the storm between her thighs. Clawing his hand, she jerked it from her, gasping. With a light moan, she bit her finger, trying to push up in her seat. A light sheen of sweat glistened over her skin, causing her dishevelled clothes to stick. 'I've needed that all night.'

Ryan slowed the car.

'Where are we?' She looked outside to see dark countryside.

'We're turning around to go back to the hotel. We passed it a few miles back.' He gave her a sheepish grin. 'I thought it better to keep going.'

Megan chuckled. 'That was probably for the best.'

He shifted uncomfortably in his seat. 'Maybe for you, but I'm not so sure about me.'

She glanced down to his lap, seeing his tight erection pressing against his pants. 'You know –' she licked her lips '– I could take care of your little problem. Or should I say, *big* problem?'

'I don't think I could handle myself if you sucked on me now. I'd drive off the side of the road and kill us both.'

'Well, then –' Megan leant towards him, drawing her finger down the centre of his chest '– I guess you will just have to pull over so I can attend to you properly.'

Ryan instantly slammed on the brakes. Megan giggled, as he reached to unzip his pants. It didn't take him long, even in his fumbling haste, to have them pulled down on his hips freeing his cock to tower from his lap. 'I've been hard since I saw you in that dress walking down the stairs. It took all my willpower not to throw you down and fuck you right there.'

'Oh, poor Ryan,' Megan teased, flicking her tongue over the tip of his cock as she lightly caressed his balls. 'Do you need me to –?'

'Yes,' he rushed, not giving her a chance to finish. 'Suck my dick like you said in the restaurant. Put it in your pretty mouth and suck all the sweet cream filling out.'

'You mean like this?' She wrapped her lips around the tip of his shaft. Her tongue moved in circles, exploring the head fully. She liked watching him squirm.

'Ah!' Ryan bucked, pushing the back of her head so that his cock slipped deeper into her mouth. She kneaded his balls, massaging them in her palm. He worked his hips up and down, pushing up as he nearly suffocated her with his passionate force. She rolled her tongue down his shaft, sucking hard as she sensed he was close. His body jerked and he pulled her hair to get her off a second before he came all over his own lap. 'Mm, sweetheart, I can't tell you how much I needed that.'

'Get us to that hotel,' Megan said. 'I have a feeling this night is just getting started.'

'Yes, ma'am.' Ryan put the car back into gear before motioning to her chest. 'You best right your gown. We might get the room for free, but I'm not sure I like the idea of the hotel clerk seeing your nipple.'

Megan looked to where he motioned and laughed, secretly pleased with his possessive tone. 'Just concentrate on getting us to our room. I can handle any amorous hotel clerks.'

'Whatever you say, sweetheart.'

Megan broke away from Ryan's mouth long enough to glance around. 'Wow, this room, ah . . .'

Ryan reached for the light switch, further illuminating their accommodation as the door shut behind them. A red and green plaid bedspread covered the queen-size bed, the only hint of accent colour in the sparse room. Aside from the pastel-green walls with one mirror, there was a small television stand on a long short dresser. He didn't let go of her, keeping her body tightly pressed to his as it had been since they'd turned the corner out of view from the front desk of the small hotel.

'It sucks,' Megan finished the thought. 'Couldn't get us a room at the lodge?'

'I didn't realise you'd be such high maintenance, needing a room at a thousand-dollars-a-night place.'

'Thousand?' Megan coughed.

'Only room they had left. I did ask.'

'I take it back. At forty dollars, this room is perfect.' Megan giggled, moving to kiss him, but he drew his face back. She tried again and this time he allowed her a small taste before pulling away. When she studied his eyes, she could barely see the bruise that had marred his features days before. Just looking at his handsome face made her giddy inside. 'It's a little late to play hard to get, isn't it?'

'We need to talk.' He let go of her but didn't back away as Megan held on.

'OK.' She licked his jaw, nibbling at it. 'What do you want to talk about? Whether we start in the shower and move to the bed? Or we start on the bed and end in the shower? For me, personally, I don't know that I'll want to get out of bed once I get into it.'

'Mm,' he groaned, as if warring with himself. 'About us. We need to talk about what's happening between us.'

'Oh, now you want a conversation.' She backed away when he didn't return her embrace.

'What's happening here, Megan?' He ran his fingers through his hair, pulling it from the ponytail and messing it up. It fell around the sides of his face in disarray. 'I need to know.'

'You were serious about coming to a hotel room to talk.' She gave a small derisive laugh, purposefully strolling across the room, pretending to examine the edge of the dresser as she ran her finger along it. A small mirror on the counter reflected her smudged lipstick and dark-lined eyes back to her. She wiped self-consciously at her cheek, fixing her makeup the best she could. Then she took out the clip that held the side of her hair up and dropped it on the dresser. Scratching her head, she made the curls tumble around her face. When she again turned her attention to Ryan, she looked to see if her smeared makeup was on his face. It wasn't.

'What is happening here?' he repeated.

'If you had shut up and kissed me, you would already have that answer.' It was meant as a joke, but she couldn't force herself to laugh.

'Meg –'

'Tell you what. You talk and I'll do what I'm doing.' Reaching behind her back, she pulled at her zipper. She loosened her gown so the bodice released its corseted hold. 'Wow, I can breathe again.'

'We have been putting off this conversation,' Ryan said, but he sounded distracted.

'I'm not stopping you from having it,' she assured him, unzipping the gown the rest of the way. It slid off her body with a loud rustle of fabric only to land on the floor. She stepped out of it, wearing the strapless bra Sasha had lent her, her best pair of dark-blue panties and Zoe's high-heel shoes. Feeling empowered, she crossed over to him. His eyes darted down to her chest and his lips parted.

She had seen him naked, had tasted his flesh and she wanted to do so again. He crossed his arms, as if trying to look stern. Megan sauntered around him, drawing her fingernails over his biceps, bumping over the light sweater. Slowly, she inched up his shirt, until his naked back was exposed. She pressed the curve of her breasts to the heat of his flesh, rubbing against him, liking the way his breathing quickened.

Megan wrapped her arms around him, sliding her fingers along his waistband until she reached the button in front. His arms were still crossed and she had complete access to his stomach. Every ridge passed beneath her soft touch, until she'd drawn her way over each taut line. Then, after unbuttoning his slacks, she pushed them gently so they slithered off his hips. Tight boxer briefs moulded his hips and ass.

Megan couldn't resist pressing her hips against the firm mounds of his butt. She skimmed over the boxers, feeling the full press of his cock already at attention. Laughing softly to herself, she knew all thoughts of talking had left him. He took a deep breath and held it. She dipped her hands beneath the material, taking his shaft in hand.

Her soft pant of approval joined his. His smell, the slight hint of soap and cologne, engulfed her senses. She liked these moments, when they didn't speak, didn't think, but merely acted on instinct. Too many times her head had to have control of her. But here, now, her body told her what to do. Instinct and desire trumped necessity and logic.

Still he didn't touch her as he rocked his hips forwards, thrusting his arousal into her hands. She leant to the side, wishing there was a mirror in front of them so she could watch him as he moved, his body so sleek with streamlined perfection. The look of his arousal was as intoxicating as his touch. Ryan had the body of a model, without the effeminate features that turned her off. He was rugged, as a man should be, and so incredibly sexy. If she were a drug addict, his body would be her prescription of choice.

Without a mirror to satisfy the desire to watch her hands on his cock, she let go and strolled around his proud form. His erection stood tall, held to his stomach by the tight boxers that still covered the bottom half of his shaft. Though not too long, it was thick, the perfect size to fit within her body.

Megan touched the tip with her finger, drawing it in circles. 'You were saying something?'

'Mm' was his groaned answer. His body jerked and his knuckles whitened as he gripped his arms tight. 'You are one sexy woman. Have I told you that?'

'A woman never tires of hearing it,' she assured him.

'Even you, Megan?'

'What? You think me so different from other women?'

'I have news for you, sweetheart.' He paused, his head rolling back on his shoulders as she continued her slow torture. 'You *are* different.'

'I'll assume that was meant to sound like a compliment.' She chuckled.

'Believe me, it was.'

A droplet of moisture wetted the tip of her finger and she glanced down. He looked about ready to come from just her teasing the ridge around the tip of his penis. She imagined the tight pressure of his boxers had to feel nice against his balls, holding them and shifting subtly with each motion of his hips.

An animalistic sound reverberated from the back of his throat. He uncrossed his arms and lifted her off the floor to carry her forcefully to the bed. After tossing her down, Ryan pushed his boxers from his hips and crawled on top. His demanding lips met hers, ravishing her mouth, even as he pushed open her thighs. A finger slipped along her wet slit, stroking her pussy through the silk panties.

His mouth worked down her throat, biting and licking a hot trail over her flesh. A finger slipped past the silken guard, easily finding home within the folds of her sex. He narrowed in on her clit, rubbing over it hard until she jerked and jolted with each sensitive pass.

'I love how you respond,' he growled, somehow manoeuvring one of her breasts free. Hot kisses found the ripe nipple, sucking and nibbling the budded flesh. His groans vibrated her, adding to the pleasure.

With the light on, she could see him clearly. Passion lined his gaze as he looked up at her from where he kissed her chest. Then, with purposeful intensity, he continued his way down her body. Dragging his tongue, he skated a trail down her tight stomach to encircle her navel. The hand against her clit pulled back, taking the panties with it. Ryan took them from her as he crawled off the bed. When she lay before him, legs parted for his full viewing pleasure, he kneeled. Without word, he jerked her body down. Her feet dropped on the floor and he kept pulling, stopping only when her butt hit the end of the bed. She lay on her back, her legs forced open wide as he licked the full length of her sex.

Ryan's hands kneaded her hips as he held her to his

mouth. Aggressively, he fucked her with his mouth, his tongue and teeth like tiny torture devices. When she was crying out, fingers replaced his tongue, thrusting inside her body. Then, unexpectedly, he slid a wet finger to her ass, probing it as his lips concentrated on her clit.

She bucked up on the bed, shocked because he'd never ventured there before. The action pushed his finger deeper within her and she gasped to discover how much she liked it. Keeping her body propped on her elbows, she slung a leg over his back, rocking into his mouth and riding his finger at the same time. Seeing his wavy dark locks bobbing against her pussy made her want to grab a camera. As a police officer, she knew it was stupid to take pictures of such things because nothing ever stayed private for long. Secrets had a way of getting discovered. But this was one image she always wanted to remember. It was the memory she'd masturbate to when their affair was over.

The fingers inside her wiggled, stimulating the nerve endings. She moaned, shaking as she came with a great force. The instant she started, Ryan pulled back and was on top of her. His hips pushed at her as he guided himself to her. With his feet still on the floor, he thrust in, filling her with his thick erection. With hands on either side of her body, he kept himself lifted above her. The sudden tightening of her muscles didn't slow him as he pumped rapidly against her, fucking her hard and deep as she came. Her breasts bounced hard on her chest with the force of his movements until, finally, he came, pulling out at the last instant to spill his seed all over her stomach.

Panted breaths filled the otherwise silent room. Then, suddenly, loud cheering accompanied pounding on the wall. Megan tried not to laugh, as she realised how loud they'd been.

'I guess trying to keep quiet finally caught up with

us,' Ryan said, grinning. He rolled over on to the bed. 'At least we don't know them.'

Megan didn't move off the bed, as she waited for her heartbeat to slow. Sweat covered her body, sticking her hair to her flesh, not to mention his semen on her stomach. Taking the end of the bedspread, she wiped his come off her flesh. 'I need a shower.'

'Give me a minute to recuperate and I'll be in there to join you.'

There was something seductive about soap gliding along wet flesh, even if it was cheap motel soap. Unfortunately, the shower stall was too small to manoeuvre in and they couldn't do much more than caress each other to arousal. By the time they finished their shower, Megan was ready to go again.

'How do you want it?' he asked, their wet bodies fused together in a locked embrace.

'How do *you* want it?' she returned the question.

'All I know is when we're not together I can't seem to stop thinking of ways I want to be with you, but the instant we start kissing I become a fumbling idiot who can't think past just ramming it home.'

'Oh, I don't know, you did all right before.' Megan thought of his mouth on her clit, sucking her to release.

'Purely selfish motivation. It was the fastest way I knew to get you where I was at.'

'So, this time is my choice?' Megan asked, arching a brow.

'Any way you want it, baby,' he said, grabbing her naked hips and pulling her to rub along his arousal.

'Anything?' She dropped her voice into a seductive murmur.

'Mm, yeah, anything at all.'

Megan pushed back and grinned. Her tone back to normal, she said, 'I want a full body massage.' It took him a moment to react. She didn't wait, as she lay down on her stomach. 'I'm waiting.'

The bed shifted as he climbed next to her. She tapped her feet lightly, the comforter a little stiff beneath her body. Warm hands grabbed a foot mid-kick, instantly massaging the arch. Megan tensed, moaning in relaxing pleasure as he did one and then the other. Next, he found her calves, kneading up her legs. A low groan left him as he worked and his touch deepened.

Megan's eyes closed as he moved higher, his gentle hands gliding over her knees. Each stroke sent a shiver along her body, a tortuous hint of what was to come. He rubbed her thighs and she tensed, confident his fingers would work their way between her legs next. Already her sex was wet with need for him and she didn't care if he finished the pleasurable massage.

She groaned, opening her legs in offering. His fingers seemed to flow over her, skimming higher until he rubbed her ass. She waited, biting her lip in anticipation. To her surprise, he skipped her pussy only to move up her back and arms. By the time he'd finished, her body was taut with need.

'Turn over,' he ordered, his voice hoarse.

Megan made a weak noise, but obeyed. Instantly, she again parted her legs, bending at the knee to let him know she was ready for him. A look of pleasure crossed his handsome features as he looked at her offering. He knelt between her legs, only to grab her arms, giving the front side the same treatment as he'd given the back. When, finally, he touched her breasts, the nipples had already hardened. Megan moaned, trying to pull him forwards with her leg muscles. He kept back, despite the thick arousal towering from his thighs.

'Ah,' she panted, pushing her breasts into his hands.

Ryan pinched her nipples, opening his mouth as if he'd like to take a bite. He held back. 'I like looking at you move,' he said, gliding his hands down to massage her stomach. He didn't spend as much time as before, instead letting his fingers roam down her thighs and back up to her breasts.

'You like watching, do you?' Megan pushed up, only to pull away from him. Though weak from his deep massage, she stood and walked over to the television. Grabbing the small card beside it, she looked through the movie list until she found one she wanted.

'Don't tell me you are bored already,' Ryan said. 'Come back to bed.'

'One second. It's too quiet in here.' Megan pressed a code into the box on top before reaching for the remote control on the dresser. Walking back towards the bed, she hit the power button on the remote, before dropping it on the floor. The sound of a woman talking filled the room, the type of airy cheesy dialogue only found in porno films. Ryan's eyes rounded slightly. Megan giggled. 'I like to watch, too.'

'I didn't think women, I mean, I'm sure there are women who ... but I never met one who liked ...'

'To see people fucking?' Megan said. 'I love it.'

'Mm, come here.' He motioned to her with his hand. It was strikingly erotic the way his hair fell around his face. 'You are so beautiful. I love the way the light shadows your flesh.'

'Wait –' she held up her hand, not taking his offered one '– we're going to play a little game. Whatever they do, we do.'

'Then I hope they have sex really soon.'

As if to answer his wish, the telltale music started, followed by light moans. Megan glanced at the television.

A busty blonde woman was on the floor on her hands and knees in front of a fireplace, her breasts so big they had to be a creation of plastic surgery. Fire glowed off her as a dark-haired vampiric-looking man came up behind her. He was naked except for a cape and fangs.

'I'm scared you'll hurt me. I know what you are, Vladimir. I saw what you did to Jules.'

'You cannot resist me, my love. I can control your mind, Kiki.'

'You don't expect me to act like that, do you?' Ryan asked, mimicking the bad porno accent. He still knelt on the bed, his hands resting at his sides.

Megan smiled, as she crawled on to the bed, facing the television as she waited on her hands and knees. Throwing her voice into a bimbo whine, she said, 'Oh, Ryan, I'm scared you'll hurt me with your vampire ways.'

Ryan chuckled. Megan arched her ass towards him, glancing over her shoulder. His hands were lifted, as if cupping her through the air. She did it again, pushing her body to him, rolling her hips in small circles.

'Why am I like this? Why can't I move? What did you do to me?'

'Because I want you like this. I told you I can control you with my mind. It happened when you let me bite you at the party.'

'No!'

Megan backed up to Ryan, bumping along his cock. Ryan groaned, saying, 'You have a great ass.'

'Yes.' Instantly, the music became louder and there was no more talking on screen, only moans as Vladimir had his way with Kiki.

With a staggered breath, Ryan mimicked some of the movements on screen. Megan watched, aroused by the game as he drew his cock to enter her. Slowly he thrust, keeping time with what was happening in the movie. She moaned at the tight fit. His fingers dipped around to her clit, rubbing it. Megan rocked her body back and forth, taking him deep. Each gentle movement slid her wet sex along his firm shaft. She ran her palm over her breast, tweaking the erect centre.

'Ryan,' she panted. The slow speed set by the television was pure torture. He touched her wherever he could reach.

Suddenly, on the screen, the couple's position changed. The man was on his back as the woman sat astride him, facing his feet.

Ryan didn't wait to be asked as he pulled out and fell on to his back. Megan climbed on top, grabbing his thighs to angle her body to the new position. She clawed at his legs, using them for leverage as she rotated her hips in small circles, even as she moved up and down. Now that she controlled the pacing, she ignored the television, only hearing the sounds of sex in her head as she closed her eyes and made her own hard and fast rhythm. Leaning forwards, she kept his cock deep inside her as she bent it, putting deliberate pressure on the root of the shaft. Ryan groaned loud and long in noisy approval, nearly screaming like the people in the movie.

Megan opened her mouth wide, but no sound came out. Frantic, she bucked wildly against him. Her body tensed, jerking as she finally met with sweet release. Ryan grabbed her hips, his finger digging into her flesh.

'I'm coming,' he cried in warning. Megan fell forwards, though it was hard to let her body release his cock from her depths. The movie continued as the onscreen couple finished up. She reached over to the side of the bed, grabbing the remote to turn down the volume. Smiling, she crawled next to him on the bed and propped herself against a pillow.

'Mm,' Ryan moaned, instead of talking.

'Liked that game, did you?' Her voice dropped into a purr.

'Mm-hmm.' Clearly beyond words, he gazed at her in what could only be adoration and amazement.

'I'm glad –' Megan rolled over and kissed his ear '– because the movie's not over and there is no way I'm going to be outdone by some bimbo named Kiki. And, when we show up Kiki and Vladimir, we'll take on the next couple.' He looked worried. Megan nodded wickedly. 'We've got an all-night pass to the channel.' She pushed up from the bed and crawled over so her lips were right above his. 'That's right, stud. You better get recuperated, because I'm not done with you yet.'

Chapter Ten

'What are you doing?' Megan watched Ryan shove glossy pieces of paper into his back pocket from the sparse hotel-room dresser. Frowning and grunting in soft irritation, she struggled to put her all-too-relaxed body back into the tight dress she'd worn the night before. Her hair was wet from a second shower, but, with only the plastic comb from the outside vending machine to pull through the locks, it was still a little tangled.

'Brochures.' He held one up. 'Your family seems to like looking at them so I thought I'd bring these back to them. They're different from the ones at the cabin.'

'Hmm,' she hummed thoughtfully. The late hour had crept up on them as they slept in and they'd missed the free breakfast provided by the hotel. Though the clerk did let them sneak a couple of cups of five-hour-old coffee with powdered creamer. The thick black brew reminded Megan of tar, but she drank it anyway. 'Brochures about what? I think I want veto power over them before we give them any more bad ideas. No museums. No amusement parks. No water parks. No miniature golf.'

'I liked the miniature golf,' Ryan said.

'No miniature golf,' she repeated.

'You're just sore because you lost.'

Megan wrinkled her nose at him. 'I still say you and Sasha cheated.'

'Only once.' He kept his eyes on the brochure in his hands, giving a crooked grin.

'What other ones do you have?' Megan turned back to the mirror, sighing as she decided it was no use trying to fix the wild mess of her hair.

'This one is about sightseeing and has some nature trails listed. It says the Rocky Mountain Front in Montana has a diverse number of species that have lived on the prairies and mountains for centuries before man came. Including bears, elks, white-tailed deer, bighorn sheep, mountain goats, moose . . .'

Megan nodded her head, hiding her smile as she heard the excitement in his voice as he talked about it. He really was interested in the little nature facts. Yet somehow, as he talked, she found what he was saying incredibly sexy. Or maybe it was the sound of his low voice. 'You don't say.'

'. . . bobcats, wolves, beavers –'

'I have a beaver you can see if you want to take in some sights.' Megan stepped closer to him, parting her legs in an unmistakably unsubtle invitation. 'I'll even draw you a map so you can follow the trail to get there.'

He arched a brow, glancing at her before continuing, 'Mules, mountain lions –'

'And I'd really like to play with your mountain lion.' She reached forwards, grabbing him by the front of his slacks. He too wore the same clothing he had the evening before. His shaft didn't stir as readily as it had through the night. 'Oh, is your lion tired?'

'He had a busy night,' Ryan defended. 'Do I have to remind you about the two-hour marathon you put me through?'

'You didn't complain last night.'

'I'm not complaining right now. Just reminding you to take it easy on my fella.' Ryan kissed the tip of her nose. 'Now, do you want to hear this brochure or not?'

'I didn't ask to hear you read it all to me.' Megan continued to play with his cock. 'But go ahead. Your smart talk turns me on.'

'Oh, does it now?' He cleared his throat.

'Besides, it doesn't matter what you say. I can turn any conversation topic into a dirty one. It's a gift.' She unbuttoned his pants, reaching in to continue massaging. Check-out was in an hour and she was going to get all the sex she could before they went back to the cabin. With her family near by, they had to be quiet when lovemaking, but at the hotel there was something freeing about keeping all the other guests up all night with their loud marathon.

'The prairie grasslands are used to graze livestock,' he read, pausing to arch a brow in challenge.

'Interesting,' she lied, before proving her point by saying, 'My lips are used to graze the length of you.'

'Many different grasses cover the plains, steppes and rolling hills.'

'Many different positions cover my body with yours.'

'OK.' The word became huskier than before as the blood began to fill the pliable flesh beneath her hand. 'On average they receive sixteen inches of rain.'

Megan laughed, tossing back her head. 'You really want me to comment on sixteen inches? Sorry, pet, I didn't bring any toys on this trip.'

'Sixteen?' Ryan gave her a look of mock horror. 'Then it's a good thing I didn't mention the forty-five-hundred-to six-thousand-feet elevation.'

'Ouch.' Megan wrinkled her nose. 'Are you done with the brochure now?'

'Well, there was a section about the wetlands I was interested in.'

Megan laughed as he picked her up and tossed her down on the messy bed. This time, they came together slowly, not bothering to strip out of their clothes. By the time she came, he was right behind her, pumping his way to the grand finale.

Afterwards, as he lay next to her on the bed, panting for breath, he lifted his hand to show the crumpled brochure. 'I told you that you were different. You are the only woman I know who's been turned on by a land survey.'

Lightly, she punched his arm. 'Tell a soul and you are a dead man, Mr Lucas. Farmers everywhere will be knocking down my door.'

'About time,' Zoe teased as Megan snuck quietly into the cabin's living room. 'Wow, sis, you look like you were up all night having –'

'Shush!' Megan frowned at her in warning, pressing her finger to her lips. The last thing she wanted was her parents seeing her come in, smelling of Ryan and looking like a dishevelled hooker. Motioning to Ryan to follow, she led the way up the stairs.

Zoe giggled. 'Don't worry. They're all outside picking wildflowers. You're safe.'

Megan sighed in relief. Taking the stairs two at a time, she almost ran into Kat on her way down the hall.

'Oh, Megan, I forgot, Kat's up there!' Zoe yelled from below.

'Kat,' Megan said.

Kat glanced at her and then behind her to where Ryan was at. 'Long night?'

Megan almost jumped to hear her sister speak. 'You could say that.'

Kat nodded, walking past them to the stairs. Megan's smile fell into a frown. It appeared as if Kat was still upset with her. Megan didn't chase after her sister as she went to the blue room to change.

Ryan shut the door behind her. 'It'll be all right. Kat can never stay mad at you for too long. She's said before that she tries, but loves you too much to –'

'I can handle my relationship with my sister,' Megan snapped.

'Excuse me?'

'I don't need your advice about Kat,' Megan said, lightening her tone, though it was still firm. 'I'll handle it. My relationship with my sister is my business.'

'I just meant –'

'Ryan, please, I don't want to talk about it.' Megan unzipped her dress, as she crossed to the bathroom to wash up. The material whooshed to the floor.

Ryan didn't answer as she cleaned her face and brushed her teeth. He didn't even try to come into the bathroom, which was fine with Megan. Any more sex and her sore, but sated, body would fall apart.

She came out refreshed, and quickly put on a fresh pair of panties and a bra. Ryan was still on the bed, his arms crossed over his chest. He hadn't moved.

When he still didn't speak, she asked, 'What do you think about suggesting horseback riding today?' She pulled on a pair of sweatpants. 'I've wanted to try that. And maybe we can go fishing tomorrow morning. Or hiking.'

'Why won't you talk to me about anything serious?' His eyes lifted to meet hers, but his body stayed still.

Megan blinked, swallowing nervously at his tone. She turned her back on him under the pretence of getting a T-shirt. Pulling the tightly fitted shirt over her head, she took a deep breath.

'I said, why –?'

'I heard what you said.' She wound her hair into a bun and secured it with a ponytail holder, leaving it a messy version of her normal hairdo. 'But I don't know what you expect me to say. I already told you I don't want to talk about my relationship with my sister. If you insist on asking, I'll have to insist on ignoring you until you stop.'

'I'm not just talking about your fight with Kat. You never talk to me about anything. It's almost like . . .' He sighed heavily.

'Like what?' She put her hands on her hips. This was not a conversation she wanted to have, not today, not after the great pressure-free night they had. Today should have been easy, light. She had started to relax and truly enjoy her vacation. Why couldn't he just go with it? Why did he have to ruin it with talk?

'Like we're not even...' He paused. Megan didn't move. Weakly, he finished, 'Friends.'

Fine. He was going to force her to have this conversation. He couldn't leave well enough alone. This was supposed to be a stress-free day. Things had finally become effortless between them. The night before had been wonderful. 'What exactly do you want from me, Ryan? I don't know you, not really. We work together – sometimes. But aside from this week, we've not spent any real time together. You have more in common with Kat than you do me.'

He didn't speak, merely sat unmoving, his arms crossed, his brow furrowed.

His silence prompted her to continue. 'We're good in the bedroom, and that's great, but we're not close friends. It's not in the cards. I'm a cop, my friends are other cops. It's the way it is.'

'Are you trying to convince yourself or me?'

'It's the way it is,' she repeated, her tone harder than before.

Ryan slowly stood. 'So that is all I am to you? Something to fuck.'

'I wouldn't have put it that harshly.' What was wrong with him? She'd actually gotten the thought into her head that they could work their little situation out. Of course, they wouldn't be married, but there was no reason why they couldn't continue to be of service to each other when they got back to the city. It wasn't like her job allowed for relationships. Seeing his face now, she knew how impossible that idea had been.

'Harsh or not, Megan. Truth is truth.'

Megan had a sinking feeling in the pit of her stomach. She knew where this conversation was headed. He wanted some sort of sentiment from her. 'Truth. Hmm, truth. Like the truth you told my parents when you said we were getting married?'

'You're the one who said you wanted to get married. You listed the traits, I fit the traits...' He threw up his hand. 'Why can't we be engaged? Why is it so impossible for you to even consider marrying me? I filled your requirements. They were your words, not mine.'

'Right. You gave me a choice.' She snorted, shaking her head in disbelief. Motioning her arms around, she said, 'I don't remember being asked if this all was OK or not.'

'The cabin? Your mom picked it out, not me.' His voice rose in anger.

'I mean Montana,' she argued. If he wanted to have it all out, she'd give it to him. 'I mean this family vacation. Only wait. This isn't *your* family, Ryan! It's *my* family. This is my life you are messing with.'

He looked like she'd slapped him. His face paled.

She lowered her voice, not wanting the others to hear them. 'I know you are holding that picture over my head to get me to go along with your ploy to integrate yourself into my family, but it's over. I know you want to replace your family and I'm sorry they're gone, but this isn't your life. This will never be your family, not like you want it to be. And I will not be blackmailed. Now, you seem reasonable for the most part and I have no choice but to appeal to your rational side.' Megan went to the bed and pulled her carry-on bag out from under it. She took out the Preying Mantis's case file. 'I have a few pictures of my own I want to show you. These aren't anything you'll see in your newspapers.'

'Megan,' he began to speak, but stopped as she opened the case file.

She threw the victim photos down on the bed, one at a time as she said their names. The women's battered lifeless faces were framed in a sea of insects. 'Janice. Lucy. Patricia. Madeline. Consuela. Constance. Shanita.' Megan pointed at them. 'Now, you look at them and you tell me if you can live with yourself if you publish that photograph of me stepping on evidence. You might earn a few bucks, but you'll ruin my reputation and my credibility before I testify for these women – women who can no longer testify for themselves. These seven were only in three years. Can you imagine what would happen if the guy got off on some technicality?'

Ryan did not look at the grotesque images too long. Megan understood. At first she could barely stomach seeing them – once average, everyday, never-hurt-any-one women taken from their families, their lives stolen to feed one man's sick obsession. But, she had forced herself to look, until their faces were burnt into her head. She had been unable to sleep until the man who killed them was captured and brought to justice.

Ryan shook his head in disbelief. 'You really have a low opinion of me, don't you?'

'I know what I know, Ryan.'

'Do you?'

'I know that I'm on this little forced leave of absence because of that crime-scene photo. I know that, every time you seem to snap a picture of me on the job, my life takes a turn for the worse. First, you ruin my career by putting that stupid photo of me taking down St Claud –'

'That was a damned good picture. The people of New York needed that picture and, like it or not, they needed *you*. They needed a hero. They needed closure to the terror this man caused and the fact that you are a woman who took down a man who preyed on women only made it that much more potent. You might not like it, Little Darling Detective, but the people needed the morale boost. Hell, your beloved department needed the image boost.'

'Image boost?' A short humourless laugh escaped her. 'I had to transfer out of homicide because I could no

longer do my job effectively. Damn reporters and photographers were following me wherever I went, with a
hard-on to see who I'd arrest next. And, if it isn't bad
enough that my work life is ruined, my personal life is
crap, too. I can't even get dates because, once the guy
finds out I'm not only a cop, but *that* cop, I become some
kind of strange trophy.'

'You were never a trophy to me.'

'This is my life, Ryan. This isn't a game.' She slammed
her fist on the bed, making the pictures jump. 'These
murders are not a game.'

'You really think that I would hurt you on purpose.
You think so little of me, even after this last week, after
all –'

'All the sex?' she interrupted.

'Wow.' The word was dead, flat. He looked like she'd
slapped him. 'That was all you felt between us, wasn't
it? I guess I knew, but I didn't want to believe it.'

'Did you feel there was more?' An unfamiliar shiver
worked over her, as she studied him. She knew his
interest in her was to fulfil a need for a family. Loneliness did strange things to people – even made them fake
an engagement to an NYPD detective.

'Apparently not.' Ryan went to the dresser and began
pulling out his clothes. 'Don't worry. I'll be gone by this
evening. Hopefully Zoe will let me return her rental for
her.'

Megan blinked in surprise. He was leaving? Just like
that? He schemed and blackmailed his way into her life
and now he just gave up after one small fight? She
opened her mouth, only to shut it. Though she had the
urge to say something, she couldn't force herself to stop
him from going.

Once his bag was packed, he reached into his back
pocket and pulled out his wallet. He took out a credit
card and his driver's licence before throwing the wallet

into the bag. 'I already paid your mother back for the flight. I'll call the airport and see if they can transfer my ticket.'

'But,' she started. It was too late, he was out the door and heading downstairs, still wearing his clothes from the evening before. Megan took a deep breath, saying to herself, 'But, I didn't mean you had to leave this second.'

'You're leaving early?' Kat demanded, hands on hips. 'Why?'

Ryan didn't meet her searching gaze as he flipped through the phonebook. 'It's over, Kat. I am clearly not meant to be with your sister. I honestly don't know what I was thinking pining over her this last year. Stupid, right?' He snorted. His hands shook with anger – anger that she could think so very little of him. 'I'm such a fucking idiot.'

'You are not an idiot,' Kat argued, her voice low. 'Whatever Megan said to you, I'm sure she was out of line. I don't know what's wrong with her lately, but someone has got to call her on her attitude.'

'Well.' Ryan gave a derisive laugh. 'Luckily it doesn't have to be me. I'm sorry, Kat. You know I care for you and we'll always be friends. I hope this doesn't change anything, but I can't do it any more. I can't hold myself for a woman who doesn't want me. I need this to be over. I need her to be out of my life. I'm going back to the city and I'm going to get a new job. I can't see her.'

'Ryan, you know whatever happens we'll still be friends,' Kat assured him.

'I know. I just can't talk about her. My heart can't take any more.' He stopped flipping through the phonebook and gave a meaningful look to where her hand rubbed her stomach. 'When you are ready to talk about it . . .'

'I'll call.' Kat nodded. Though it was small, he saw her give him the first real smile he'd seen since Megan blurted her secret.

'Don't torture Megan too long over it. She does feel bad.'

'She should.' Kat sighed. 'I thought you didn't care.'

'I'm really trying not to.' Ryan reached for the phone. 'You'll ask Zoe for the car?'

'Yeah, if you are sure.'

'No.' Ryan glanced up the stairwell. Megan still had not come down. He hoped that she'd stop him, say she was sorry. She didn't. 'I'm not, but she is.'

'Is there something you need to tell us, Megan?' Beatrice said, eyeing her eldest daughter.

Megan glanced at her mother, not answering as she went to the refrigerator to grab a beer. It was early to begin drinking, but, if ever there was a time she wanted to be drunk, now, during her family's inquisition as to why Ryan just drove off in the middle of their vacation, was it.

A very tiny part of her didn't expect him to actually leave. The larger, more pragmatic part of her nature suspected he would. After the show of packing, he'd be too proud to stay unless she begged him. Megan wasn't the type of woman to beg. But, even so, a ripple of doubt and regret shuddered through her as she watched him drive away. Their eyes locked for the briefest of seconds when he put the car into gear. He didn't say a word, having already said his goodbyes to her family as she hid in her room, resting on the bed next to the case file.

She wanted to believe he wouldn't ruin the reputation he'd made so public, but there was no way to be sure. With anyone else, Megan always seemed to just know. But, with Ryan, she couldn't always predict what he would do, or what he wanted. He took her by surprise and that wasn't something she knew how to handle.

'Megan?' her mother insisted.

'Nope, can't think of anything.' She opened the beer

bottle by hitting the cap against the edge of the counter so it popped off.

'Did you two have a fight?' Beatrice's voice rose and fell in confusion. 'I just don't understand. Is it something we did?'

'I don't think she wants to talk about it, Mom,' Sasha said softly. 'Let's just leave her alone.'

'This isn't how it's supposed to happen,' Beatrice insisted. 'I read the tea leaves and...' Stopping she glanced around, as if she'd said too much.

'No, Mom, it wasn't you.' Megan wasn't in the mood to hear about her mother's stupid tea leaves. Life could not be predicted by a drink. 'It wasn't anything. He just needed to go back. He had to work.'

'But...' Beatrice looked helplessly around.

Megan walked towards the deck. 'I need some air. I'll be outside.'

As she shut the door, she heard her mother say, 'But that's not what Ryan said. He said the engagement was off.'

Megan froze. He'd told her family the truth? Well, part of the truth anyway. Stiffly, she walked across the deck to the railing.

'I don't get you.'

Megan spun round, startled, nearly dropping her beer as she saw Kat sitting on a chair near the side of the cabin. She'd been hidden from view from within. 'What do you mean?'

'When did you become so cold?' Kat stood and crossed to join her at the rail. They looked out over the prairie to the distant mountains, but the distance had lost its beauty.

'Shit, Kat, is this about your damned pregnancy? I'm sorry I said anything. I'm sorry I stole your moment of glory. I'm sorry, I'm sorry, I'm sorry!' Megan hit the bottom of her beer bottle down on the wooden rail to punctuate her words.

'Don't give me that sarcastic apology crap. I know you don't mean it and it's insulting.' Kat touched her stomach. 'And did you really call this my moment of glory? There was no moment. Do you think I want to be pregnant?'

Kat gasped. Megan froze, her eyes round as she turned to her sister. Kat had her hand over her mouth as she stared forwards.

'I . . .' Kat shook her head. 'I didn't mean that.'

'Yes, you did.' Megan saw the hesitant truth on her sister's face. It was so clear to her she had to wonder if it had been there all along. Maybe if she hadn't been so wrapped up in Ryan and her sex life, she'd have seen it sooner.

'I didn't fully mean it,' Kat whispered. 'Omigod, don't tell Vincent I said I didn't want to be pregnant. Please, Megan, don't tell him. He won't understand. He'll think I don't want to have his baby. He'll think I have doubts about our marriage, about my love for him. He won't understand.'

'I won't say anything, I promise.' Megan touched her arm.

Kat jerked back. 'Don't think that makes what you did OK.'

'I said I'm sorry.'

'Did you say you're sorry to Ryan?' Kat put her hands on her hips. 'And, if you did, did you say it like you meant it?'

'I don't want to talk about Ryan.' Megan took a long drink of her beer, gasping slightly at the bubbly feeling in her throat. 'What about you and not wanting this baby? Want to discuss that?'

'My situation is not that simple, but no. I don't feel like telling you right now. I'm still irritated with you for telling the rest of the family. I don't know that I've forgiven you.'

'Well, I'm irritated with you for encouraging Ryan and I don't know that I've forgiven you for that.'

'Fine.' Kat put her hand on the rail and stared forwards.

'Fine.' Megan agreed, as she too looked into the distance. She knew Kat's anger towards her was just a projection of her own insecurity over her pregnancy, an insecurity that would be fixed with a little time in Vincent's arms as her sister got used to the idea of being a mother. Once that happened, Kat would attack motherhood with the same fierce dedication she did everything in her life. Figuring out Kat was easy enough. Then why couldn't she figure out Ryan? Why was he so difficult?

They didn't say another word, embracing their mutual need for silent contemplation. Kat would come to her, when she was ready, not before. To force a conversation would only do more harm to their recently strained relationship. Sometimes, as sisters, the easiest things to hear were the ones that weren't said.

East Village, New York City, New York
The late hour cast dark shadows over the brick front of his apartment building, but Ryan didn't hurry inside, feeling almost as if he'd truly lost once the last leg of his journey home was over. He promised himself when he left for Montana that he would give his heart until the vacation was over before letting his mind take over. By walking in that front door, the vacation would be officially over.

A soft flick sounded, only a little louder than the surrounding city. Even though the street looked barren for the most part, no one was every really alone in the city – at least not physically. There were always eight million other people around to fill the void. Ryan wasn't surprised by the sound, or by the temporary glow of fire from a lighter, shining like a tiny beacon in the shadows. A figure moved, one he didn't notice before in his contemplation. The flame turned into a bright hot speck of light, dancing in the night, evidence of a burning cigarette.

'I saw you walking down the street.' Diederick's accent gave him away as he spoke in low tones. 'I thought I'd wait to join you.'

As Diederick stepped into the streetlight, he dropped his cigarette hand slightly, the other hand was thrust in his pocket as he strolled forwards. He looked like a television commercial – an elegant mysterious man in a tux and white scarf, slowly puffing on a cigarette in a world where troubles did not exist. Ryan wanted to live in that uncomplicated world.

'I've been here for at least five minutes,' Ryan answered. 'You were hiding all this time?'

'More like ten,' Diederick corrected. 'But I did not wish to disturb you.'

'Oh?'

'You look at this place like it represents the end of the world.' Diederick motioned to the front of their apartment building. 'I come here to escape the end.'

Ryan arched a brow, glancing up and down over his friend's rich attire. 'Yeah, looks like you are in hell.'

'I've been in the States long enough to know this sarcasm.' Diederick laughed. 'And hell comes in many forms. What form is yours?'

'A woman.'

'Ah, the worst kind.' Diederick nodded. 'What she do? Try to make you her little, ah, *futzä-schläcker*?

'Her what?'

'*Futzä-schläcker*. How you say, the dog on the lap, always licking the ladies' ah . . .' Diederick motioned down to his crotch.

'I'm going to pretend that does not translate right,' Ryan said dryly.

Diederick chuckled, waving his cigarette back and forth. 'So then she tried to light fire on you?'

Ryan frowned, confused.

'Light you . . .' He muttered to himself in his native tongue. 'Ah . . .'

'You mean arouse me with sex?' Ryan asked, giving a small laugh.

'No,' his friend shook his head, 'with the, ah, match and the fire and burning.' He reached into his pocket and flipped the top of his fine engraved silver cigarette lighter. As it flamed, he motioned towards Ryan. 'Put fire on you.'

'Ah, no, she didn't try to murder me,' Ryan said.

'Then I would not worry. There is still hope.' Diederick put the lighter back. 'Only when they try to kill you do you start to think, maybe she is not the one for me to love, no?'

Ryan laughed, despite his tired jet-lagged state and sour depressed mood.

'See, it can always be worse,' Diederick said.

'So, you had a woman try to light you on fire?'

'*Ja*, a couple times.' Diederick threw his cigarette down and stepped on the end. 'In some countries, it's not so illegal as it is here in America.'

'I'd ask what you did to them –' Ryan picked his bag off the ground and began walking inside '– but I'm too tired to hear the story right now.'

'Another time, then,' Diederick agreed. 'And you must tell me what it is this woman did to make you be in hell.'

'I would, but, as soon as I step through that door, it's over. And I plan on never thinking about her again. I'm putting it all behind me and moving on.'

Diederick didn't answer, only laughed as he held open the door. Ryan thought he'd feel different at the official end of his pursuit of Megan, but he merely felt worse. All hope he'd carried was gone, vanished as he passed the threshold. He'd given everything he had the last year to win her and it wasn't good enough. *He* wasn't good enough. The loss of a dream, his dream of her, was a painful lump to swallow, but swallow he did. It was time to move on with his life.

'Do you know what you need?' Diederick asked, as they walked up the stairs single file. 'You need to purge this woman from you. We should find you a prostitute to do this.'

'I doubt there is a woman in this city who could draw my interest,' Ryan said. It wasn't a lie. Megan was still in Montana with her family. 'I think I'm done with all women for a while.'

'That is sad,' Diederick said. 'Then you must come with me to Romania. We will take my father's jet. I know this place.'

'Ugh, don't mention flying.' Ryan's head spun just thinking of it.

'Drink the orange juice and it'll be better. In four days we will leave. I have business in Germany.'

'I thought you said Romania.'

'The place I know is in Romania, but my business is in Germany.' Diederick shrugged when Ryan looked back at him, as if the two countries were just right around the corner from each other. They'd made it down the hall to Ryan's door. As Ryan made a move to walk inside, Diederick slapped him on the back. 'Don't worry, my friend. You will enjoy it!'

He shut the door. Once again alone, the small smile faded from Ryan's face. He set his bag on the floor, mindful of his camera he'd tucked inside during the car ride from the airport. Not bothering to unpack, he walked towards his bedroom, too tired to even shower. As he moved to lie down, he swiped at the picture of Megan on his dresser, knocking it into the trash without daring to gaze at the likeness of her pretty face. Tomorrow he would purge her image from his home and his heart, but tonight, he just wanted to sleep and never wake up.

Chapter Eleven

One week later...

The second week of vacation was a far cry from the first and Megan discovered that there was a limit to spending consecutive time with her family cooped up in the same house – especially when all of the sisters seemed to be in a bad mood. Zoe was fighting her boss. Sasha, they discovered in a strange outburst, had a problem with a boyfriend they never knew existed. Bickering and snide remarks had been prevalent, especially at the end. Oddly, their mother seemed to enjoy it, making comments about how it was just like when they were kids.

Though Megan crammed in every activity her family was up for and more, it was only a temporary fix to her main problem – the problem where Ryan wouldn't get out of her head. Whenever she got a second to think, she found herself straining to remember every detail since she first saw his camera flash out of the corner of her eye as she tackled Jersey St Claud. To her surprise, it was fairly easy. At first, she tried to chalk it up to her police training, but, never one to lie to herself, she knew it was more than that. She'd looked forward to seeing him, even if it was only to avoid him.

Now, standing in the middle of her apartment, all family gone and nothing but empty time staring her in the face, she felt very alone and perhaps a little scared as well. Even if she wanted to, the only way she could talk to Ryan was to ask Kat where he lived. And, to do that, she would have to talk to her sister – something Kat didn't seem willing to do. Her other option was to call the station and ask someone in the department to look up his file, which didn't seem a very bright idea. Either she'd never hear the end to the teasing, or the captain would panic and think she'd lost her mind and was going to kill Ryan for taking the picture.

She slowly spun in a circle, studying her apartment. It was unloved, unlived in and suddenly very depressing. Her life had never bothered her before but take away the business, the work and the crime fighting and she was left with an empty apartment and a few posters on the wall. Poetry was never her thing, but even she could see the strange collation of the barely decorated home and her life. Without the job, she was a barely decorated person – empty, alone, neglected. And the saddest part of all was that she had done it to herself. No one forced her to live this way, to put her personal life on hold. Other cops still managed to try to have a life outside work. They might be lousy at it with drinking problems and failed marriages, but they were out there, endeavouring to feed the human inside themselves, the part that wasn't the cop.

Megan blinked, stopping in shock as she lifted her hand to her face. Drawing her fingers back wet, she realised tears slipped over her cheeks. She couldn't remember the last time she'd cried, not even as a child. The hard shell had taken over, until the woman inside her was buried so deep she had all but disappeared.

'What have I done?' she whispered, thinking of Ryan.

So what if he blackmailed her? He was something tangible in her world. He had been hers, hadn't he? If only for a short time, when they were together, he had been hers. Why had it taken her so long to see it? She thought of his face, of the hints over the past year only now becoming clear. Somehow, with the publication of the Little Darling Detective photo, she'd filed him away in her head as a nuisance and never gave him a chance to be anything else. She ignored her attraction to him, denied it, just as she denied any part of her that needed a life outside being a detective. But, all along, he'd been right there, smiling at her, begging her for her attention. And she'd thrown it in his face repeatedly. Yet, still he tried, never giving up on her.

'Never giving up until now,' Megan said, still not moving, barely making a sound in her dim empty apartment. The hour was late yet the pulse of the city echoed faintly from behind her window. This wasn't like Montana, the endless silence, the peace, Ryan. No, the city was thriving, lonely and even a little cruel. 'Oh, fuck. What have I done?'

Shivering, she crossed to her couch and curled up into a ball. More tears slid over her cheek. It took getting him and losing him to make her realise she even wanted him. She was a stubborn know-it-all fool and she'd lost the first thing in her life she might actually want more than her career. When she closed her eyes, she saw his face, the brief last glance, the hurt, the disbelief, the anger. People didn't easily recover from what she had done. She let him go. And, now that he was gone, she knew there was a chance he'd never come back.

'Oh, fuck. What have I done?'

'I'm sorry. I never meant to hurt you. I never meant to boss you around or say things I shouldn't have or be mean. I love you and I didn't mean to hurt you. Please, forgive me, or I'll . . .' Megan paused in her rushed apology, unsure how to proceed. She'd been on the verge of saying, 'Or I'll beat the shit out of you if you don't', but somehow that didn't seem the way the apology thing was done. 'Or I'll apologise over and over again until you do.'

'That's OK, Megs,' Kat drawled, stepping back to open her front door. 'This first one was painful enough to watch. I'm not sure I can listen through it again.'

'Then, you forgive me?' Megan rushed inside, grabbing Kat in a big hug. Her sister looked adorable in her ivory stretch-lace camisole. Its high ruffled neckline and satin-ribbon trim had a Victorian feel that was contradicted by the bright-red-highlighted bangs framing her face. The full white skirt also had lace trim along the bottom edge, high enough to show off her bare feet. 'I'm so glad. I'm so sorry, Kat, I don't know how it happened, or why I am the way I am, but I'm sorry. I didn't mean to boss you around, or order food for you when you can talk for yourself, or not call you back when you leave fifty messages on my phone in one night just because you can't sleep and want to talk. I have taken so much for granted, like having you as a sister. In my mind, you would always be there when I needed or wanted to come around, but that's not how life works, is it? People disappear and you can't find them, and I don't want that to happen with you. I don't what to go months without seeing you, or being here for you, or –'

'Megan,' Kat said, pushing her away with a small laugh. 'I accepted the apology, now do me a favour and stop apologising.'

'Oh, yeah, sorry.' Megan nodded, somewhat nervous. This was new ground for her and she'd been so worried Kat wouldn't listen, would slam the door in her face like she felt she deserved.

'You look like you could use a drink,' Kat said, motioning towards the kitchen. 'Come on, let's see what I've got.'

Megan followed, tugging on the drawstrings to her hooded grey knit shirt. Cropped, it fell to just under her breasts with a white tank top showing from beneath. With the grey stretch pants and running shoes, the outfit was the only thing she could force herself to put on. Her period had started, making the effects of her mild depression all that more out of character.

'Or is this rushed heartfelt apology the result of too much drinking?' Kat paused by the entryway, leading to the hall that would take them across to the kitchen. 'Do you need to sober up? Should I put on coffee instead?'

'I haven't drunk since we came back,' Megan admitted. 'But coffee sounds perfect. I didn't sleep too well last night.'

'So you are sober?'

'Completely.'

'Have you eaten? You're paler than normal.'

'Sure, I...' Megan frowned. 'I can't remember, honestly. I was so worried you wouldn't let me say what I needed to and I am really –'

'Ah!' Kat held up her hand to keep another apology from coming out. 'Fair warning, you start up again and I might just go all hormonal on you. Pregnant women do that, you know.'

'Oh, I know. I worked this case where a pregnant woman found her boyfriend cheating on her with her cousin and her sister. She grabbed a shotgun and waited until they were all three in bed together before –'

'How about we save the cop stories for, um, let's say after my morning sickness is gone.' After flipping the switch to turn on the kitchen light, Kat moved to the cupboard. Like the rest of the house, the room was white from the walls to the appliances, even the floor. There were touches of red where Kat had started to decorate with cherry-blossom wall hangings and matching towels. The room was pristine, the type of state-of-the-art kitchen Zoe would have loved to have in her home. Since Kat wasn't much for cooking and Vincent was never home, it was never used.

A box of crackers was on the counter and Megan picked them up. 'So are you very sick?'

'I think it's jetlag hanging on. I didn't feel terrible until we got on the plane.'

'Should you even be flying when you're pregnant?' Megan frowned.

'I have no clue.' Kat stopped what she was doing, leaving the cupboard open as she faced her sister. 'I didn't know I was pregnant before we left. I snuck a test from the grocery store once we got there. I thought maybe my menstrual cycle was messed up. I never expected the thing to truly say I was having a baby.'

'How late were you?'

'Ah –' Kat glanced away, giving a sheepish smile '– month and a half.'

'And you didn't think to test it before then?'

'I didn't want to.' Kat turned, pulled a tin of coffee grounds down and set it on the counter. She took the empty coffee pot and filled it with water.

Megan studied the appliance's many buttons and odd space-age shape. 'This coffee pot looks like a time portal.'

'Don't even try it, sis.' Kat lifted the lid and filled the back. 'No matter how much you want it to, my coffee pot will not bring you back to the eighties.'

'I'm not stuck in the eighties.'

Kat giggled. 'Tell that to the movie posters on your living-room walls. I bet you still have those spandex tights you wore in high school.'

'Leave the posters alone,' Megan said. 'And I never once wore spandex.'

'Uh-huh, do I need to get out the pictures?'

'That was Halloween and you know it. Quit trying to bait me.' Megan grimaced. 'Now, about you. What's going on? Why are you so scared to be pregnant? Are you worried about Vincent? Has he said or done something?'

'No, Vincent's great. He's the best husband a girl could ever have, even if he forgets the time, knows a little too much about giant fire ants and milks poisonous spiders as a hobby.' She gave a small humourless laugh, continuing to make coffee as she talked. 'It's one hundred per cent me. I'm not ready. What do I know about being a mom? I'm selfish and as distracted as my husband. Who'll get the kid to school on time? And what's worse? The kid being raised by someone like our flaky mom raised us? Or Vincent's parents, plastic-surgery Mimi and

Big Vincent with the cellular phone glued to the side of his head? Can you imagine all the ways the kid's going to get screwed up?'

'OK, it's my turn to tell *you* to shut up. You are going to make a great mother. You are not our mom and Vincent is definitely not his socialite parents. So you need to shut up, stop worrying about it, relax and know that a baby born out of the love you and Vincent feel for each other can't be screwed up.' Megan crossed over and hugged her sister around the shoulders. 'Trust me, I know everything, remember. I'm always right.'

Kat laughed. 'You really think we'll be good parents?'

'I know so.' Megan sighed. 'And, if you ever start acting too much like mom, I promise to smack you over the head.'

'Perfect.' Putting the tin back into the cupboard, Kat cleared her throat. 'It's your turn. What's up with you?'

Megan's face fell and she sighed. 'I suck.'

'What brought about this sudden insight?' Kat smirked. 'I could have told you that.'

Megan tried to smile, but the effort was weak. She knew her sister was joking, but she wasn't in the mood. She'd spent the last week beating herself up. 'I'm serious.'

'No, I think you're just a little lost, what with being off work.' Kat grabbed her box of crackers and walked out a door. Instead of back to the hallway, the door led into a dining room. An elegant scrolled-ironwork chandelier hung over a polished dark-wood table. Sophisticated hand-carved details accented the high-backed chairs. 'You've had too much time to think.'

Kat opened a panelled door on the china cabinet and Kat took out two stone coasters and set them on the table, before taking a seat at the head of the table as they waited for the coffee to brew. Megan sat next to her, leaning back in the chair. 'I still can't believe you live here.'

'It's growing on me and don't change the subject. You're about to tell me why you're beating yourself up.'

'I already told you in my apology.' It wasn't a complete lie.

'Uh-huh, yeah, I'm flattered,' Kat answered dryly, unconvinced. 'And I'm new to your planet.'

'Fine. I fucked up and it wasn't just with you.'

Kat lifted a brow, the box of crackers untouched next to her. 'Go on.'

'Ryan,' Megan mumbled, leaning forwards to rest her head on her arms so she didn't have to look her sister in the eye. 'I treated him like shit and I need you to tell me how to find him so I can apologise, only I have a feeling he won't want to see me.'

'Yep, you're probably right.' Kat nodded.

Megan's heart dropped. She hadn't expected agreement; in fact, she had counted against it.

'I have a confession. When Ryan and I first came up with this idea, I pushed it because I wanted to prove to you that you weren't always right. The man has cared for you since the first moment he saw you and he's a really good guy.'

'He blackmailed me into dating him.'

'I wouldn't call it blackmail. At best, he tricked you into noticing him and, if you ask me, it was a damn good plan. It worked, didn't it? I just can't believe you went along with it, especially as far as Montana.'

'I had to. He took a picture of me stepping on a museum artefact. With St Claud's trial coming up and me on the witness list, I can't have it going public.' Megan lifted her head. 'I think the coffee's done.'

'I don't know anything about trials and pictures.' Kat began to stand, but Megan motioned her down and got up herself. 'What I do know is that Ryan really liked you, Megan, and you hurt him. Bad.'

Go ahead, rub it in, Megan thought, as she started opening cupboards in search of a coffee mug.

'Right of the sink,' Kat called. With the directions, Megan went right to the mugs and pulled one out. 'French vanilla creamer is in the fridge.'

Megan peered into the refrigerator. 'I don't see it.'

'Look for a metal creamer pitcher near the back right. The cleaning lady keeps pouring it in there. I think she does it to take home the extra creamer.' The sound of the plastic cracker wrapper punctuated Kat's words. 'I keep telling her to stop, but she doesn't listen.'

'Your housekeeper steals creamer from you?' Megan poured a little into her mug.

'Yeah, can you arrest her for me? It's not like she does the grocery shopping.'

'Creamer theft really isn't high on NYPD's list of crimes to investigate –' she shut the refrigerator door and crossed to pour the coffee '– but I'll see what I can do.'

'Thanks, sweetie.' Kat gave her a playful smile as she walked back into the room. 'So what happened between you two?'

'I don't suppose I can pretend not to know what you are talking about?'

'Ryan.'

'Ah, right.' Megan sat back down. Putting her mug on a coaster, she pointed at Kat's empty coaster and frowned. 'Did you want a cup?'

'No, I grabbed it out of habit. No caffeine for me. And you, missy, talk.'

'He accused me of never talking to him about anything important. That I was just using him for sex.'

'That's not a horrific thing to be used for.'

'Yeah, the sex was great.' Megan sighed. 'I do miss the release. I mean, you know how some men are just really good at it. Like they can read ...' Her voice tapered off into a moan.

'Vincent is like that. A mind reader or would that be a body reader?'

'Both.' They shared a heavy sigh. Megan continued,

'Our, or rather *my*, communication skills were horrible. Or maybe they weren't horrible as much as untrue and very harsh. He said I acted like we weren't even friends and I agreed with him and said we weren't friends because we didn't know each other.'

'You've known him a year,' Kat interrupted.

'This might not make sense, but I didn't see it. I separated what we were in my mind. Thinking back, I can see how he thought we were friends. I can even see how he might have hinted at being more.'

'You should have told him this before he left Montana.'

'I want to tell him now, but I need to find him first.'

'Megan, I don't know that he wants to see you. It will not be easy. He told me when he left he...' Kat paused.

'What? Whatever it is, I can take it. I need to know.'

'He basically said he needed to wash his hands of you. I've never seen him that angry.' Kat reached out, touching Megan's hands. 'I'm sorry, Megan. But I don't think he'll entertain a relationship with you. He already told Mom and Dad the engagement is off. And, even though they refused to talk about it the last week in Montana, the family knows not to expect him around. I don't think he even wants to see me right now.'

'Kat, he might not want to see me, but I can't leave it like this. Even if he...' Megan took a deep breath, feeling the tears well in her eyes. 'Even if he doesn't want me like that again. I need to see him. I need to tell him I didn't mean what I said.'

'Maybe time...'

'No, not with this.' Megan pulled her hands away and ran them over her hair to the bun at her nape. 'I said things, accused him of not giving a crap about Jersey St Claud's victims. Accused him of blackmailing me with a picture so he could replace the family he lost.'

'Megan, no,' Kat gasped, jumping to her feet in shock. 'You didn't mention his family.'

'What?' Megan's breath caught in her throat.

'He wouldn't have told you, but...' Kat shook her head, turning away.

'Kat, what?' Her whole body shook violently.

'His parents were murdered. It was his first semester in college. He'd left a week before it happened to go to school or else he probably would have died with them. His dad's boss was a friend of the family and called him to ask if everything was all right at home since his dad hadn't been to work. Ryan found them.' Kat turned her troubled gaze to Megan's. 'He knows firsthand what it's like to be part of the victim's family. If you accused him of not caring about the Preying Mantis's victims...'

'Little Darling Detective,' Megan whispered. 'That's what he kept talking about, the city needing closure to the murders. He said I was the hero they needed.'

'He never really said it, but I know he thought of that picture he took of you taking down St Claud as the pinnacle of his career. He took the job doing crime-scene photography to be closer to you. Perhaps that picture did have something to do with his initial attraction, but I never would have encouraged him if I thought he was a bad guy. He was just too shy to approach you outright at first. It's hard for him to let people get too close.'

'You never said...'

'Why would I?' Kat asked. 'I shouldn't be saying it now. I promised him I wouldn't tell you. He didn't want your pity, Megan. He wanted your attention. Your affection. Your love and acceptance. He wanted you to see him just as he is, not pity him because of what happened to his parents. Maybe it's the cop thing. Maybe you make him feel safe. Or maybe it's just that he thinks you'll understand because of what you've seen. I only tell you all this now because it's gone too far. You've said too much. I'm sorry, Megan, but I can't let you hurt him any more. I understand that look on his face now and why he won't return my phone calls. What you said devastated him.'

'I didn't know,' Megan whispered.

'Please, Megan, leave him be. If you must apologise, do it and then leave him in peace.' A tear slipped over Kat's face. 'Especially if you doubt you can truly love him forever and ever, heart and soul, don't even try it. Ryan isn't like your cop buddies. He doesn't hide from his emotions. He's deep and he feels things deeply. He's not hardened like you can be. I love you, sis, but this is one thing you've really messed up.'

Megan looked at Kat, seeing the pleading in her sister's eyes. She nodded once. The gesture was small and all she could manage. Kat was right. She'd been a bitch to Ryan and she didn't deserve his forgiveness. Still, she owed him an apology.

'I promise to let his actions guide mine,' Megan said. 'If he looks upset, I'll leave. I just need to know where he lives. I need to find him.'

The dark-red silk peasant shirt with the smocked bust fluttered against her arms as she stood outside Ryan's apartment building. She'd borrowed the clothes from her sister. It had taken some coaxing, but Kat finally let her use them. The grey workout outfit wasn't exactly what she wanted to be wearing when she faced Ryan. She knew by the look on Kat's face that her sister still held a small hope that she'd work things out with Ryan, despite how Kat begged her not to hurt him again.

Wiping her sweaty palms over her denim-covered hips, she took a step forwards. The three-storey apartment was exactly the type of place she imagined Ryan living. Old, quaint, with two trees guarding the entrance, the stone face had artistic appeal. As she stepped inside the small front lobby, the wood floors creaked. Mailboxes fitted along one side wall, leading the way to a narrow hall. In front of her was a narrow stairwell, next to a worn round table and two folding chairs. A stack of magazines had been left.

'Can I help you?' a man came from the hall, as if he'd been lurking in the shadows, watching the front door. His wrinkled face had the appearance of hard leather, the whites of his eyes were bloodshot and his short hair showed small lines where he'd combed it back. In his hands, he carried a baseball bat. Though he wasn't threatening with it, Megan's stomach tensed.

Not wanting to deal with what she could only assume was a drunk, she said, 'No, I'm just visiting a friend. Thank you anyway.'

'I don't have you on my approved list of friends,' the man insisted, when she tried to dismiss him by walking towards the stairwell.

Kat had told her where to find Ryan's apartment. Unfortunately, her sister forgot about the bodyguard she'd have to get past. If she'd known, Megan would have brought her badge.

The apartment door at the base of the stairwell opened. An elderly woman poked her head out and looked directly at Megan, clutching knitting needles in her hands like knives. Her wide eyes echoed the look of her rounded hairdo.

'You,' the woman said, her voice shaking.

Megan glanced behind her and back. With a slight smile, she nodded once. 'Me.'

'Leave her be, William.' The woman's face wrinkled into a scowl and she slammed the door shut.

'You can pass,' William said, stepping back into his shadowed hall. 'But be warned, I'm watching you.'

Megan shook her head, musing to herself, 'That's some sort of a security system they have. Creaky boards, a grandma with knitting needles and the crazy guy lurking in the hallway.'

The light from below cast her shadow along the dim walls. Each step lasted an eternity and she imagined this was how men on death row must feel, walking towards a fate that had very little chance of ending in their favour. Finally, she made the top, finding a lonely hall stretched out before her. Going to the first door on the right, she lifted her hand, hesitating before knocking softly.

Behind her, the door opened. 'He's not there.'

Megan turned at the sound. The woman was younger than Megan would have suspected by her voice. Pulling a long knitted brown jacket around her thin frame, she crossed her arms. Behind her, birds chirped noisily, the sounds varied and too numerous to count how many.

'Ryan's not home. He's out.'

'Do you know when I might expect him back?' Megan asked.

In a fury of movement, a grey parrot landed on the woman's shoulder, squawking, 'God bless you. *Gesundheit.*'

'Hush, Bullet,' the woman said.

'Good boy, good boy,' Bullet answered.

'Yes, good boy.' The woman scratched the parrot's neck. 'Ryan's not here.'

'I'll try back later,' Megan said.

'I could give him a message when I see him,' the woman offered. 'Like a name.'

'Detective Matthews.' Megan did not know why she gave the formal title over her given name. Part of her hoped the woman would be intimidated by it.

'Ah, you are that cop he took the picture of,' the woman said. 'I'll tell him you stopped by when he gets back from his honeymoon.'

Megan stiffened. 'He hasn't come back from Montana?'

'Montana?' The woman laughed. 'No, Montana was work. He took Rosa to Europe. Do you know Rosa? They were married right here on the roof just as soon as he finished that photography assignment in Montana. A guy, Harry, from our apartment building performed the ceremony by moonlight. It was very romantic. Ryan said

he never wanted to be parted from her again and proposed. Diederick who lives on the top floor went with
him, as he is from Switzerland and knows the area. I
believe Romania was mentioned a few times. Who
knows where those lovebirds are?'

'God bless you. *Gesundheit.*'

'Is there a message?' the woman asked, ignoring the
bird. 'Are you all right?'

'Huh? Fine.' Megan turned to go. Married? Ryan was
married? She studied the woman for a sign that she was
lying, but what motivation would the bird lady have to
lie about her neighbour getting married? Had she hurt
Ryan so badly that he ran back and married on old
girlfriend? Or had Megan been the other woman to his
relationship? It didn't make sense.

Without realising she'd walked down the stairs, she
glanced around to find herself in the lobby. The door
opened and the old woman popped her head out. She
began to close the door.

'Excuse me,' Megan said. 'Your upstairs neighbour –'

'Don't know her,' the old woman said. 'Only know she
rescues abandoned birds. Leave your card in her mailbox.'

'No, not the lady with the birds. I mean the other
neighbour, Ryan Lucas.'

'Oh, Ryan? Yeah, sweet kid, both him and his new
wife. If you are here for the wedding, you already missed
it. They're in Eastern Europe on their honeymoon. I think
she has family there. Sweet kids.'

'Oh.' Megan glanced up the stairwell. Inside, her heart
squeezed tightly in her chest and she felt nauseous. 'I
guess I'm too late.'

Dazed, she walked out of the apartment into the
bright sunlight. Even though it was warm, she shivered.
Ryan was married? How was this possible? It had only
been a little over a week. Not sure what to do, she
automatically waved for a cab.

* * *

Margie petted Bullet's back, making kissy noises at him as she walked down to the lobby. Seeing Mrs Hartman, she asked, sounding distracted, 'Is she gone?'

'Yes.' Mrs Hartman joined her in walking to the front window, as they watched Megan Matthews get into a cab and drive off. 'Why do you think she came to pay our Ryan a visit?'

'Whatever the reason, her being here will only cause him more hurt. I'm just glad Ryan already left with Diederick. That poor boy doesn't need this woman toying with him any more. I know her kind. They only come back when it suits them, when their life isn't what they want it to be. She comes so Ryan can nurse her ego and then, when she thinks something better comes along, she'll tear his heart out again without thought.' Margie sighed. 'It's a good thing you called to let me know she was here. I told her there was a wedding and that they're gone.'

'Hopefully the news will be the end of her,' Mrs Hartman said, still looking outside, though Megan's cab had driven off. 'It broke my heart to watch him throw away all the pictures he took of her. It's like a piece of him is missing.'

'He handed me the box and asked me to burn them.' Margie clucked her tongue, scratching Bullet's neck. 'Normally, he's so optimistic. That one did a number on him and she'll only do it again.'

'Let's not tell Ryan about this. It's better if he doesn't see her. She knows she's lost him now. She'll leave him be. I saw it in her face. We won't be seeing her again.' Mrs Hartman waved her hand towards her apartment door. 'Bring that little guy and come have some cookies. I just baked a batch of oatmeal raisin.'

'It's a good thing Ryan has us,' Margie said.

'That's right. We take care of our own. The boy will finally find his much deserved happiness.'

Chapter Twelve

The pain filtering through Megan was unbearable, not so unlike the time a bullet grazed her side, only worse because it shot through her chest and stayed. Her period stopped and yet she was still weepy, almost unable to get off her couch as she watched movie after endless movie. Nothing took her mind off Ryan for long and she was left feeling miserable and alone. A werewolf came on and she remembered how Ryan's hair was brown like the onscreen beast. If it was a documentary on animals, she'd think of how Ryan took pictures and knew bear trivia. And if there was a love story – forget about it.

The news of Ryan's marriage left her stunned. Ryan and Rosa, even their names sounded cute together. She just bet they were perfect – happy, loving, making baby noises at each other with stupid little pet names like muffin-pie and sweetie-kins. Megan snorted grumpily at the thought.

Hearing noise at her door, she glanced at it, not moving from her couch. Her doorknob jiggled and she automatically reached under her seat cushion for her gun. The familiar grip of the standard-issue 9mm hand-gun slid into her hand.

'Megan?' Zoe called out, coming into view as she pulled the spare set of keys from the door. Her sister's eyes found her on the couch, glancing down at her hand. 'Oh, please, don't tell me you were going to shoot me. It was Kat's idea I come over and check on you. Shoot her, not me.'

'Ever hear of knocking?' Megan pulled her hand out and shoved it under her cheek, not bothering to sit up.

'Yeah, but I also know you'd have the door blockaded

in about three seconds if you didn't want me coming in.' Zoe laughed and shut the door. 'Good thing I did come over. You look like ass.'

'Don't come in here looking all breezy and pretty raining on my depression.' Megan motioned over Zoe's outfit. The pretty chartreuse and charcoal silk dress had a deep V neck, a contracted hem and half-length sleeves.

'I almost didn't believe there was cause for worry, Megs,' Zoe said. 'After all, men never affected you, even in high school when you caught Jake what's-his-name cheating on you with that cheerleader.'

Megan sighed, pushing herself up on the couch. 'Why should I care about him? Besides, Kristy Skankyton gave him crabs.'

'Skankyton?' Zoe mused.

'What? She was a skanky whore. Why do you think Jake liked her? Why do you think the whole football team liked her? All at once in the boys' locker room?'

'OK, maybe I was wrong. You seem bitter.' Zoe walked over to the television and pushed the volume down. Then, frowning slightly as she stepped over broken DVDs on Megan's floor, she moved to the end of the couch to sit. 'Didn't feel like paying the late fees?'

'They pissed me off.' Megan ran her fingers through her hair, getting them snagged in the tangled mess. 'Stupid, unrealistic, happy couples.'

Zoe leant over and picked up a broken half. 'Happy? This chick dies in the end leaving the man alone and depressed.'

'Really? It didn't start that way. Huh, maybe I'll rent that one again and fast forward to the ending.'

'Ah, nice to meet you, Ms Bitterton.' Zoe tossed the broken piece on the floor, back into the pile.

'I'm not bitter. Stop saying that.' Megan began to lift her arms in a stretch, only to frown and think better of it. Instead, she crossed them over her chest. 'Look, if you're all going to come over here to do the "let's cheer up the depressed sister and make her shower and eat" bit that we did to Kat when she couldn't work it out with Vincent, then I'm telling you now, I will shoot you all.'

'Don't make me take away your gun.'

'Go ahead. I have a Glock 40 cal in the bathroom and a 9mm auto in the bedroom.'

'And this is why I came alone,' Zoe mumbled. 'It's a not-so-sneaky sneak attack. See, if we all came, you'd get hard-headed and resistant. This way, I can threaten to call our mother if you don't get off your butt and into a shower. You not only look like ass, you smell like it too.'

'Go to hell,' Megan mumbled, fully intent on lying back down.

'Mom will bring the tea,' Zoe threatened, all the while smiling sweetly. 'I'll make sure of it.'

Megan glared at her. 'I hate you.'

'You hate the world right now, so I won't let that go to my head.'

'I want to punch you in the head right now,' Megan pouted, knowing full well she'd never hurt her sister.

Zoe knew it, too. Wryly, she drawled, 'That's real mature.'

Megan made a weak noise. 'I just want to sit here.'

'Wallowing in self-pity?'

'You don't understand.'

'What? That you are in love? You messed up and are now feeling sorry for yourself instead of being the aggressive Megan I know and love. The Megan who goes for what she wants?' Zoe arched a brow. 'Mm, no, I guess I don't understand at all.'

'It's not that simple.' Megan took a deep breath and held it against the pain inside her.

'Just apologise. Tell him how you feel.' Zoe moved closer, running her hand over Megan's back.

'This isn't a damn romance novel.'

'Hey, you leave my slight addiction to books out of this,' Zoe ordered.

'Slight?'

Leaning over, Zoe pinched Megan's outer thigh. 'Shut up! It is slight.'

'Whatever.' Megan tried to suppress her laugh.

'We all saw him look at you, Megan.' Her sister clearly wasn't going to let her get out of the conversation.

'He's married, Zoe.' It almost killed her to say the words out loud. It made them all the more real. 'He came back from Montana, got married and is now on his honeymoon with his wife, Rosa.'

'Rosa?' Zoe sounded sceptical. 'And you got this info where?'

'I'm a cop.' Megan dropped her head. 'I know, Zoe, and it hurts. I've seen people who've gone crazy when they can't have who they want and I never really got it before, but I do now.'

'Don't talk like that, Megs. You're not crazy, you are in love. But you are right. Love isn't rational, it's not planned, it can't be controlled or forced. It's not even one of your mysteries to solve. It just is.'

'If I wanted philosophy, I'd have asked Sasha.' Even as she said it, Megan gave her sister a small smile. 'If you want to make me feel better, help me come up with ways to hurt Rosa.'

'All right, that's it.' Zoe stood up. 'Enough. You are better than this. Get your smelly butt into the shower. I'm supposed to get you over to Kat's for a surprise cheer-up party and makeover. And, if you don't hurry, I'll call Mom and tell her about it.'

Megan grumbled.

'Kat bought wine.'

She grumbled again.

'And beer,' Zoe added. 'Lots and lots of beer.'

'Fine.' Megan made a face. 'But no happy-couple movies.'

'Only exploding bullet-flying fun,' Zoe teased.

'Promise?' Megan gave a sheepish grin.

'Yeah, yeah, promise. But, if you start scratching your crotch and belching, I'm calling Mom. This is a party with your lady sisters, not your macho cop buddies.'

Buuuurrp!

Kat fell over laughing as Sasha finished. Sasha just grinned. 'I told you I learnt something in college.'

'Oh, how things degenerate fast,' Zoe moaned.

'Ah, come on, Zoe, try it. You might like being vulgar,' Kat said.

Megan cuddled back into Kat's white cushy couch, curled in a burgundy knit blanket. For the first time since Ryan walked away in Montana, she felt some semblance of happy. All that was missing was Ella to make the night perfect.

'I should have known you'd turn this into a Megan night.' Zoe laughed. 'I was such a sucker when you told me this was a ladies night makeover party.'

'What?' Kat stood, showing off her tight vinyl police uniform with the too-small shirt, high-cut shorts and utility belt. 'I call this a makeover.'

'I don't think stripper was too far of a leap for you,' Sasha mused. She wore a militant black leather domina-trix costume, complete with shiny cap and whip.

'And bossy not too far for you, college girl,' Megan said, kicking her bare foot out at Sasha who sat on the floor.

'I can't believe you didn't put on your outfit.' Kat pouted. She was the only one not drinking, but didn't seem to care.

Megan sat up, revealing her plaid pyjama pants and tight tank top. She grabbed the old-fashioned nurse's uniform and held it up for inspection. 'Do I look like a compassionate caregiver?'

'You might turn into one, if you put on your superheroine costume,' Kat said under her breath, but not so quiet they couldn't hear.

'Super like me?' Zoe jumped up, dropping her quilted blanket as she put her fists on her hips, lifting her chin. A long cape fluttered behind her tight spandex bodysuit. The bright colours were hard to look at for too long. 'Super chef!'

'Super slut,' Sasha mumbled, giggling.

'Ha, ha,' Zoe answered, sitting back down and tugging the quilt around her shoulders.

'Why don't you go get us more food, super chef?' Megan handed an empty dip bowl to Zoe. 'And don't forget the chips.'

Zoe got to her feet, grumbling. 'This isn't chef work, it's waitressing.'

'Ah, but super chef can do anything,' Sasha said.

The doorbell rang, a long drowning series of tones.

'Like answer the door,' Kat said.

Zoe looked down in shock. 'What? I'm not answering the door like this!'

'Go on. It's probably just the male stripper Kat ordered.' Sasha laughed.

'You ordered a male stripper?' Megan sat up straighter, somewhat shocked.

Sasha laughed harder.

'Megan, you go get it. We're not dressed.' Zoe ran towards the kitchen with the empty dip bowl.

Sighing, and somewhat curious, Megan got up, trailing her blanket behind her. Kat said, 'I can't believe you actually hired a stripper. I was joking about that.'

'The whores are in the other room waiting for you,' Megan said, swinging open the door to look out into the hall. No one was there. 'Hello?' Leaning forwards, she glanced down the hall, but saw no one.

'Megan?' Kat called.

'Um, do you have another door?' Megan shut the front door, frowning.

'What?' Kat came up behind her.

'No one's there. I'm going to go help Zoe in the kitchen. You should have Vincent check the doorbell. It might be faulty.'

Ryan took a deep breath. She didn't see him. He never imagined Megan would be at Kat's house so late in the evening. When he heard her voice, all he could think to do was hide behind the thick plastic plant in the corner. Lucky for him, she didn't search too hard, just peeked her head out the door. Not so lucky for him, he'd seen her and it was like a shock of cold to his soul. He hadn't been ready. He told himself he'd have time to prepare for her, and perhaps an inordinate amount of alcohol.

She looked beautiful, her long dark hair pulled into pigtails, hanging over her shoulders at each side of her neck. By her clothes, she was staying the night with her sister. Funny, she'd never done that before. At least she was happy, judging by the quizzical smile on her face. Her words confused him, but more than likely she was just teasing her sisters by calling them whores.

As the door to Kat's home shut, he reached out and pushed the elevator button. The gift he'd bought in Romania for his friend could wait, as could the pictures he took. The door opened again, just as the elevator dinged. He made a run for it and hit the button for the lobby floor several times.

'Megan!' Kat yelled. 'There's someone out there.'

Megan turned on her way to the kitchen, spurred into action by the sound of Kat's startled voice. Without thought, she ran past Kat into the hall. The elevator was closing and she ran towards it, darting out her hand between the metal doors. They tapped her fingers before the sensors picked up her movement and forced the doors to open. Her lips parted, her body tensed ready to face the intruder that caused her sister to panic. Then, seeing him, she froze.

'Ryan,' she whispered, surprised to see him. Her extended hand remained lifted between the doors.

'I can come back when you're gone.' He didn't move, as his body pressed against the rail along the back of the small area.

'Do you hate me that much?' She tried to give a small laugh, but the combination of liquor and panic made it hard to think and the laugh never made it past her mouth. She didn't expect to see him so soon after discovering . . .

Megan couldn't even force her brain to remember what she'd discovered. He was here now, before her, his hair and light shadowing of a beard scruffy yet irresistibly handsome.

'I don't hate you, Megan.' The soft words were almost impossible to hear. Megan trembled, her eyes drawn to his mouth. 'I should leave –'

Megan pushed forwards, letting the elevator close behind her as she rushed him. She didn't think, just acted on instinct. He didn't hate her. She'd been living in the fear that he'd never think kindly of her again. Not hating didn't mean love, it didn't even mean he liked her, but it was something and her hazy mind seized hold.

Ryan didn't move, didn't try to escape as she pressed her mouth to his. Megan grabbed the rail on either side of them. The elevator jolted into motion. She sighed against his lips, as they didn't readily part to let her tongue pass. The familiar smell of him, the press of his tight frame as she trapped him along her body, made her desire for him focus hotly between her thighs.

'Megan,' he said, pulling his head back slightly. 'Stop.'

She heard him, but didn't want to listen. Breathing hard, she leant away, keeping her hips forwards so they stayed pressed along his growing erection. He said stop with his mouth, but his body had another message for her.

'I've missed touching you,' she admitted.

'Megan...' He hesitated.

The elevator continued down. Soon the doors would open and he'd walk away. She didn't want that. There was no time to talk. She was in her pyjamas and her sisters would worry if she didn't go back up.

'I know,' she whispered, lightly touching the side of his face. 'We can't be. I know this and I'm sorry I tried to tempt you. It will not happen again. This was the last time. I promise.'

She drew her hips back. Ryan moved aside and she dropped her hand to let him pass. Facing the mirrored back, she saw her face, the pigtails Sasha had talked her into trying and the overdone black eyeliner Kat had applied when doing her makeup. Though overdone, her sisters had done a good job in their call-girl makeover – all except the nightclothes she wore instead of a nurse's uniform.

Seeing movement in the mirror, she glanced at Ryan's reflection. His back was towards her as he pushed a button on the wall. She turned, curious to see what he was up to. The elevator slowed and the doors opened on the thirteenth floor, too far from the bottom to be his stop. Meeting her gaze through the polished metal panels, he reached his hand towards her. 'The last time, I understand.'

Knowing they had a silent agreement, she eagerly went to him. Her hand slipped into his. He glanced either way before pulling her with him.

'Where are we going?' she asked, as they passed a closed apartment door.

'The elevators have security cameras. I don't want to put you in an awkward position again. But I overheard the security guards on my way up. They're rewiring the stairwell's security system.' He paused at the end of the hall, leading her to the carpeted platform above and below long rows of stairs.

When the door closed behind them, he dropped her hand and turned to face her. Megan tilted her head to the side. 'Ryan, I wanted to say ... well, I'm not sure what I wanted to say. There were things but right now I can't think of them. My sisters are having a slumber party upstairs and they did my hair and we've been drinking and I don't think I'm explaining the things I want to.'

His eyes cast downwards briefly before meeting hers straight on. 'We never were good at just talking, were we?'

'No.' She shook her head.

He cupped her cheek. 'I got it. This is the last time.'

'OK,' Megan whispered, but that wasn't what she wanted to say. His warm fingers slid down her cheek to her neck, glancing over the strap of her tank top only to follow the line of the bodice towards the top curves of her breasts.

'We might be bad at words, but we're good at this part.'

Megan nodded, unable to form a coherent thought. In the back of her mind, a nagging idea tried to surface. There was something she needed to remember, but couldn't think of what it was. Did it really matter? Ryan was here and he didn't look like he hated her. A slow smile curled on his features, but didn't fully reach his serious eyes.

Damn, but he could still make her legs weak with just one look. The rough, sleep-tousled look of his hair drew her hands. She grabbed hold, pulling him forwards. Their lips touched, melding in instant passion. He wasn't too muscled, like bodybuilders, but very toned. Megan moaned, as his hands slid up her back, keeping her body locked against his. The thin material of her pyjamas was no match for the stiff denim-clad erection rocking alongside her stomach. Ryan's hands dipped beneath her waistband, squeezing her ass.

Megan turned her face, gasping as she reached to push off her pants, taking the cotton underwear down with them. They fell to the floor, leaving her ass bare. 'I don't want to rush this, but I don't want my sisters to worry and someone could come along.'

'Mmm-hmm,' he agreed, working on his zipper. Megan reached to help him, kissing him as she tugged down his pants. Ryan pulled her tank top off her shoulder, stretching it so he could reach her breast. 'We'll be very –' he kissed her lightly '– very quiet.'

Ryan stepped forwards, trapping her to the wall. Her body settled into his familiar one. The hard length of his cock pressed against her, as his hands roamed down over her hips only to reach between her legs. Her thighs tightened and he stroked her clit, rubbing it in small circles before parting her slick folds. Just the thought of him made her wet and to feel him was as close to heaven as she'd ever get. And then she realised something. Over the last year, Ryan's presence always brightened whatever situation she was in.

'I love the way you smell.' He took a deep breath, kissing down her throat, groaning in appreciation.

His words kept her from saying what was on her mind, from telling him how he made her feel. Everything she'd been feeling since she realised her emotions couldn't be put into words. She'd tried, practised what she wanted to say to him if she saw him again, but none of those words formed together now.

Ryan sucked her nipple between his teeth, and Megan squirmed. Reaching down, she wrapped her fingers around his stiff arousal. She stroked the length of him, moaning softly. His finger worked along the rim of her body, dipping inside her sex, working slowly in and out of her opening, rubbing her sweet spot. Focusing his efforts, he twirled the tip of his finger over the sensitive bud. She clamped her thighs down hard on his hand.

'There isn't much time.' She meant the words as more of a reminder to herself. Her stomach tightened and she bit her lip to keep from moaning too loudly. Ryan reached around, grabbing her ass. The motion drew her cheeks apart. Megan lifted her leg to the side, opening herself up to him. 'I need you, Ryan, please.'

He knew just want her body wanted, always knew how to touch her as if sensing her needs and magnifying them with his own. When Ryan looked at her, she felt like they were the only things in the world. She refused to think of anything else but the moment, a moment she never wanted to end.

Megan held on to his shoulders as he lifted her up. The wall pressed into her back, hard and unforgiving, as the tip of his cock found her entrance. Ryan made a weak noise as he slid into her body. Gasping, she pressed her back into the wall, trying to get leverage as he controlled the pace. With aching slowness, he worked his hips back and forth, staying deep inside her.

'Nothing makes sense when I'm with you,' he whispered.

Megan knew exactly what he meant. 'This position is too hard. Lie on the floor.'

Ryan instantly set her on her feet. They knelt together. He leant back on the small platform, his upper back hitting the bottom of the stairs leading up to the next floor. Megan crawled over him, straddling his thighs. Pulling her hips forwards, Ryan moaned. Their bodies joined once more, his cock seated deeper than before.

As she rode him, he stroked her sex, circling the sensitive bud. Each press sent wonderfully erotic sensations through her. She ran her hands over him, touching his chest and arms, amazed each time they came together at how wonderful he could make her feel. No matter how often they had sex, she never got tired of it. Ryan knew all the right ways to touch her, the right pressure to use. And knowing this was the last time made it all the more bittersweet.

Though she fought her climax, her orgasm hit her hard, slamming into her like a hurricane. Her whole body tensed and her breath caught. Ryan grunted and they couldn't have timed their releases more perfectly.

Megan tried to hold on to it, tried not to catch her breath, tried not to let her heartbeat slow. But, as the seconds ticked by, and her body came down from the rush of the climax, she had no choice but to get up. She moved to get dressed. It was really over. What could she say? How could she convince him to give her another chance? Then, the thought that tried to surface in her foggy brain pushed through. He was married.

'What have we done?' she whispered.

'What?' Ryan asked. 'I didn't hear that.'

'I said, I'm sorry. I didn't mean for this to happen. I –'

'Wow, let's not.' Ryan moved behind her and she heard his zipper as he dressed. She pulled on her pyjama pants, tightening the drawstring. He continued, 'I think I know what you want to say but, instead of a bunch of apologising or explanations or fighting, how about we just leave it at it's over. I think we both know that this, whatever it is between us, will never work out. We were both wrong about a lot of things. You said that a man with all those qualities you listed would make you happy and I thought being that man would make us both happy.'

'Ryan . . .' Megan turned. He stood before her dressed. Everything she wanted to say meant nothing. Her eyes turned to the floor and she saw a gift bag. She hadn't paid attention to it before, but now she asked, 'What's that?'

'A gift for Kat. I went to Romania with someone from my building and picked it up for her while I was there.'

Someone from your building? she thought. Don't you mean Rosa?

'It's Vampire wine,' he said. 'A cabernet sauvignon. I thought she'd like the novelty of it coming direct from Transylvania though I think you can get it here in the States. I know everyone thinks Italy is the best wine country, but Transylvanians can hold their own.'

Megan smiled briefly. She found it endearing when he started over-explaining – like with the bears in Montana. It was almost a nervous tick.

'I couldn't resist buying myself a bottle of each. Luckily, we had a private jet at our disposal so getting it home wasn't a problem. Their merlot and chardonnay were excellent. And –' he paused '– I'm rambling, aren't I?'

I like it, she thought. I like listening to you talk about trivial stuff. I like when you tell stories and when your eyes glaze in thought. I like you, Ryan. I want to be with you. But I can't. Because of Rosa. Rosa, your wife. Rosa, your rich wife if a private jet is any indication. Though the fact she lives in your building doesn't make sense if she owns a jet. She's probably beautiful, too.

Ryan looked at her expectantly. Instead of saying what she thought, she nodded. 'A little. I never really got the fascination with vampires. They kill people, have no soul, drink blood and live forever as monsters. None of that sounds too appealing to me.'

Especially not right now, her mind whispered. Not with the pain of a breaking heart. Who would want to live forever with such an empty feeling?

'Oh, I don't know.' Ryan picked up the bag, his tone lightening as he fell into easy conversation. 'There's something sadly beautiful about the concept. Watching worlds fade around you only to rebuild into something else, immortal and eternal. I've always been fascinated by the idea – not so much that I'm going to wear a vial of blood around my neck, let alone drink my breakfast. I like bacon and eggs too much.'

'I shouldn't have said that about –' Megan tried again to apologise, not caring that they spoke of other things. The weight of what she wanted to tell him bore down on her.

'Shh.' He shook his head. After touching her face for a second, he let go and turned to walk down the stairs. 'Goodbye, Megan.'

Megan watched him disappear around a corner and heard him continue down. Part of her begged to run after him, to tell him how she felt regardless of Rosa, of the past, of the apology he refused to hear. Swallowing over the lump in her throat, she turned to the door leading to the thirteenth floor. Her feet hit silently against the carpeted hall. It was late and no one was around. The apartments were quiet as she walked past a couple of doors. No one would ever know the secret passion that had taken place in the stairwell.

At the elevator, she pushed the button that would take her to the top, back to Kat's home. Once there, she found the front door open and her sisters inside changed from their stripper uniforms into pyjamas.

'What was it?' Sasha asked.

'Someone who was lost. I gave him directions,' Megan lied. 'Sorry it took so long. I didn't mean to make you worry.'

'Well, you are just in time for the movie to start,' Zoe said, grinning. 'Nothing but action adventure, just like I promised.'

Megan forced a smile, shoving Ryan to the back of her mind. 'Perfect.'

Zoe and Sasha headed back to the living room. Megan moved to follow, but Kat's hand on her arm stopped her.

'Ryan?' she asked. 'I know it was him. I saw him run into the elevator. I screamed because it scared me, but it was him, wasn't it?'

'Don't worry, I didn't hurt him. I just said I was sorry

and let him go. It's over.' Megan didn't move until Kat drew her hand away. 'Can we just leave it at that?'

'Megan –'

'Don't, Kat. Just don't. I don't want to talk about this with you. You asked me to leave him be and I am. It's for the best and I know why you asked me.' Megan said no more as she went to join her other sisters in front of the television.

Ryan cradled Kat's present against his body as he left the building and Megan in it. The strange combination of a sated body and broken heart filled him. He knew what Megan was going to say, but he really didn't feel like listening to her apologise for not wanting to be with him for more than sex. She didn't have to be sorry for not loving him and it was never his intention to make her feel bad about it.

'The last time,' he told himself, looking up the side of the building. His heart squeezed in his chest. Feeling the doorman's eyes on him, watching him through the front glass door, he nodded in the man's direction. The man didn't return the gesture and Ryan felt extremely alone.

Chapter Thirteen

Megan stood, watching the flurry of movement in the police station around her. She smelt the familiar stale air that reeked of coffee, paper and a lingering hint of Axel's cheap cologne. The captain had called her the night before to tell her to come back to work. Just like that, her vacation was over. She was back in her old clothes – the black slacks, white linen button-down shirt and black fitted suit jacket. Her hair was pulled back to the nape of her neck, wound into a perfect bun. The familiar weight of her gun was in her shoulder holster, pressed against her side. But, despite these well-known comforts, all was not the same.

She watched the movement around her like a play, nodding at those who greeted her and welcomed her back. Megan even heard her voice answering her fellow police officers, saying all the right things, making jokes and taking them.

'Eh, Matthews, vacation did you some good,' Officer Gates said. 'Why don't you take us next time you decide to spend a month on the beach?'

'Do I look like I've been on the beach? Besides, you in a thong gives me nightmares.' Megan laughed.

'I'll let that slide, because this is your first day, but don't think I don't know you want this.' Gates rubbed his protruding belly.

'Careful, boys.' As Axel walked towards her, the smell of his cologne became pungent. 'We wouldn't want to be arrested for sexual harassment.'

'You'd have to be sexual to even be a candidate,' Megan answered.

'Ouch, Matthews.' Axel put his hand over his heart. He

lowered his voice, saying, 'Is that any way to treat the man who carried your caseload.'

Megan's expression didn't change, but the man had a point. She should take it easy on him. 'Pile my desk, I'll return the favour.'

'Already done, slick.' Axel pointed his fingers, shooting at her with his pretend guns while making soft gunfire noises. Megan instantly glanced at her desk. Three giant stacks of files were piled on it. 'Don't worry, I saved you all the fun stuff.'

Megan suppressed a groan, mumbling, 'Asshole.'

'I love it when you talk dirty, Matthews.' Axel laughed.

Seeing Captain Turner's office door open, she watched a man in a cheap business suit walk out. The captain frowned from behind his desk. He didn't look happy, but, then again, he never did. Before she could move, he looked up and saw her.

'Matthews,' he yelled, not bothering to get up from his desk. Megan instantly stiffened, her body filling with the familiar stress of work. He motioned with his hand for her to come to his office and she obeyed, automatically walking into his office then shutting the door. 'Welcome back, Matthews.'

'Thanks, I –' she started to answer.

'Here –' the captain handed her a file '– I need you to go over this. Trial date was moved up. Johnson's not available and you were second on the scene. Be at the courthouse at two.'

Megan flipped open the file. It was one of her old homicide cases, one in the sea of many she'd worked on.

'Oh, and that photographer, Lucas, played ball. Nothing was in the paper when you were gone, the museum thieves were caught and I finally have one of my best detectives back on the job.'

Megan gave a slight smile. 'Yeah, he turned out to be all right.'

'It's too bad he's quitting. Only two of the new pho-tographers are working out. But, what can we do?'

'Ryan, I mean, Lucas is quitting?'

'No.'

Megan began to sigh in relief.

'He already quit, gave his notice a little over a week ago. We're waiting for him to drop off a full backup copy of all his work for our files.' The captain picked up his coffee cup to take a drink, frowned into the empty depths and set it back down.

'The picture could still show up,' Megan said weakly.

'I don't think so. He seems like a straight shooter.' The captain again made a move towards his cup, only to stop himself mid-action.

'Would you like me to get you coffee?' Megan asked.

'What?' He frowned. 'No, stuff tastes like ash anyway.'

'You were saying something about the photogra-phers?' she asked.

'What? Oh, Lucas. It's too bad we're losing him. He's dependable and we can call him at any hour.' The captain sighed heavily, motioning to the file he'd given her. 'I need you in court for this case and then I want you on desk duty until the St Claud trial. I think Axel left a few files on your desk.'

Megan bit the inside of her lip to keep from comment-ing. A few files?

'I'll only pull you off desk if I need you. I don't have to tell you there is a lot of pressure on this one, Matthews.'

Megan stood up, knowing by his tone that their con-versation was over. 'I'm on it, Captain.'

'This is for work,' Megan told herself, nervously smooth-ing down the front of her loose black slacks. She'd gone so far as to buy a new navy-blue ribbed knit shirt with a semi-sheer overlay. The fitted sleeves, wide scoop neck with chiffon trim and gathered bust was what the saleslady called runway chic. It was a little overdone for what she normally purchased, but she had an uncontrollable urge to look pretty.

Her hair fell in long waves down her back and she wished that she had pulled it into a bun. Maybe the new shirt and non-work hairdo was too much. Maybe she should turn around, run down the stairs and out of his building before anyone saw her – like the crazy man with the bat.

What if someone at the department discovered she'd deleted a few of Ryan's pictures that she needed to finish the stack of files on her desk? That she'd planned the necessity of this meeting in a late-night fit of loneliness and need? She missed Ryan, missed seeing him, hearing him, smelling him. Was that so wrong?

'Yes, when Ryan is married,' she mumbled to herself. 'Just get the files and get out. This is a stupid idea.'

Taking a deep breath, she thought of what she planned to say. *The data was corrupted. I need the pictures for my file. How are you doing? I miss you. Please don't quit. Come back to work so I can see you.*

Why did he have to be married? Why had she been such a schmuck? Every moralistic code she lived by screamed at her, compounding her guilt about what had happened in the thirteenth-floor stairwell of Kat's apartment building. The feeling warred with the pleasure she'd felt being in his arms.

'I'm just here to pick up the pictures,' she whispered, taking small steps towards the door. 'Pictures.' Megan took another deep breath and knocked. 'Pictures.'

'You didn't have to knock . . .' Ryan's words ground to a halt as his eyes met hers. 'Megan, what are you . . . ?'

'Pictures,' she said softly. He looked so good. She couldn't help but stare at his face.

'Ryan? Is that Diederick with the groceries?' a woman called from within the depths of his apartment. 'Tell him to get in here. I'm starving. This baby ain't gonna feed itself.'

Baby? Megan made a weak noise and began to back away from his door. Ryan looked handsome in his jeans and plain white T-shirt, just as he always did. The tousled easygoing look suited him and made her heart flutter in her chest. What was she doing here? 'I really needed to talk to you, but I see you're busy. I can come back.'

The expression on her face must have worried him because he frowned and leant towards her. 'Megan, what is it? What's wrong? Oh, man, you're not pregnant, are you?'

'No.' She gulped, shocked by the question. 'What? No. I'm not pregnant.'

'Oh, wow, sorry. You showing up out of the blue nearly a month after we were in Montana and I just thought that maybe you came to tell me ...' He sighed, flustered as he searched for the right words. 'Since we weren't all that careful in Montana, or really any time we ... Well, if you're not, that's good. I mean, it's for the best.'

She didn't answer.

'You still have that look. Like you have bad news to tell me, but don't know how to say it.' He kept his voice quiet, as if hiding his words from the people inside. She couldn't say she blamed him. 'You didn't come here to tell me you have some sort of disease, did you?'

Megan grimaced. Did the disease of a broken heart count?

'No, no, it's nothing like that.' She tried to peek over his shoulder as she heard footsteps.

'Then what is so important?' he asked.

'Diederick, did you forget the –?' The woman appeared next to him. She was in her early twenties, with a pretty smile and laidback appearance that matched Ryan's. Her white long-sleeve undershirt was printed with fake tattoos and she wore a pale-green T-shirt over it. 'Oh, hello. I thought you were someone else.'

Megan watched, but the woman didn't wrap her arms lovingly around him, didn't kiss his cheek or do any number of things Megan imagined a new wife would do.

'Rosa, this is –' Ryan began.

'Detective Matthews,' Megan finished holding out her hand. 'I just came by to speak to –' she couldn't force herself to say 'your husband' '– Ryan about some crime-scene photographs he took for us.'

'Oh, ick,' Rosa said, tossing her curly dark hair. 'Let me know when Diederick and Pete get here with the food, will ya?'

Ryan waited for Rosa to leave before speaking. 'Your department should have almost all of them. I emailed the ones they said were urgent.'

'You did?' Megan tried to act innocent as she remembered deleting the email messages.

'I'm sorry you had to come here. I'm sure you just missed the email. Is there a specific photo you need? I told my contact at the department – a Mrs Daniels – that all anyone had to do was call me and I'd send whatever was needed, if it was needed before I could get a hard copy turned in.'

Megan glanced over his shoulder, wishing he'd invite her in and yet knowing it was better he didn't. To see him with Rosa, together as the happy newlyweds, would surely kill her.

'But, while you're here, I'll just give you the master copy of everything, if you don't mind taking it in for me since you're heading there eventually anyway. I told the captain I'd drop the backup off when I pick up my last cheque.'

'Yeah, I heard you were quitting.'

'It's for the best. The paper has offered me a staff position with better hours and less crime.'

They still stood in his doorway, Ryan leaning against the door without inviting her in and Megan standing in the hall not asking him to. 'We'll be sorry to see you go. The guys have nothing but good things to say about your work.'

'It's time. But thank you for saying so.'

'Here,' Megan reached into her pocket and grabbed a piece of paper. 'These are the file numbers we need. I'll be happy to take the disk in for you. It's not a problem at all.'

Ryan nodded, hesitating before taking the paper from her. He seemed careful not to touch her outstretched hand. 'I'll send them right over.'

'OK.' Her voice sounded shrill, even to her own ears. 'Thank you.'

'Was that all?'

'Yes. But you're busy. I can come by tomorrow and pick them up then.'

'Yeah, we're having a building party. It's my turn to host.'

Megan nodded. 'OK, then. Bye. Thanks.' She moved to go, only to stop as Ryan began to shut the door. Turning, she blurted, 'Why did you have to marry her?'

'What?' He looked shocked.

'Her,' Megan demanded quietly, motioning behind him. 'Rosa. Why did you have to be with her? You belong with me. I'm the one, Ryan. I'm . . .' She shrugged, feeling teary and afraid. 'It's me. You couldn't have waited one week for me to come to my senses?'

'Why shouldn't I be with someone else? Suddenly, you want me now that you think you can't have me?' He glanced behind him before pulling the door shut so they were alone in the hall. 'What kind of crap is that?'

'Think?' Megan seized upon the one word. 'You said now that I *think* I can't have you.'

He looked away, as if searching for a response. His mouth worked, but nothing came out.

'Am I wrong, Ryan? Do I have a chance to make it up to you?' She took a step towards him.

'You know everything,' he said. 'Don't you know the answer to this?'

'No, no, I thought I did, but I don't. I'm no good at relationships.' She lifted her hand, wanting to touch him, but needing permission. 'In Montana, so much was said. I'm sorry for most of it. I'm an idiot. I don't know anything. I didn't realise what I felt. But, when you drove away, I felt my heart breaking. I didn't even know my heart could break. I went to work and hearing that you weren't going to be there ruined it for me. I like seeing you at the crime scenes, however morbid that might sound. When we first met, I wrote you off as a nuisance because of that picture you took of me taking down St Claud. I didn't realise you published it for more than recognition and money. I didn't know there could be another reason, especially the reason Kat said.'

'She told you about my parents?' His face hardened.

'Don't be mad at her. She was trying to make me understand. That photograph, when it came out, ruined my life. Or I thought it did. Or at the time it did.' Megan shook her head, beginning to pace back and forth in the small hall. 'My work was all I had and being moved from homicide to catching burglars was a step down for me. Then, you took my picture at the crime scene when I stepped on that stupid rock.'

'You mean the priceless carving of the Aztec god?' he interjected.

Megan grimaced. 'Yeah, that would be the rock.'

'Go on.' He crossed his arms over his chest.

'You took that picture and all I could think was how you were going to ruin my life again. So, when you showed up as my fiancé, I just knew it was to blackmail me. Only, I wasn't sure why. I assumed it was to get in good with my family because you didn't have one.' Megan made a weak noise, her eyes darting to his steady gaze. 'I didn't mean it like that. I told you, I'm no good at these things.'

'What? Apologies?'

'Yeah, those.'

'Go on. I'm listening.'

'Oh . . .' Megan blinked, trying to remember what she'd been saying. Nothing was as articulate as she'd endlessly practised. Her body shook with nerves, making it hard to concentrate. Somehow, she knew this was her chance to get everything she wanted to say out. 'Where was I?'

'You think I blackmailed you to get into your family.'

'Right.' She pointed at him to punctuate the word. 'You had that picture and I was so sure you were using it for leverage.'

'I wouldn't do that, Megan. If this is to get the picture back –'

'No, it's not, I swear.' She made a move towards him, only to hold back. 'I know you wouldn't do that. What I'm trying to tell you is I suspected you endlessly, adding motivations where there weren't any. I suspected the worst when, in fact, the only thing I should have suspected was the way I truly feel about you.'

'And how is that?'

Did he lean closer to her? She couldn't be sure. Her world was spinning around her, a rush of emotion that centred on him. How could she say the words? Her voice cracked and she tried her best to get them out, but they wouldn't come.

'Megan?' He touched her cheek, gently running the backs of his fingers along her neck.

'I love you,' she whispered. 'I want to take everything back. I want to rewind time and go back to Montana, to when we were engaged, to before you . . .'

'Me?'

'Rosa.'

'Me and Rosa?'

Megan nodded. 'Before.'

'Rosa is married to Pete. There isn't a me and Rosa.' This time she was sure he was closer. Her nerves snapped with the electric heat from his body. 'There has never been a me and Rosa.'

'No you and Rosa?' Sweet relief flooded her. She'd hoped, prayed for such a thing. 'But your neighbours said . . .'

'My neighbours?' Ryan frowned, glancing at his door.

'When I came, they said you were on your honeymoon in Romania and you said you were in Romania when I saw you at Kat's.'

'Who said this?'

Megan motioned towards the door across the hall from his. 'The woman with the birds and the lady downstairs.'

'A moment, please.' Ryan pushed open his door. 'Margie, Rosa, Mrs Hartman, can you come here for a moment?'

Rosa was the first to appear.

'Are we married, Rosa?' he asked.

'No, not so long as Pete behaves himself.' Rosa winked at him.

'Thank you,' Ryan said, nodding.

Rosa laughed, tossing her hand. 'I love your strangeness, Ryan. Don't ever change or I'll no longer be your friend.'

A smile crept over Megan's face. 'So, you're not married?'

'Margie?' Ryan called.

'Ryan, you don't have to do this,' Megan said under her breath. 'So long as it's not true, I don't care why they said it. Please, just tell me I have a chance to make it up to you. That's all I'm asking for is a chance. Let me take you out on a date. I'll do –'

'Ye –' Margie, the woman who had the birds skidded to a stop as she saw Megan. Without having to be asked, she said, 'Yes, I did and I did it to protect you from her. And I'd do it again.'

'Why would I need protection from my fiancée?' he asked.

'Engaged?' Megan gasped.

He smiled, turning to her. 'Engaged.'

'Quick, shut the door, Margie. Let them be,' said the older woman who could only be Mrs Hartman.

'They're hoping I forget to yell at them for meddling in my life. Though they did mean well, it wasn't their place to lie to you and try to protect me.' He chuckled, a knowing sound, before raising his voice. 'Even if they now listen from the other side of the door so they can hear what we're talking about.'

A thud sounded at his claim followed by the unmistakable drumming of footsteps.

'You said engaged?' Megan didn't dare to hope, but how could she not?

'To you.' Ryan leant his mouth to hers.

'Really?' Megan wound her arms around his neck, pressing her lips tightly to his to keep him from answering. She moaned against his mouth, having missed the feel of his body against hers. The tight muscles of his chest welcomed her and his arms held her waist as he lifted her feet off the floor.

He was the first to draw back. 'Yes, really. You see, I told myself the next woman I was with would be "the one". I'm looking for marriage, kids, the whole familial package.'

Megan laughed, remembering the words she'd told him that night in the alleyway when he'd asked her out on a date to her parents' house. 'And how do you know you've found the right woman?'

'She'll be stubborn, wilful, frustrating as hell . . .' Ryan paused, kissing the tip of her nose.

'I like her already.' She arched a brow. 'And . . . ?'

'Tough yet sweet, beautiful, sexy, big eyes that melt me with just the thought of them.' He kissed each of her temples by her eyes. 'So long as she is you, I know I'll be happy.'

'And the details are irrelevant?' she echoed the past words.

'No, wrong. The details will be the most important part. I want to live and remember each and every second of our life together.' Ryan cupped her face. 'I love you, Megan. I want to always love you.'

'I have a confession,' she said. 'I didn't fight your coming to Montana harder because I secretly wanted you to be there with me. I would never have admitted it then, but I know it now. I'm a cop. There is no way you could have blackmailed me, if I didn't let you.'

'I've got a confession as well.' Ryan grabbed her arms and turned her towards the wall, intent on trapping her against it.

'What?'

'The motorcycle wasn't mine.' He moaned softly, his eyes shining bright as he pressed into her body. The fullness of his arousal rocked into her, stirring her already piqued desires. 'I don't own a bike, have never owned one. I lied about it because I wanted to be with you. Can you forgive me for pretending to fit your list?'

'No.' She shook her head, feigning a scowl. 'But you can spend all of our married life making it up to me.'

Ryan nipped at her jaw, only to breathe heavily against her as he nuzzled her throat. 'So you give in to me. What was it? My sexy boyish charm? My suave manners?'

'It's the details.' Megan leant up to kiss him, only to draw back. 'I wasn't lying when I said I suck at relationships. So I have to ask, are you sure about this? About us? Because I can't lose you again. And you better be sure, because I'm licensed to carry a gun.'

'I'm not worried. I've been told the secret to happy marriages.'

'Are you going to share it? Or do I have to beat it out of you?'

'Easy there, Detective Matthews.' Ryan gave her a sultry smile.

Megan flipped him around, changing their roles as she trapped him to the wall. 'Let me guess. The secret is ...' She ran her hand down between them, letting it cup his arousal pressing against his jeans.

'Nope. Not even close.'

'It's not?' She quirked a brow, drawing her hand away and holding it to the side where he could see it. 'Are you sure? Because sex is the one thing we actually get right.'

'Your father says the key to a happy marriage is to run away each time a wife menstruates.' He laughed. 'He recommended I take up a once-a-month hobby. With as many women as he has in the family, I figured he'd be the one to know.'

Megan slapped him playfully on the chest and pushed back. She looked at his door. 'I'd ask you to invite me in, but I'm not sure I could hold a straight conversation with your neighbours. And, yet, I don't want to leave you either.'

'This –' he touched her cheek briefly '– is a problem I can solve.' Ryan opened the door to his apartment. His hand slid from her face, reaching down to grab hers. Leading her inside, he loudly cleared his throat. 'Anyone in here wanting my forgiveness for anything, leave now and all will be forgotten.'

Mrs Hartman and Margie glanced at each other, quickly standing from his couch. Margie shuffled past them, not saying anything, barely even looking in their direction. Mrs Hartman wasn't so modest, as she stopped, eyed Megan and said, 'Hurt him and I'll take a hit out on you. Ryan, sweetheart, come down when you two are done talking. I've baked a fresh batch of cookies.'

'Cookies?' Rosa asked, excited. 'Why didn't you say you made cookies?' She rushed to the door, patting Ryan on the arm as she passed. 'Get your nookie, Ryan, I'm going to eat your share of the cookies. Nice to meet you, detective. Don't arrest any of us. Oh, and, Ryan, make sure you ask her about fixing those tickets for me since you won't do it.'

'Tickets?' Megan asked.

'Parking tickets. She has a, um, few,' Ryan answered, turning his attention to the redhead on his couch who hadn't moved. She was on a cellular phone.

'If you ask me as a favour, I might see what I can do.' Megan looked him over, her blood rushing in her veins as her heart beat faster.

'She has twenty-nine.' Ryan chuckled. 'She's been begging me to help her for some time, but I told her I can't as a photographer.'

'Where did everyone go?' a brunette said as she came in from the back of the apartment.

'I asked them to go,' Ryan said. 'Mary, I'd like you to meet Megan.'

'Megan?' Mary asked, suddenly smiling. 'You're her, aren't you? Ryan's detective?'

Megan nodded weakly.

'It's a pleasure,' Mary said. Then, frowning, she looked over to the redhead. 'Ginger, come on. Ryan needs his privacy.'

'I already told you the price, now you either take it or leave it. I don't come cheap. If you want cheap, you can get your ass down to a back alley for some of that discount puntang,' Ginger said into the phone, lifting one manicured nail in Mary's direction in a silent motion to hold on for a second while she negotiated.

'Sorry,' Mary said under her breath. 'She's in, ah, sales.'

Megan didn't say anything. Mary rushed to Ginger

and whispered frantically at her. The redhead stopped talking, turned to stare at Megan for a brief second before saying weakly, 'I'll, ah, talk to you later, Mom. I have to go.'

'Ginger, this is –' Ryan began.

'Lovely to meet you, detective,' Ginger rushed, smiling prettily. 'We must be going.'

Ryan shut the door behind the women and they were finally alone. Megan studied him carefully, and asked, 'Are you the only man in this building?'

'No, Pete, Rosa's husband, is at work and we didn't expect him to join the building party until later. Diederick, our resident millionaire, volunteered to buy the groceries and, since he's rich, we let him so long as he promised to buy normal food. William is busy patrolling our halls. He's kind of like our security system.'

'Oh, yeah, I think I met him. The guy with the baseball bat?'

Ryan nodded. 'Yes, that's William. He's harmless. And finally there was an unemployed singer named Harry, but he moved out this week. He finally got his big break singing show tunes in some lounge in Las Vegas.'

'Old ladies threatening cops downstairs. Parking-ticket bandits upstairs. Suspicious millionaires who live beneath their means. And call girls who try to solicit their own mothers for ... I don't even want to go there.' She strolled around his apartment. Tidy and neat, his living room and open kitchen had more appeal than her own. Framed artistic photographs dominated the visual wall space. They were of children laughing, couples walking, friends talking, even a couple kissing in Central Park. 'You live in a regular crime nest, Mr Lucas.'

'If you ask me nicely, I'll let you be the Queen of the Crime Nest.' Ryan chuckled.

'OK.'

'OK?'

'I'll move in,' Megan said. 'We can live here. I like it.'

'Really?'

'Why? Don't you like it here?' She twirled around, holding her hands to the side to encompass the room. 'Because I hate house shopping and my place is a real disaster. Besides, did I hear right? The lady downstairs bakes?'

'We get our daily dose of cookies. And she makes a tremendous lasagne and garlic bread. With Mrs Hartman around, none of us ever starves. We all pitch in for groceries to help her out.'

'Wow, what else does this building have to offer?' Megan asked, quirking a brow as she watched him.

'Well, of course, you've met the crazy guy who paces the halls and acts as our security.' Ryan shaded his eyes.

'Not exactly what I had in mind.' Megan moved to sit on his couch.

'And what did you have in mind?'

Megan ran her fingers through her hair. 'Oddly, I think I might miss your blackmailing me. Power looks really sexy on you.'

'I never thought I had the power.' Ryan chuckled. 'As far as I've known, it's you who's held the power over me. One look and I was yours.'

'Get your camera,' she ordered, standing.

'What?'

'Get your camera,' Megan repeated. She pulled at her new shirt, lifting it over her head. Tossing it aside, she stood in her navy lace halter bra. 'It's time for a photo shoot.'

Even as he obeyed, moving to his camera bag on the kitchen bar, he looked unsure. His eyes roamed down over legs as she pushed the pants from her hips. 'What exactly am I shooting?'

'More blackmail photos.' Megan kicked her pants aside, waiting for him to take out his camera. The boy short panties matched the butterfly lace halter. Both were new, bought on the dim hope Ryan would see them. But, instead of the guilt she thought she would feel at this moment, there was only happiness. Standing before him, more vulnerable and emotionally exposed than she'd ever been in her life, she placed her hands on her hips. 'You need to know I trust you and this is the only way I can think of to prove that I do.'

His hands shook as he began to lift the camera, only to lower it again. 'You don't have to prove anything, Megan.'

She sat on his soft brown couch, only to lie across the seat. Extending her arm, she rested it behind her head as one leg dangled off the side to the floor. 'Take the pictures, Ryan.'

It never took much to become aroused by him. Even the thought of him could make her stomach tighten and her knees weak. She'd trained herself to be hard to it, but, now that she accepted him in her life, Megan couldn't suppress what she felt. Her breathing deepened as she watched him lift the camera. She studied his eyes noting the focused look he normally got when working, only this time there was a telltale distraction in his movements. The camera moved, as if focused close to her body even though he stood several feet away. Knowing he looked, the lens magnifying her flesh for him so he could see every detail, made her pussy wet and her body ache with need.

The soft click of the shutter release caused her to squirm. Ryan walked slowly towards her, leisurely snapping pictures. Megan rolled up, reaching behind her back to unfastened her bra. The tight material released its hold, allowing her breasts to move freely beneath the material. She lay down once more, pushing the strap of the bra off her shoulder. Ryan made a weak noise and the soft clicking became more frequent. She repeated the action on the other side, until the lacy material lay over her in scant protection.

Ryan neared, breathing hard but no longer shaking.

He stood above her, bumping into the arm of the couch with his leg. Instantly, he lifted a knee, not bothering to look as he rested it on the couch arm. Megan gave him a slight smile, staring at the lens as she drew her foot up his inner thigh.

'Ah.' he sighed, his hips rotating slightly as she neared his cock. Finding it full, she wiggled her toes against him. 'Mm.'

Arching her back, she ran her hands up her stomach, dipping them beneath the loose bra so she could massage her breasts.

'You are so beautiful,' Ryan said, the words low and hoarse.

Her rubbing caress pushed her bra up, exposing her breasts to his lens. Her toes pushed insistently, massaging his firm arousal. Then, dropping her foot, she couldn't seem to stop her words, as she looked directly at him and said, 'I love you, Ryan.'

He smiled, lowering the camera to the side to look at her. 'I love you, too.'

'Come here.' She adjusted her hips, allowing her thighs to open in invitation.

Ryan set the camera on the floor. He shrugged off his shirt and tossed it aside before unfastening his jeans. He pushed them from his hips, taking the boxers with them. Then, he ran his hands down her legs, his fingers tickling as they lightly stroked her flesh. Megan took her bra all the way off and dropped it near where he'd set the camera. Grabbing her panties, he tugged them down, undressing her completely.

The contact of his body against hers sent heat shivering its way through her. The cloth material of his couch softly moulded to her as his weight pressed her down. She enjoyed looking at him, the passionate light in his eyes, the seductive tilt of his lips, the way his muscled chest lifted and fell with his rapid breath.

She ran her hands over his arms, exploring every inch

of him she could reach. Hair tickled the backs of her hands as she pulled at his neck, gently urging his mouth to hers. Ryan didn't resist, kissing her deeply as his hips settled next to hers. There wasn't enough room to sprawl out, so Megan placed one foot on the floor and hooked the other over the back of the couch.

The wet heat of his mouth ventured to her neck, licking a passionate trail along the tender flesh of her throat, over the ridge of her collarbone, across her chest, only to stop to pull a full breast between his lips. Sucking excitedly, he made small animalistic noises in the back of his throat. He braced his weight, gaining leverage to stroke between her thighs. His fingers glided over the tight bud he found hidden within the slick folds. His knee slipped off the side of the couch, but he quickly righted himself.

'We need more room,' Megan said, her eyes closed as she writhed against him.

He groaned an answer, but she didn't understand what he said as he switched to suck her neglected nipple between his teeth, biting gently. A thick finger glided down her slit, only to thrust inside her ready body. 'Turn over.'

Ryan pulled away. Megan moved to her hands and knees, her fingers digging into the arm of the couch, clutching the soft brown material. The stiff probe of his cock excited her, causing a thrill of pleasure to ripple over her as he looked for entry. He forced himself back and forth along her sex, pushing so that when he found what he was looking for his body moved into hers. Ryan groaned in pleasure, taking her by the hips. Megan eagerly accepted him as he rocked forwards, filling her with his thick arousal.

He controlled her actions, making her ride him in shallow movements as he stayed buried deep. Megan stroked her own clit, torn between the pleasure it caused and the aching in her nipples as they begged for attention. Gradually, he increased the pace, lengthening the thrusts.

Megan clenched him, loving the way he grunted with the tight press of her muscles around his cock. She did it again and again, making him lose his pace as he jolted within her. The tremors started and she knew she was close.

'Not yet,' she demanded, sensing he was close. Even as she ordered him to hold back, she intentionally squeezed him. 'I'm almost there. Don't stop.' She pushed back hard, rolling her hips in circles as she urged him to stay deep. 'Almost. Oh. Don't stop. Coming. Coming.'

Her body tensed as she met her release, riding out the pleasure as Ryan continued to move. Then, suddenly, he pulled out so as not to come inside her as he finished with a soft cry. Her limbs weak, she lowered her body to the couch. Ryan stretched next to her, his naked body tight along hers, as he cradled her back to his chest. A light sheen of sweat glued their flesh together, but neither of them cared.

'I told you this was something we always seem to get right.' Megan giggled. Smiling as his fingers danced lightly along her hip.

'The other stuff will come in time,' he assured her. 'So long as we always talk about what's going on. No more tricks or games.'

'Well, a few games,' she corrected.

He laughed. 'Yes, of course, a few games.'

'You never did say you were sorry for telling everyone we were engaged before we really were.'

'That's because I'm not sorry.' He kissed her neck.

She chuckled, content to be in his arms. 'Me neither. I'm glad you did it.'

'You didn't need to get back to work, did you?' He stiffened somewhat, as if just thinking of it. 'You did come over for pictures. There wasn't an emergency, was there?'

'No, I, ah . . .'

'What?' He touched her face, cupping her cheek as he forced her to look at him.

'I deleted the pictures you sent so I'd have an excuse to come and see you.' She blushed, glancing away before forcing herself to meet his steady gaze.

'I figured it might be something like that.' He kissed the side of her mouth where he could reach. 'I already got a confirmation from the department that they were all received.'

Megan's eyes widened. 'You knew when I came here?'

'You are not the only one who can be cunning, my darling, sweet beautiful Detective Matthews. I'll have to keep my wits sharp. I have a feeling that loving you will keep me on my toes.'

'At least you'll never get bored.' She turned away, the strain on her neck not allowing her to continue looking at him.

'With you? Never.'

'Being with a cop isn't easy,' she warned.

'You already told me, you're licensed to carry a gun.'

'That and we work horrible hours, become wrapped up in cases. We are moody and authoritative and –'

'Sh,' he interrupted. 'I'll take my chances.'

'Don't say I didn't warn you.'

'Well, I think it's worth it.' His fingers stayed possessively beneath her breasts, keeping her close. 'Besides, I heard this rumour somewhere that cops come with accessories.'

Megan laughed. Her sisters often teased her about that very thing. 'What? You like the handcuffs?'

'Only when I'm naughty.' Ryan placed little kisses along the back of her ear.

Megan sat up and leant over to get his camera. Lifting it, she pointed it at him and pushed the shutter release button. Ryan laughed, adjusting his shoulders on the couch. Not really paying attention to how she framed the photographs, so much as she made sure to cover every inch of upper body, she manoeuvred herself so she was straddling his thighs.

'I love you, Ryan Lucas,' she said, watching his face in the small viewfinder. 'And I want you to know, you have a family now. Forever and ever. We'll never leave you. I'll never leave you. I promise.'

Chapter Fourteen

'I knew everything would turn out for the best.' Beatrice grinned, as she looked into the teacups, divining Megan and Ryan's future. The sisters had finally talked her out of the pantsuits, with Kat using her 'allowance' from her rich husband to purchase their mother some new clothes. The woman actually looked good in the three-quarter-sleeve tunic and light denim jeans. Loose and flowing, the material fluttered as she moved.

'You did not,' Megan said, her tone sceptical as she threw an ace of spades playing card down on the table. It was her last card in her hand, as she played Gin Rummy with her family. 'Gin.'

Megan grinned, as she felt Ryan's fingers creeping along the small of her back, dipping beneath the grey T-shirt she'd stolen from his side of the closet. Across the front, it read 'Panic Man' and had a stick figure drawing of a man running from a tornado. Turning to him, she placed her hand on his knee and nuzzled his throat briefly before moving to add up her score for the tally sheet.

'Oh!' Sasha cried. Ms College Student was in an NYU T-shirt that looked as if it had at least two previous owners before finding its way into her closet. 'Mom, why couldn't you have predicted that for me? I was about to go out.' She set her handful of cards on the table, a straight run of hearts. If she'd played them, Sasha would have had the most points. Instead, according to the rules, she lost points for all the cards in her hand.

'I don't use my gifts to cheat,' Beatrice said.

'I believe your gifts, Mom.' Vincent grabbed the deck

and began shuffling. His combed hair was slicked back from his face, as if still damp from a shower.

'Thank you, Vincent.' Beatrice nodded at him.

'He does not.' Kat laughed, jolting her husband lightly in the ribs with her finger. He grunted, shooting her a stern look that hardly appeared threatening. For once, her hair was highlighted with a natural-looking dark brown, though the feathery magenta clip on top more than made up for the lack of her usual unnatural colour. Floral embroidery around the neckline of her sheer magenta shirt showed phoenixes with long tails reaching down to from an almost V-like shape. The loose material completely hid the small swell of Kat's belly.

'I do too,' Vincent said. 'It's how we met.'

'We met because of her meddling,' Kat corrected, tugging at his lightweight black cashmere sweater.

Megan was glad to see her sister had come to terms with being pregnant. After Megan and Zoe dragged her to a doctor, and Sasha bought her six books on pregnancy from a used bookstore, Kat had been much more relaxed. She'd even received a short note from Ella, who gave her wholehearted congratulations. No one else had got a letter, though Ella did occasionally call their parents to check in.

Vincent paused in his shuffling to give his wife a kiss. 'Either way, I'm a believer.'

'Stop,' Zoe protested. Pushing up from the table, she grabbed a bowl. 'Please remember some of us don't have warm bodies to go home to.'

Vincent chuckled and went back to shuffling the cards. 'Want me to set you up on a date?'

'Uh, no, I think I'll pass,' Zoe answered, walking to the kitchen. She had raided Kat's closet as soon as their pregnant sister had outgrown some of her tighter clothes, staking claim to the fitted mesh tunic she now wore along with some of Kat's other shirts. 'I've seen the guys you work with. Ancient is not my thing.'

'Since when?' Sasha teased.

'Ew!' Zoe yelled from the kitchen.

'You've been staring at that cup grinning for a while, my dear,' Douglas said, adjusting his glasses. 'Why don't you share?'

Megan exchanged a secretive look with her father. She knew the man was only humouring his wife, or at least she was pretty sure that was what he was doing.

Ryan leant close to her ear, nipping gently at it under the pretence of whispering to her. Megan laughed. It has been two months since she'd moved in and sex had not even started to get old. The second they walked in their apartment door, they couldn't keep their hands off each other.

'Actually,' their mother said, 'I think I'm going to make a confession.'

'I knew I was adopted,' Sasha said. 'Thank the gods.'

Beatrice gave her a disapproving look. 'Thirty hours of labour pains you gave me, smart mouth.'

'Sorry, Mom.' Sasha hung her head, trying not to laugh.

Beatrice turned to Megan, serious. Megan's smile fell somewhat. Nervous, she asked, 'What? Are you telling me *I'm* adopted?'

'I knew your engagement to Ryan was a fake when we went to Montana.' Beatrice gave a meaningful look at Ryan and Megan. 'That's why I pushed for the trip so fast. I've felt bad for lying about not being able to read your first tea-leaves reading to you, Ryan, but I thought not telling everyone else the truth would make it easier for you to woo our Megan.'

'Kat, you told her!' Megan tried to kick her sister's leg under the table, not once believing her mother had actually read the truth of it in the teacups.

Kat pulled away, shaking her head. 'I swear, Megs, I didn't say a thing.'

'Sasha?' Megan waited as Sasha shook her head before turning to Zoe who came from the kitchen.

'I didn't say a thing to her,' Zoe said. 'She probably overheard us talking.

'I don't know why you girls refuse to believe. I have hoped for years that one of you would embrace this family's gift, or at least show some interest in your potential.' Their mother sighed loudly, shaking her head.

'You can teach me,' Ryan said diplomatically.

'Sorry, you're male,' Beatrice answered. 'Men can't possess the gift.'

'Maybe a granddaughter will,' Vincent offered, only to get a dirty grimace from his wife.

Beatrice brightened at the thought. 'I didn't think of that. You know, Kat, if you have a girl, I'd be willing to –'

'Mom? You were saying about our readings?' Megan interrupted, saving Kat's unborn baby from years of lessons into the art of tasseography.

'Oh, right, you should get married in Las Vegas,' Beatrice said. 'It'll bring you luck and I have coupons.'

After an abrupt silence, they all laughed.

'I'm serious,' Beatrice protested.

Megan glanced at Ryan. He gave a slight shrug. Turning to her mother, she said, 'OK, then, Vegas it is. Works for us.'

'Wonderful, I'll book the flight!' Beatrice announced.

'Aside from Las Vegas,' Ryan interrupted. 'You were saying something about a confession.'

'Oh, right.' Beatrice nodded. 'I saw in the first reading that you had yet to actually get together and the engagement wasn't real, but it could be. So I took you to an isolated place and now look.' Lifting her hands to the side, she sighed. 'Happy, happy, happy.'

'I still think Kat told you. She never could keep a secret,' Megan said.

'I can too!' Kat tossed the card Vincent dealt her at Megan's head. 'I keep secrets from you all the time.'

'Oh, yeah, prove it then,' Megan challenged. 'Tell me a secret you've been keeping.'

'All right.' Kat met her steady gaze. 'I knew Ryan wasn't married when Zoe told me about it at the slumber party we had for you. I also knew he'd take you back if you played your cards right. And I also knew the only way you'd learn your lesson and really apologise was if you thought Ryan was completely lost to you. It was the only way you, Ms Know-It-All Detective, would let your guard down long enough to say what was really in your heart.'

'You never could back away from a challenge,' Sasha agreed.

'You were in on it?' Megan frowned. 'And you didn't tell me?'

'We all were,' Zoe said. 'Except for Mom.'

'I already knew on my own,' Beatrice said, motioning to the teacups. 'I didn't need to be told.'

'And,' Kat continued, as if no one had spoken, 'I knew Ryan was coming over that night to drop off my Romanian gift. I knew it was him ringing the doorbell and, when you said no one was there, I knew he'd be hiding from you so I screamed like I was in trouble and sent you after him.'

'That's why you got those stripper – er, I mean costumes.' Megan thought of the sexy nurse's uniform her sisters had tried to get her to wear.

'Wait,' Ryan said softly. He leant into her. 'Costume? What costume?'

Megan smirked at him, not answering.

'I thought you two would talk it out that night, but clearly you were still too hard headed at that point.' Kat grinned. 'So I let you stew.'

'That's horrible,' Megan said.

'Yes.' Kat didn't flinch. 'But necessary, Megs.'

Megan sighed. It was all done with now. And, whereas she didn't like to be manipulated, she couldn't really find fault with Kat's logic. It was true. She *was* hard-headed and it was quite possible that, without the true fear of not being able to have Ryan, she might have dragged her feet in apologising completely to him. It was only when she had nothing to lose, that she put it all on the line.

'I'm so glad that's out in the open now.' Kat sighed. 'I hated to do it to you, Megan. But, you see, you're not the only one who knows their sisters.'

Megan slowly stood, moving to walk around the table.

'Don't hit her, Megan,' Sasha said. 'She's pregnant.'

Kat stood, facing her. Megan gave her a wry smile. 'Thanks, Kat. Just don't ever do it again.'

Kat nodded, her features falling in relief as Megan hugged her.

Sasha gave a nervous laugh. 'I don't know what you did to mellow Megan out, Ryan, but, whatever it is, keep doing it.'

'I plan on it.' Ryan gave his fiancée a meaningful private look, full of sexual tension.

Megan rejoined him at the table. 'So, as long as confession time is over, how about we play cards?'

'Sounds good to me,' Zoe said.

'And this time I'm going to kick your butt, Miss Megan,' Sasha warned.

As Vincent dealt, everyone became quiet as they adjusted their cards. Leaning towards Megan, Ryan whispered, 'So, um, what was this about a costume?'

Megan laughed. Kissing him lightly on the lips, she answered, 'Don't worry, sweetheart, I promise to show you later.

Epilogue

Rosa and Pete, deciding marriage wasn't for them, separated after a month, starting what the other tenants of the building felt was a renewal of their old habit of off again, on again living. However, after discovering Harry wasn't technically capable of legally binding couples in matrimony, they decided to get married for real. The second ceremony was performed by a friend of a friend who ordered his licence online. They're positive this time it's forever.

William the Pacer is still happily patrolling the floors of the East Village apartment building and is only too happy to talk shop with his fellow enforcer of the law, Detective Matthews, who he has taken to saluting every time he sees her. Megan gave him a plastic badge. It's his most treasured possession.

Margie and Mrs Hartman formally apologised for their little deceit. Mrs Hartman with a plateful of chocolate no-bake cookies and Margie with a baby African Grey parrot named Clara. The bird was politely given back with a promise to visit it often. Margie was relieved to have the beloved pet returned.

Mary still maintains that Ginger is in 'sales'. Ginger maintains that she's a beautician. And Megan pretends to believe them both, though she's secretly trying to get Ginger out of the call-girl lifestyle.

The first time Megan met Diederick Meier the Third, he came on to her. As soon as he realised she was Ryan's woman, he jokingly offered to buy her from his friend. Megan threatened to have him arrested and they've been great friends ever since. He is still leading his secretive double life.

Jersey St Claud smiled throughout his whole trial, as if enjoying the attention of the spotlight, before being found guilty and sentenced to six consecutive life sentences without the possibility of parole. Megan had never been so glad to step out of a courtroom in her life as she did the day she finished testifying at the Preying Mantis's trial. To celebrate, she took a nice long bath by candlelight with Ryan in their clawfoot tub, away from the annoying camera flash of his fellow reporters. Though her picture did again appear in the newspaper, it was never one taken by Ryan. Those he saved for their private stash.

Megan and Ryan really did get married in Las Vegas. Beatrice couldn't have been happier, until she saw Megan and her sister bridesmaids dressed in tight cop uniforms complete with hot pants, tight blue halter tops and suspiciously shaped rubber batons. Kat's naked belly protruded, with the words 'Flower Girl' painted across her stomach in a sea of swirly flowers. Vincent protested that the baby might be a boy, but his logic fell on deaf ears. Even Ella made it home for the ceremony.

Douglas merely laughed at his daughters, proud to give his eldest away to such a fine young man. With the groom stood Diederick, the only one from their apartment building who could make the journey, and Vincent. Ryan and his groomsmen wore baggy black and white striped jumpsuits with a ball and chain dragging from the lock on their ankles.